Everfall
Great Sea
Hill Country
Lanalia
South Land
Clear Water

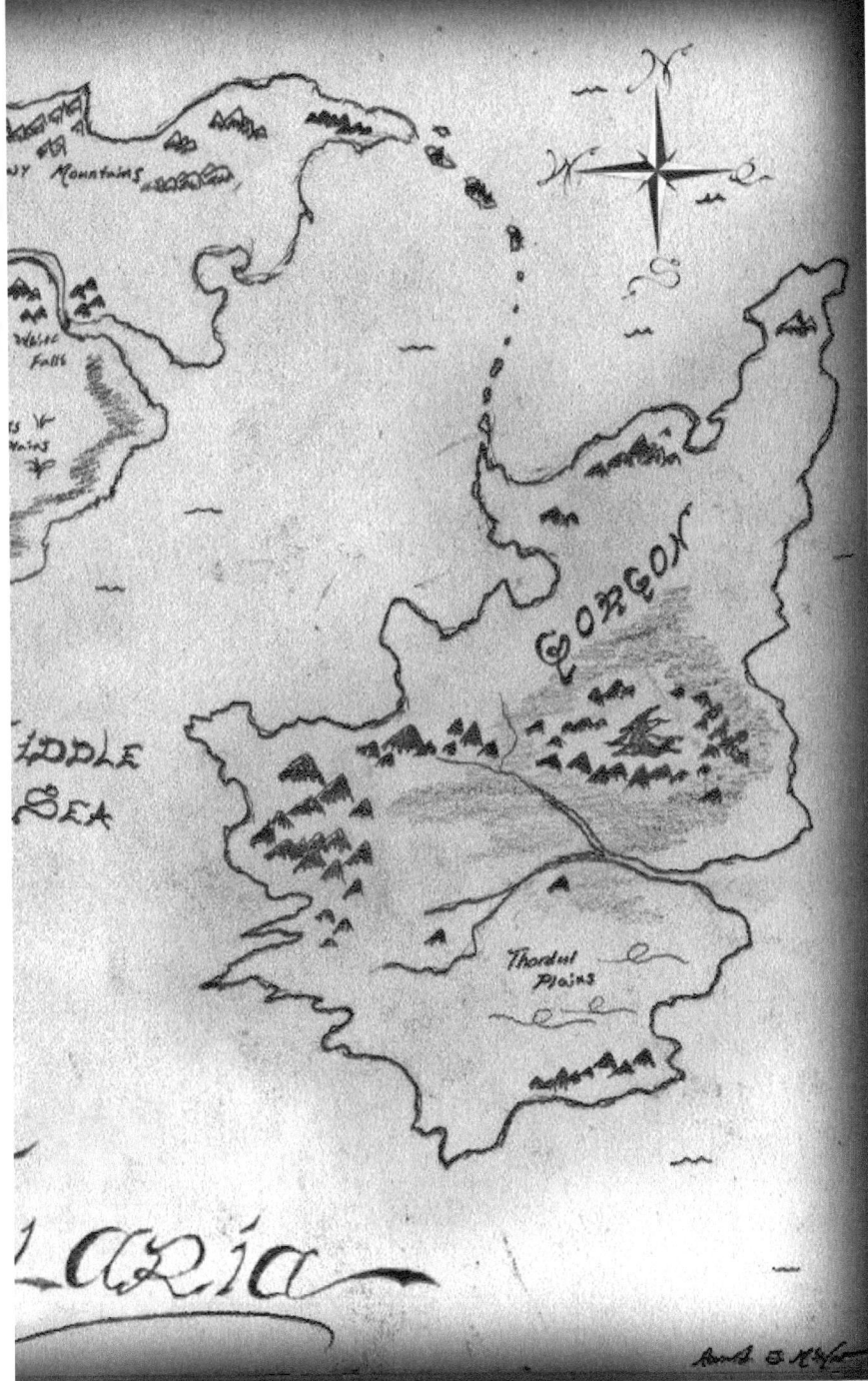

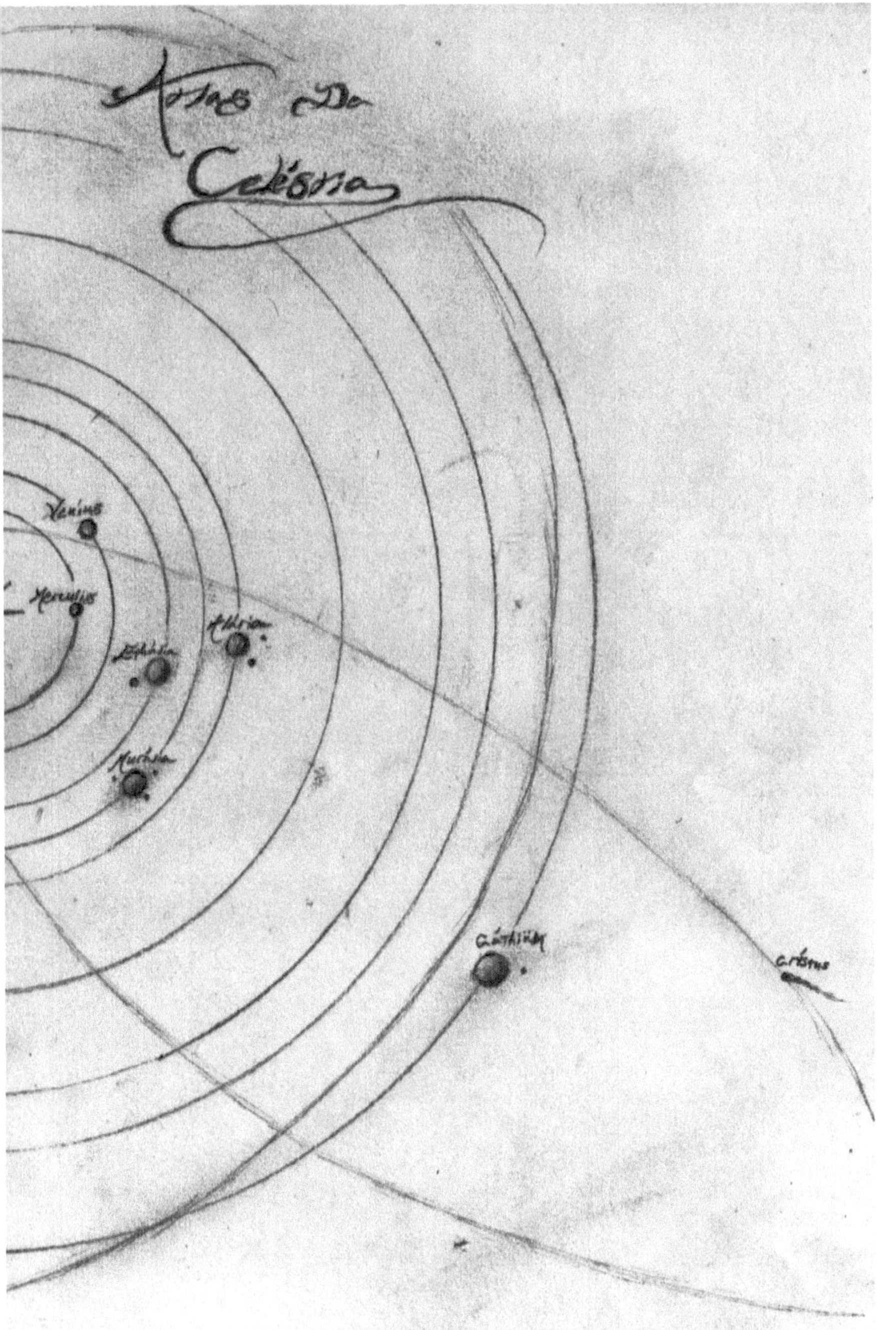

Astras Da Celéstia
Mercurius

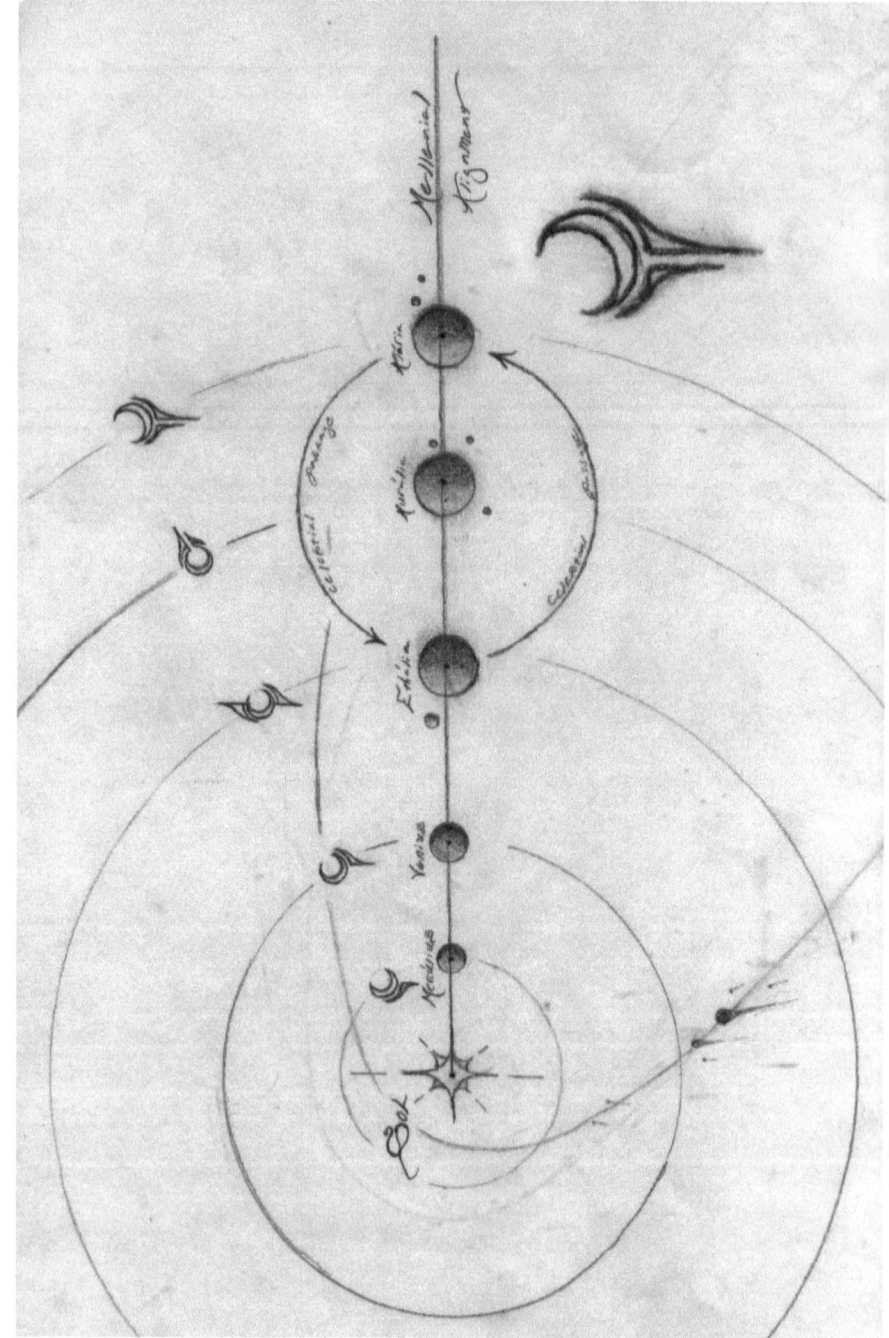

Lux Æterna

Ronald J. McNutt

ISBN: 978-0-9892843-2-5

www.luxaeternabook.com

Lux Æterna

Written by my hand
in the year of our Lord 2012

Ronald James McNutt
April 10th, 2012

This book is dedicated to my loving wife Patricia who has always been
a constant source of encouragement.

Special Thanks to my mother Marlene Griefenstine, Zack Cole, Joshua
Flott, and Josh Hutfles. Your imaginations have inspired many and
have led to such wonderful tales.

To the One who is maker of us all, you are the light within all men.
There are none like you, there are none beside you; you are worthy of
all praise and to you be the glory forever.

Lux Æterna

Ronald J. McNutt

Chapter	Page No.

Lux Æterna

Ronald J. McNutt

List of Illustrations

Ronald J. McNutt

Part I

"You are not what your eyes can see but what your heart believes."

Inceptus
Prologue

Of passion and virtue, betrayal and great loss, of
endless ruins scattered against the stars forever cast into
the endless sea of eternal night, of a world now vanished
save only in legend do I now speak. Far beyond the
horizon and out into the infinite sky, between the cold red
sphere of Mars and the grandeur of mighty Jupiter with its
moons, lay a field of ancient debris floating lonely and
forgotten in the dark silence of space. These desolate ruins
drift together even now in their tireless circle around the
sun. Yet before the eyes of Men beheld the blue skies of
Earth and dirtied their feet with its rich, black soil they
lifted their eyes toward different horizons and trod the
ground of another world.

Here young lovers once ran through green fields and
rested upon thick grass to stare upwards at the clouds and
starry heavens. They daydreamed of a future that never
was. The featureless boulders and shadowy rocks, which
now float adrift between the worlds, were once great
oceans, mountains, fields, rivers and vast forests. This
same quiet desolation was once wrapped in a brilliant sky
filled with life and reflected the glory of the sun as it

danced upon the waves of the sea. The leaves of the trees were luminous as they swayed in a gentle summer wind. It was a world of allurement and mystery, where the beginning of Men first displayed the splendor of their Creator and beheld the work of His hands in all its vast array. It was a world of peace and beauty until the shadow of the great Enemy covered the land filling it with violence and war.

Even now, though all is still and silent as the grave, the voices of the fallen and their cries of battle echo out into the vastness of space telling the story of both victory and defeat: a battle which shook the very pillars of Heaven and sent rolling thunder through the cosmos causing even the stars to reel back in astonishment.

Alária it was called and it shined out into the darkness radiating its glorious light as the fifth in line from the Sun along with its celestial brothers. It was the home of Men until its end.

Nothing now remains of its former glory. No monument. No song. Only shadows and dust far, far away. Yet if one were to search the endless rubble and debris, if one were to lose his whole life sifting through the blackened sand and every solitary island of stone, there may be something; an unlikely and seemingly simple object standing alone against the darkness of space bearing testament that there was once here something more than refuse and dust. For along the outer edge of the debris glides an asteroid like all the rest save for a large, dark precipice and a shimmering light upon it that reflects the light of the sun. It is the smooth and mirrored surface of a sword unlike any other. It was driven hard into the rock with strong hands long ago. Upon its hilt hangs a small silver leaf from a frail silver chain and together they look out toward the stars.

This is the account of that sword, the men who wielded it against evil, a planet destroyed and a bridge between worlds.

I.

Lux Æterna

Eternal Light

In the beginning, an eternal Spirit moved through endless darkness. From it a great light shined out and Darkness fled in terror. In fear and wonderment he watched from afar as Alária was revealed, suspended like a green pearl in the vast, starry expanse. Darkness did not understand the light and feared it. For in time before time, it perceived nothing greater than himself and here was something new, far beyond imagining. Of course, this was not always so. In his age-long and silent wandering through the void, Darkness had forgotten, or perhaps chose to forget, that he too was created by the same being that it now gazed upon with fear and trembling.

Light Enduring created Darkness to support the light and contrast with it as an artist who blends his paint upon a canvass. But Darkness had looked out into the void and saw with angelic eyes no end to its expanse and wandered far out into it. His thoughts became bent to the mystery like an addiction. He would wander farther and farther from Light Enduring out into the void seeking others like himself. But finding none, thought that perhaps the void itself was the greater power and Light Enduring was but a mar in its beautiful emptiness. In his folly, Darkness' heart began to worship the void and this consumed its mind. He began to hate the Light. Being far away from the Creator, his thoughts became corrupted with pride and his heart was darkened as black as his outer countenance. Finally, he set out into the void intending never to return.

It was thus that Darkness began a lonely and endless sojourn. After many ages passed in the silence and finding nothing in the void, Darkness forgot about the Light, and his thoughts began to exalt himself, his pride becoming king of its mind, forcing out all memory of his creation and purpose.

Presently, from across the abyss, Darkness sat perched upon a high, dim precipice with black wings unfolded in silent brooding, watching with farsighted eyes all that Light was doing far off in the fathomless depths of emptiness. Each new creation He set His hand to was an abomination to his pride and the holy expanse where he felt he alone was ruler.

Darkness was not prevented from entering the creation, however, and soon his mind haunted the shadows of the world and looked as an even more marvelous thing happened. Light entered into the dust of the ground and, from it, splendorous and beautiful beings were made. Creatures which grew up from the ground, swam in the sea, or flew in the air. The final one to be made, the chief creation, took dominion over all others. He walked with majesty and bore the glory of Light Himself who walked beside them. Darkness saw with intrigue this new creature brought to life with divine breath, yet marked with astonishment the seeming carelessness of their Creator as the new creature appeared frail and puny compared to the fierce and wild world it was loosed into. Light Enduring created many of them and, to Darkness' disgust, they walked upright with strength and dignity as Light Enduring shined upon them.

Darkness perceived their lives were made to endure as the Light Himself was made imperishable and made to grow in beauty as the ages passed. They called themselves Men and the fairness and beauty of those first made surpassed all who came later in the long years to follow. In the dim morning of the world, they awoke. On that first cool, misty dawn their eyes beheld their Creator standing strong and firm in the shape of a man yet wrapped with light as one would wear a garment. His head was crowned with glory and beyond Him a sea of stars floated in the endless abyss of the night sky. As their eyes adjusted, Men perceived they were not alone and many others like themselves stood near and other things as well. Their Creator taught them about the world and all manner of ways of living. They listened intently to all He would say for they could sense that they were once a part of his very being somehow made separate and yet complete. They longed for His presence and He in turn longed for them as they were an extension of His very substance.

Darkness became increasingly more jealous with every new expression of the Enduring Light's craftsmanship. Rage tormented its soul as day and night Men grew in the place of honor he himself once possessed. Groping in the dark his massive hand came to rest on a rocky mass of black stone, an undesired and desolate rock cast far out from the rest of creation. For a moment, Darkness felt akin to it and felt sympathy toward it; feeling cast out and forgotten. This was the last time he would ever feel such a feeling. The rock could not speak nor sympathize and the moment was quickly gone.

Suddenly his fury rose to such fierceness that he grasped the rock and with all his might flung it toward the world Light had created. Darkness perceived Light Enduring turn with a look of scorn. Just as quickly as Darkness' anger had come, it fled, replaced with panic and the fear of Light's face as it realized it was not forgotten, nor hidden from the Light in the dark. The Light turned His face back toward his creation, now filled with concern for that which He created. But like the rays of dawn which grow steadily brighter as the day approaches, so did His countenance. Soon He was like before, giving no heed to Darkness or his wrath. This angered Darkness worse than before and he turned his mind to how else he may destroy Men and their glory.

It was then that his wicked imagination conceived a sinister plot and into his mind came the thought of having beings of his own, agents to carry out his own malevolent will. Though made without creation, for the power of creation was held by Light Enduring alone, Darkness found he could divide his great power into lesser beings and give to these beings portions of his own power and will. Reserving the greatest powers for himself, he made many such malignant spirits. They were mighty indeed, and Darkness sent them to the glowing green sphere of Alária to inhabit the shadows and search out a way that Men might be corrupted. Darkness knew that Light

Enduring was an imperishable, inextinguishable flame, yet His creations may be found with fault as they had wills of their own and may be deceived.

II.

Primus Basileus et Incipiens de Malorum

*The Beginning of Evil and the Anointing
of the First King*

The world was young and life filled every crevasse that water and light could reach. Light Enduring walked among the forests and explored the deep seas. From the start He looked at the doings of Men for they had begun great works; works of renown remembered now only in legend. They built grand cities with magnificent towers and homes made of stone cut from living rock, molded and fashioned with intricate designs and laid with tools of iron and strong hands. They built roads spanning for miles in every direction from their capital, its foundations being placed where the first of Men were born and stretching as far as the Middle Sea.

Bright and dazzling stars illuminated the night sky. Men looked to these for signs and used them for navigation and the making of calendars. They marked with astonishing accuracy the symmetry and balance of the celestial bodies as they passed on their endless circuits through the heavens. In those days, one could not help but stand amazed at the stars. So bright were they that as the first written words were being created Men could read by their light. They became skilled in every work: masonry, metallurgy, the taming of animals for work and food and the growing of crops. Though some became more familiar with one task or another, all held a great love and passion for the arts. Marvelous paintings and intricate carvings on stonework and woodwork were common. Songs were made and voices rang out in the still forests and open plains. Songs of things they had seen or hoped for, but mainly of past history as a way to remember and learn. It was not long before stringed instruments accompanied their songs and delighted all who could hear.

They were happy in those days and the land was laid open for adventure and exploration in every direction. They were men of courage and passion, climbing the highest mountains and navigating across the farthest seas to admire and seek out the land given to them. Of them, a line of kings was born. Families of honor and wisdom. Noble in heart and action. They could inspire and lead and in their minds was the Enduring Light through which they could commune with the Great Creator.

In those days, men and women matured differently even as the land itself was different. They did not stoop with age and depravity, nor did their flesh hang about them like old rags as time ebbed by. Their eyes were bright and clear. Their ears came to a sharp corner, marvelously acute and their strength was unparalleled. They moved with grace and easiness. Though their physical appearance was different than modern man, it was their heart which made the real difference, and it is the heart of Men which gives life or takes it away.

Leánder and Ahriman were among the first to awake in the forest at the beginning of time with the First Men. They looked so alike that they were called brothers. In the years to come they would share the name of Lanálian, which in their language means 'endless forest,' for that is what they perceived surrounded them in the beginning. However as they began to explore guided by the wise instruction of the Light, they found themselves to be in a vast and wide country with striking mountain peaks in the west sloping down into a dark forest stretching many miles to either side. To the east lay a peaceful hill country leading into fair grassy plains ending in sandy shores against a wide sea. This sea was later explored by the first mariners and was named the Middle Sea for another land was discovered in the east, a land of shadows and mist with lofty, snowcapped mountain peaks and deep valleys where shifting mountains split the earth's foundations. Gorgon, it was named, which means 'many shadows', and it remained uninhabited for a long time.

Many mighty birds were found there nesting in the high cliffs and arid, yet fertile plains stretched away southward ending in a small band of mountains against the sea. A great mariner named Thordul was the first to master the wind using sails to cover unheard of distances. It was he who first explored the land of Gorgon. Its southern plains held his name as he and his men were the first to set foot there. In his mighty sailing ship Thordul's company explored many other places and navigated vast uncharted seas, sailing finally east of Gorgon into the Great Sea and out of history.

To the south of the Lanálian Forest was found a narrow gap of land between the waters connecting the lower south lands. These lands were rich in fertile soil and flowing streams, though the soil there was not as deep as that of the north causing the trees there to stand much lower and smaller. They were of a more tropical family with long pointed leaves and fernlike branches. A second-generation man named Deiriador, who learned the art of sailing from Thordul, settled this land, sailing from the grass plains of Lanália with his wife and children. He was a simple man and named the various parts of the country after what he saw, hence the name of the great lake located far inland he named Clear Water, the river that spilled into it was called Winding River and the entire continent itself he named simply Sound Land which later generations slurred together into one word: 'Southland.'

Leánder and Ahriman were the finest hunters among all the others. It was they who laid the foundation for the first great city on the western shores of the forested mountains. They inspired other men and woman to design marvelous sculptures to line the streets, works of iron and other more precious metals studded every corner and supported every beam.

The great city was situated on a high, rounded hill surrounded by a forest looking south across a wide bay. In the middle they erected an impressive white stone tower. Its height seemed impossible. Many thought that it would topple during its construction, but through wise planning, the use of tempered steel and cunning stonework, the tower reached hundreds of feet into the sky. Those far away at sea or even inland could see its beacon for miles with unaided eyes. Great lanterns were placed in its summit which burned white with an inextinguishable fire, the like of which not many understood apart from the two brothers. They surrounded the city with high stone walls built as thick as seven men standing abreast. Walls that were meant to last and stand firm against the powerful storms that would come sweeping in from across the Great Sea. The people built their homes inside the walls and upon the hill with the same white stone as the Tower of Light.

As the years passed and the great works of the city were accomplished, Ahriman found himself with a longing to explore the rest of the vast world. He began to venture far out into the unexplored wilderness and hunt giant game; animals and beasts heard of now only in stories. His course took him further and further away, and his brother would often worry when he would fail to return after many months. Of course, he would return and inspire many as he told his wild tales.

Darkness was patient, and he seemed ever present among the shadows then, noting carefully the wonderings of Ahriman through his evil agents reporting all they saw and heard.

While Ahriman was away on one such adventure, Leánder was left alone to lead the people as they continued to build and grow the city. Leánder had found ways of growing crops in the sand and built roads far into the forest with the help of men of the second and third generations.

Leánder did many marvelous works while his brother was away, however the story of Leánder and Lorwin is the most renown.

*   *   *

It was late in the day in early autumn. The forest trees surrounding the White City were arrayed in blazing colors of red and gold spangled with the last remnants of green on their large wide leaves when Leánder, walking alone through the forest, heard a voice singing on the wind. He stood enchanted for a long time fearing that the rustle of leaves at his feet would disturb the singer. Finally, after what seemed like an eternity, he dared to move and seek out this strange enchantment. He walked as quietly as he could through the slanting rays of the fading sun fearing to disturb the angelic voice from her melody. He entered a small open field and stood in silent amazement. The sky and all the air around him was aglow with a soft golden light as the setting sun played off the distant clouds and lit the dim autumn forest. The first of the fireflies were rising from the tall yellow grass like gentle embers from a golden fire, and there before him in the middle of the field by a slow stream sat a woman more beautiful than any other. She was indeed the fairest work Light Enduring had made and her clear voice sang out into the forest with praises to his glory.

Leánder dared not move fearing to end this magical sight and he stood there drinking in the sight of her. As the last of the sunlight faded her song grew softer as though it was her voice that gave light to the world. The forest itself

and all the woodland creatures stood still as her last notes faded and only gradually did they resume their normal behavior.

Sensing a presence, she looked up at Leánder standing awestruck across the field. She rose as he walked to her, and their meeting was like the mingling of water as their hearts reached out toward one another and found a kindred spirit. They stood there in the twilight until the stars shone brightly in the sky above. Leánder wished with all his heart that that moment would last forever.

Leánder spoke gently to himself, "*May this place be ever as beautiful as this night, that all may remember this meeting and the beauty that was once here.*"

She was Lorwin, also among the First and filled with wisdom and nobility, yet seldom seen 'til then for her heart was in the forest where she loved to sing to her Creator. As they made their way out of the forest toward the city however, she knew that her life would be forever changed. Yet she greeted it gladly as long as it meant she would be with Leánder. Leánder was filled with unspeakable happiness as he delighted in his new bride. Her beauty won great renown among people and all spoke well of them. Leánder laid plans to build a grand hall of stone across from the White Tower for them to live in and spent day and night on its construction. Indeed, it was nearly as beautiful as the White Tower itself, its only lack being the creative touch Ahriman could have bestowed. His absence was felt as a constant burden by his brother.

Much to everyone's dismay, something peculiar happened to the forest surrounding the city not long after the wedding. As everyone prepared for the winter, the wind grew no colder and nights did not bring frost nor did the snow fall. Instead, the trees bloomed with new leaves but they were colored a brilliant gold, red or purple, spangled with dazzling green soon to fall with an effervescent fragrance to the earth below. In the night, they would glow with a gentle golden light as though releasing the sunlight they bathed in during the day. The air itself stayed warm in the day, yet cool as autumn at night.

Heavy snow could still be seen falling in the mountains far away. It was then that Leánder spoke of his words concerning the forest when he first met his bride. Henceforth the White City was named Everfall after the unchanging season.

Darkness was patient. he watched silently as all Men, especially Leánder and Ahriman, grew in glory until its ill-content could wait no longer. Creeping through the shadows of the forest, he found Ahriman hunting alone far away from his home. In pursuit of a deer he stumbled into the darkest recesses of a woods. He noticed for the first time how oddly still the forest was. He stood there in the stillness and listened. No sound of bird, no rustle of field mice or angry squirrels high in the trees. Not a leaf moved. The only sound was of his heavy breathing and the sound of his heart still racing from the chase. He was suddenly very tired with an unnatural heaviness he could not explain. His strong shoulders slumped and his head began to bow as he closed his eyes even as he stood. Unknowingly he was falling deeper and deeper into an evil trap set to destroy him. He struggled to stay awake and with a great effort took a few steps back the way he came but all effort was futile. After only three steps he fell heavily to the ground amidst the shadows and Darkness closed in about him.

He lay there a long time in a dreamless silence. Finally, after what seemed like an eternity, he heard the sound of a voice. Deep and strong, yet coupled with an unknown feeling. Being one of the First Men, he did not know evil, yet his soul could sense its wrongness. Despite this he could not help but listen and what he heard was quite unexpected.

"Ahriman, your brother is better than you," whispered a voice.

Ahriman tried to speak but found no words. He was afraid.

"Your brother will be a great king among men and already everyone of this world worships him and his new wife for their glory. You're a coward," spoke the voice mockingly. "You're a coward for not standing up to him when you know you would make a better leader. Shouldn't you possess the most beautiful women, Master Hunter, and not your doting brother?"

Images and memories suddenly filled Ahriman's mind of times when his brother was hailed by all the people after the building of the first great city, for the songs he would sing, and for his skill as a hunter. His thoughts drifted also to times when his brother refused to listen to his ideas and ignored his suggestions. A flicker of anger sparked to life in his heart as he considered these things.

The voice softened again, just above a whisper. "*You* should be the one who stands in glory and have all the people bow down to *your* will."

"I have no such power," replied Ahriman, surprised that

he could now speak and finding his courage again. "Nor would I wish for it if it were presented. Glory is for Light Enduring alone."

"Is it?" Ahriman heard the voice ask as though it were a whisper in his ear. "And why not for you? What do you think he thinks of you anyway?"

"We are his children, the sons of his creation."

Cold fury rose in the voice. *"Sons of his creation* you say? A *son* I doubt but a *child* certainly. Fumbling about as you go, feeble and weak. Why, I could crush your body with one finger and what could you do to stand against me?"

Ahriman felt a vast evil presence growing closer in the darkness, yet stood boldly.

"No words have you? You have nothing to say to me? Let me show you a vision of what will become of your future sonship," and with that Ahriman was caught up in sights and visions the likes of which he had never imagined. Stars flew by followed by comets and rocks of all shapes and sizes, great round orbs made entirely of clouds and with majestic rings of immeasurable size. All the while he flew with impossible speed toward a world that he perceived he knew. It was a world of land and sea, lined with silver clouds and capped with ice at the poles. He thought that the vision would end there but it flew beyond and to another world, beyond and further out from Sol riding on its silent celestial track. This was Alária, the land of his making and the land of his home where he now lay under a spell.

"This is the world that you know, and now let me show you what will be." Out of the darkness in between the stars came a light blazing with an evil fire toward the planet. Ahriman's jaw slackened and his blood ran cold as terror and amazement gripped him. The blazing light took the shape of a shooting star, the kind he had seen on so many nights in the clear skies over the White City, yet this was different. *Much* different. As it streaked by Aláría's furthest moon he could see that it was much bigger and gaining speed as it drew closer to his home planet. The silence was deafening in Ahriman's ears as it approached. As it grew closer it took on the shape of a winged dragon made entirely of red and yellow flame, bright as the sun at mid-day with clawed feet which grasped and crushed his home.

Ahriman made to scream into the silence, but his voice was lost to the hurricane of violence which the monster brought as it neared. Suddenly, it impacted the planet and white flashed forever in every direction. Ahriman's body shook with so much ferocity that he thought he would be torn apart in the shock wave. As he opened his eyes again the sight he saw caused him to forget his own pain. He saw his world being torn apart in the silence. Such destruction he had never imagined in his wildest dreams and he did not believe it now though he was seeing it. Great pieces of land and sea ejected out into space and the hot foundations of the planet's core exploded outwards in all directions. Oceans, land and sky blended together and then dispersed like shattered crystal out into the darkness until nothing remained. At this, Ahriman could take no more and his eyes dimmed. As his consciousness faded, he heard the voice speaking quietly, just above a whisper.

"*This* is power and it is in my hand to wield it. If your

maker is so powerful, then I invite you to stop me. This is the place I will await you," and with that Ahriman's last image was of a dark and misty shore, lost in shadow against high black cliffs and cloudy skies. A place he had never seen before.

*   *   *

Dew and sweat covered his body as he awoke. It was late morning and he was stiff after having lain prostrate on the cool ground throughout the night. He sat up and scratched his hair and face before standing, feeling his joints loosen. The wind blew through the tops of the tall pines and all was peaceful. He wondered why he had fallen asleep there to begin with. As the trees swayed with the wind a pinecone fell from above and as it fell it seemed to slow and was replaced by the image of a fiery comet. As it impacted the ground it thundered deeply yet quietly as if awaking a distant memory or forgotten dream. Suddenly the vision came rushing back to him and he reeled back at the sight. Fear and agony gripped him as he turned and ran through the forest.

He ran and ran as fast as his legs could carry him. He ran until sweat poured from his body and his muscles screamed for relief yet on he pressed. He tore through the forest and out into the open country. He ran through the scorching heat of the summer sun, his body on fire as he made for the city. But he was a long way off. He had spent many months away and had traveled far, too far, and now every mile seemed to take an endless eternity to cross. He had to tell Leánder. He had to warn the people of their impending doom and of this nameless foe who assailed him in the forest. It would be a long time before he was home again...

*   *   *

It was late evening and the sun was spent as Leánder walked upon an upper terrace of his stone home looking upward as the first stars were beginning to appear. In recent days he had come to know for the first time what worry truly was. He longed to know what had become of his brother. He had spent endless hours here as he looked for any sign of Ahriman but all that met his eyes were endless trees swaying in the wind. Now however, something was different. Something *felt* different. He looked out across the forest as it rested in the evening twilight and through the trees he could see torches and firelight appear through the leaves. Someone was coming and at great haste.

He rushed down into the main hall but before he could reach the door it burst open and was thrown against its hinges. Four men poured in through the door with a fifth supported on the shoulders of the last two. Fear and concern was in their eyes and across their countenances as they brought him in and lay him upon a bed in an adjoining room. They laid him down gently and with great care, yet to Ahriman the sudden softness of the pillows startled him and for a moment he was clearheaded and his eyes opened wide. He grabbed his brother's collar and pulled him down urgently.

"It's coming!" he shouted. "It's *coming!*" he shouted again.

"Shhhhh my brother," began Leánder as he wiped the hair from his brother's stricken face. His emotions tore at him and he marveled at what may have happened.

Ahriman grabbed his brother's hand and sunk into the pillows as fatigue overwhelmed him once more. "The dragon..." he said finally, his eyes closing. "...the dragon is coming..." and with that he fell away into a deep sleep.

Days passed and still Ahriman slept. Leánder and Lorwin tended to him day and night and they wondered at the meaning of this coming dragon. Yet no one could say. Finally, on the morning of the fourth day, Ahriman stirred. Opening his eyes, he found himself in a room he was not familiar with. He was covered with fine white linen blankets and bathed with the tender light of morning as it poured in through the high stone windows. There was the fragrance of fall in the air and this puzzled him for the last he remembered it was early spring. Faintly he heard whispering voices outside, a man and a woman. Through the arched doorway he recognized one of them.

"Brother..." he tried to say, but he found that his throat was parched and he was barely able to speak above a whisper.

Leánder rushed into the room to his brother's side. For the first time in days, Ahriman looked peaceful and the evil visions of his dreams had passed.

"Lorwin, bring water."

"Lorwin?" asked Ahriman. "You have some explaining to do brother," he said trying to smile.

"Yes, I suppose I do," replied Leánder returning the smile. "But I am not the only one," he said alluding to the vision.

For a second there was fear in Ahriman's eyes as he recalled the vision but it quickly passed.

"Not now," said Leánder. "Rest now and we will speak later. You need to rest and regain your strength. You've been asleep for a long time." As he spoke Lorwin appeared at the door carrying an ornate jar of water. As she entered Ahriman drank in the sight of her. There was no woman more beautiful than she. He did not let it show however, and kept the thought hidden out of respect for his brother for he loved him and was happy for him.

Lorwin poured water into a clean drinking glass and passed it to Ahriman. The feeling of drinking cool water was invigorating and he drank until he nearly coughed. When he finished he looked at Leánder and his countenance changed suddenly to being very serious.

"We must talk," he began.

"Yes. Rest now a little while longer and when you're ready we will discuss everything."

Ahriman nodded and they left him to rest.

*   *   *

That day was a day of many revelations. Dark clouds had gathered and it was raining as many brave men gathered in Leánder's hall. They sat in a circle around an open stone hearth while Ahriman explained his adventure and then the vision the Enemy had shown him. He explained everything according to what he saw, leaving out nothing. As he did so, fear crept in like the cold rain and began to grip those who listened. At length, he finished his tale and he took his seat among them.

The men were silent as they considered his words and the words of the Enemy. As the rain pattered against the stone outside and the fire glowed, deep creases appeared on the faces of many of the men as they struggled to understand the possibilities. Nothing like this had ever happened before and they were at a loss. Finally, having resolved the issue in his own mind, Leánder stood and every eye suddenly fixed on him as he walked toward the fire. He starred into the flames for a short moment as he considered his words.

"Brothers," he began gently, "Men of the Light," he said stronger. "The meaning of these words are hidden from me, yet it is clear that an enemy is upon us and he brings evil and darkness. Even so, do not let yourselves be drawn into fear for we are children of Light Enduring. We were made from eternal strength and goodness, fearsome ourselves, and have not been ignorant of danger. We were told from the beginning that we must be vigilant against evil, though we did not know then what it was. Now it is here. We must be men of courage and trust that Light Enduring will not abandon us in our time of need. He is stronger than any darkness. He is wiser than any plan we could imagine. It is in Him we must trust, and commit to him our faith and honor. We must seek him first, and then act according to his command." He finished and took his seat once more.

The faces in the room were now a mixture of courage and fear. His words had penetrated their minds, but not all hearts were moved. Another was about to speak, but as he began to stand Ahriman rose and strode to the center, first looking at Leánder, then to the others.

"My brother's words are true. We should be encouraged that the Light will not abandon us in our time of need. But if I may encourage you toward one end, it would be to act swiftly and strike down this Enemy as quickly as possible before his power has a chance to spread and bring about this calamity. If we do not, rest assured our days of peace will be over and darkness will consume Alária. I propose that we raise an army so grand and fearsome that any evil will flee before it so that our borders remain secure."

"Here-here!" said many of them, finding encouragement in his words.

"I must advise caution, my brother," spoke Leánder. "We must consult the Light before setting off on such a quest. The consequences are far too great to risk rushing into the unexpected."

"I agree brother," replied Ahriman. "And that is why we shall wait upon the Light while we raise our army. I am confident that He shall answer us before it is completed."

Another man now spoke up, "Light Enduring is not subject to the times set forth by men. If in His wisdom he tarries longer than it takes for us to build our forces, what then? Will we raise our banners and set out on our own?"

"We will not be alone for we will always have each other. And as children of the Light I trust that He is always with us even as He is now and will guide us on our way whatever we choose," said Ahriman.

"In your words I hear wisdom, but in my heart I...I sense danger. In raising an army I feel a deep sense of foreboding in my soul," spoke Leánder. Many of the men near him also nodded in agreement. Ahriman would not be dissuaded however, and the majority vote ruled in favor of creating an army.

The first fighting force for the purpose of war was to be created. Undaunted, Leánder still convinced many of them to wait, for a time, until they had consulted the Light. This displeased Ahriman greatly as he longed to set out against their enemy as quickly as possible. The visions he had suffered caused a fear inside him which tore at his soul, yet he kept this hidden from his brother and the council.

In the days that followed, word was sent throughout all Everfall and the surrounding countryside. Men turned out by the thousands to begin the preparations for war. Leánder, however, spent much of his time alone seeking the guidance of Light as he walked the paths of the forest. Days turned to weeks and weeks turned into months.

The city was transformed as men worked day and night to mold steel and make armor and fighting weapons. They bent all their creative genius toward their various arts and the splendor of their first soldiers was a marvel to them all as they stood shining in the sun in their glorious armor. The young men standing beside their fathers in full battle array and shining in the sun were an inspiration to them all.

They impressed even Leánder, who still could not shake his apprehensions about such a force. He contented himself with solemn walks through the paths of the forest as he sought to allay his anxious thoughts.

Many had turned to him for guidance and direction and vowed to follow him whether he decided to stay in

Everfall or go off to battle this nameless foe. Each day he walked farther and farther until he could no longer hear the sound of training which was now a daily occurrence just outside the city wall. Upon returning from one of these lonely walks, he met his brother along the pathway leading to the city. Ahriman explained the organization of the men who had volunteered and how he had broken them down into battalions, regiments, companies and individual squads. He explained the role of the commanders and the captains and how each component worked together or even separately if they had to. He seemed very pleased with his work, yet something was not quite right.

"All this time," began Ahriman, "we have trained and made weapons. We have grown strong and no adversary can match us in strength, yet you do not approve and spend your time away from us."

Leánder considered his words as he was never one prone to speaking rashly. "Brother, we face an enemy far greater than any of us have dared to imagine. You have trained well and have become fearsome indeed, yet I have a foreboding in my heart I cannot explain. I fear that this will all lead to ruin and your own downfall if you set out upon this quest now."

"I do not understand you brother," replied Ahriman. "You speak of this danger yet you do nothing about it. You can feel it coming just as I can. In the air, in the water, even in the sunlight. Everything is tainted with some far reaching evil and we cannot stand by and let it destroy everything we have come to hold dear."

"I am with you on that," Leánder replied, looking into the eyes of his brother as they walked slowly on, "even still, I wish to hear from the Light what we are to do. Perhaps there is some strategy or insight we should know before rushing off into uncertainty."

"The only uncertainty, brother, is whether you will come with us. Your presence would greatly encourage the men... and me."

There was a long, heavy pause. "I cannot. Not until I have heard from the Light. When I do, I will do as He commands, for there is no victory without Him."

"This is true, yet His voice has been seldom heard in recent years," said Ahriman in a low tone. "Seek Him out and tell me what you find. But do it quickly. We set out at the onset of spring, seven days from now."

"He will speak to us in His own time, brother," said Leánder gently, placing his hand on Ahriman's shoulder. They emerged from the dense forest along a hillside facing the city and there Leánder's gaze fell on an impressive sight. There before him was every volunteer; training and exercising, learning orders and commands, and carrying banners of numerous shapes and sizes. In all, more than twenty thousand men had come from the surrounding countryside to rally behind the call of Ahriman. Now that their day of departure was close at hand they trained even harder. Their strength and beauty touched Leánder deeply, yet there was still something which bothered him. Something out of place he could not quite grasp, and this darkened his spirit.

*　　　　　　*　　　　　　*

The days came and went quicker than the summer tide and on the dawn of the seventh day the forces of Ahriman gathered together in the square beneath the White Tower in full battle attire. Their silver armor and shields mirrored the sun. Their spears were so numerous the wooden shafts looked like a leafless forest among the men. Tall banners waved in the morning air identifying each company, named after the captain's family who led it. They were awesome to behold and Ahriman looked on them from a balcony mid-way up the tower then addressed them. He spoke of their courage and bravery. He spoke of the good things which awaited them after their victory and how they would be home within a year.

One year. When Leánder heard that his face fell as he listened. He felt a sense of foreboding that he would never see many of his friends again and many more would be much, much longer in returning...if they returned at all. Some vast evil awaited them, of that he was certain, yet he didn't have the words to convince them. His pleas fell on deaf ears as they answered Ahriman's call. Many joined for adventure, others out of a sense of duty, others still out of loyalty to Ahriman whose words were like a spring of encouragement with the promise of valor and honor. Whatever their reasons, they were going and there was nothing Leánder could do about it.

The city gate was opened wide and the long precession began to march out into the unknown at the heralding of women and falling petals. There were many tears shed that day as they waved goodbye, little knowing that for most of them it would be the last they would ever see of home. They marched out in all their glory. At their head was

Ahriman, riding tall on a dark horse. As he passed through the city, Leánder was waiting for him. He stood beside the road and met the gaze of his brother as he rode by slowly. Their eyes met, and he lifted his hand to Ahriman and they grasped arms firmly. Ahriman saw clearly the anguish in his brother's eyes though he tried not to show it. In that brief second he wondered if Leánder was right and if this was all just a fool's errand, but he was already committed. There was no turning back now and they both new it. Neither one said goodbye. Neither one said 'I'll miss you' or 'I love you brother.' Leánder did not say 'do not go,' nor Ahriman 'come with me,' yet in that one brief look it was all said in their eyes. Then it was over.

The precession moved on and they lost each other's hand. Ahriman turned his face to the horizon and Leánder looked on after him. He stood there for a long, long time as soldier after soldier passed by. Yet they were not just soldiers. He knew almost every single one by name. There had been time to know each person. To be familiar with them and love them. Such was their time...

Finally, as the last one passed, Lorwin appeared at his side. Taking his hand in hers, she led him inside where, to his astonishment, a large crowd of people had gathered and were waiting for him.

"They are here for you," spoke Lorwin softly into his ear.

A large man with a friendly face stepped out in front and spoke loudly so that all could hear.

"We follow the house of Leánder and where you go we will follow," he said.

"My friends," began Leánder, holding back his tears,

"as long as we have each other we have more than enough and need not go anywhere. But our departed brothers may soon need our help and so I implore you to be ready for anything the future may bring."

"We will go wherever Light Enduring leads you," someone said, and many shouted in agreement.

"Go home now..." spoke Leánder softly.

*   *   *

The city seemed empty in the days which followed. The streets were silent in the absence of hammering blacksmiths and training soldiers. Women did not look up from the ground as they walked along in silent longing. Leánder continued to seek the Light during his walks in the evening, yet his heart was no longer in it. He worried for his brother and wondered what would become of him and those who followed. There were times he was angry, sad, or lost somewhere in the mist between. Why did Light Enduring not answer him? Why was He silent when he needed Him the most? *I do not understand*, thought Leánder. His faith seemed to run all but dry as those who remained looked to him for answers he did not have.

Finally, after many weeks, he was walking along a path now well-trodden by him and was passing by the place where he first met his beautiful bride. It was late in the evening and seemed to be much the same as on that day he met her as she sung her praises to her King. *The King...Light Enduring...* Leánder shook his head darkly and clenched his fists.

"I don't understand!" he shouted into the darkening

woods, suddenly giving way to his frustration. "You said you'd be there for me!" No one answered. Only the steady babbling of the stream and the chirping of crickets met him. He felt the last embers of his faith begin to flicker out. He lowered his head and ran his fingers through is hair, raising his face toward the evening sky. It was then that he noticed the first of the fireflies begin to illuminate the shadows with their warm light. Soon it was followed by another and another. As he watched, the entire forest was illuminated with their gentle light, twinkling quietly as they silently called out to one another. Had it not been for his overwhelming sense of abandonment, he would have thought the sight was beautiful, but such emotion was lost to his darkened heart. He let his face fall to the ground and he closed his eyes.

He felt something against his hand and he opened his eyes. There on his right hand was something unexpected. A firefly had landed on his finger. As he looked, he saw that it was much different from the rest. Instead of burning with a yellow light, it glowed with a brilliant blue, something he had never seen before. It blinked out and disappeared.

Then, across some distance in the forest, among the countless yellow fireflies illuminating the twilight, he noticed it again. It burned with its bright blue light and then faded into the darkness once more. This stole his thoughts as he had never seen a blue firefly before and his curiosity got the better of him. He walked toward where he had seen it, but it was gone. Suddenly, he saw it again a little further off and he followed after it. He followed its blinking light as it made its way up the stream toward a shadowy crevasse which disappeared behind great boulders.

As Leánder passed beyond the rocks and into the darker shadows he felt a cool breeze of air gently pass. It was much colder than usual, revealing his breath and chilling his skin. The firefly seemed to glow brighter in the cool air however, and it seemed strangely attracted to it as it flew towards its source. As Leánder walked along the stony ground the narrow, a rocky crevasse opened to reveal a great wall of moss and foliage hanging from the cliffs. The firefly glowed again and then disappeared into the leaves. Leánder thought at first that there was nothing but stone behind the tangle of foliage but as he reached his hand through the leaves and parted the vines, a pale silver light shone through onto his face. Amazed, he parted the vines further and felt frosty air wash over him followed by drifting snowflakes which quickly melted as they passed into the warm forest. Stepping through, he found himself looking down a long rocky corridor and a faint light beyond.

The blue firefly he had followed illuminated the walls as it traveled down the tunnel and was soon followed by many more as they became disturbed by his foot falls. Emerging on the other side, Leánder came out into a midnight clear, standing upon a low precipice which led down to a gentle snowy plain and a large starlit lake. Beyond, a grand forest lay caught in the middle of winter with snow lying heavy upon the tree branches. *A single moon,* he thought looking up. Something glittered upon the lake and as it did, Leánder was suddenly surrounded by the blue fireflies as they swirled around him and then slowly drifted down and across the plain. They led him to the shore where the snow gave over to an icy shore. In the middle of the lake, an island of stone waited for him with something shimmering in the moonlight on its top. Looking around at the sky above and the still reflection of the stars below, it looked as though he was standing at the edge of a sea of stars. If he were to simply step out from the shore, he felt as though he would float out among them.

Just then, a bright blue firefly parted from its fellows and flew past him over the lake toward the island, beckoning him to follow. He stepped out cautiously into the water. He felt the freezing water soak through the leather of his shoes but it was not entirely unpleasant. Although it was cold, he found it shallow and he slowly walked out into it.

The reflection of the stars was disturbed by his wake as he made his way. Climbing up to the top of the stone island he saw the firefly land on something before buzzing off. Drawing nearer, he saw it was the hilt of a sword standing upright, the end of its blade buried in the rock. Behind him, the firefly flew slowly to the top of a large rock hidden in shadow and looked down upon Leánder as he approached the sword. Without a sound and as smoothly as the moonlight glistened off the still water, it glowed faintly and took her true shape, unnoticed by Leánder. She sat silently and studied him with careful eyes.

Leánder took in the sight of the sword. Who placed it here he did not know, but somehow he felt he was meant to find it.

It was of magnificent design, unlike any other. Its smooth and mirrored surface shimmered with the night sky as it stood out against the sea of stars. As he gazed upon it, the view held a heavy weight of significance but the meaning was lost to him. Perhaps, somehow, it was a sign of things to come. He hesitated as he thought, but then approached slowly. Just then, he suddenly felt as though he was being watched.

He turned, and there before him in the shadows was a large pair of eyes reflecting the moonlight.

"Who are you?" he asked quietly, not knowing what to expect.

The eyes blinked, and for a moment there seemed to be only darkness. But then the two reflections of the moon returned like the burning of two candles.

"One who has waited long..." came the voice. It was that of a woman, feminine yet strong.

"For what?" asked Leánder perplexed.

There was another moment as the eyes studied him.

"For the Light to reveal the King of Alária."

"You speak of the Light, yet you conceal yourself in darkness. Who are you?" he asked again.

The eyes closed again and again there was only darkness. Then, there in the shadow something began to glow quietly. Like small blue streams of liquid light, a shape began to form, first at the shoulders, and then above and below as her fullness took shape. The pale blue light emanating from her skin illuminated the surrounding shadows. Sitting there upon a stone was a creature he had never seen before. She had the appearance of a woman, but her pale blue skin and large delicate wings revealed that she was something much different. She wore a simple white cloth which covered her ornately tattooed skin and a dark belt with a short dagger at her side. At her full height, he thought she would barely come up to his waist, yet when she reopened her eyes there was a fierceness there he hoped not to experience.

"I am Fáylínn," she said. "I and the other FáLlűmin have been the stewards of Ethália since the beginning. We heard the voice of the Light and have prepared that which He has instructed," she said, gesturing to the sword.

"Ethália?" he asked. "How far have I come from my own country?"

Fáylínn looked up to the sky and pointed toward a bright green star hanging silently against the backdrop of night. "That is your home," she said softly. "Yet in time to be, this will be also."

"You speak of the doom my brother has foretold, when Alária will be no more. Do you not?"

"I do. But the door between our worlds *must* be defended. If it is not, and evil finds its way here, none will escape."

Leánder turned and looked at the blade. It was impressive indeed, but then he sighed heavily. His face fell, his dark emotions returning.

"I have lost much in recent days. I could not keep my brothers from departing, nor do I know how to comfort those who stay. The strength and peace I once felt is gone. The Light... I have not heard His council in a long time," he said with heaviness.

"It is not with your ears that you must hear," she said. He looked up and realized that her mouth did not move as she spoke the words.

"How can this be?" he asked with a surprised tone.

In his mind he could hear her words. "We are so much more than what we see." She looked up at the moon. "Even the moon in all its glory shines only with the light from the sun. So are we, as we shine with the light of the Great One. This you cannot see with your eyes, just as you cannot see the wind as it blows through the trees. Yet the wind is there. He is all around us in all things. In the sky, the tree, the rock, the water." She paused and returned her gaze to him. "The sword is forged from metal from both our worlds. Heated in a crucible hotter than dragons' breath and hammered with a force stronger than the mountains. Yet for all its finery, it is only a symbol of what is already within you."

"A symbol?" asked Leánder not understanding.

"Sometimes a man needs a symbol to bring out the strength within him. Let this one be yours," she said gently.

He turned back to the sword and moved toward it. Behind him Fáylínn faded once more to a small blue light and flew off into the dark forest leaving him alone once more. He looked at it sidelong, wondering. He reached out to grasp it, yet as his fingers tightened around the handle everything became very, very still. Time itself seemed to stop.

Images suddenly flooded his mind and he felt as though he were floating above where he stood. He saw the ground fall away from him and the silver clouds above rush past in a cold wind as he was catapulted into the sky. The stars seemed crisp and clear and he found himself looking down on two worlds, each hanging like a green and blue sapphire against black velvet. Somehow, he knew one was his home, the other was where he had just stood, and that he had crossed the gap between the two. Many other visions were shown to him also. Some things that were. Some things that are. And some things yet to be...

*　　　　　　　*　　　　　　　*

A colored leaf lighted on his face as he awoke. He found himself lying in the forest, his clothing clean and his body rested as if he had had the most wonderful night of sleep. He felt a weight upon his chest and, looking down, found something wrapped in a long cloth of dark purple velvet beneath his folded hands. He stood and the cloth fell away. There in his hand was the sword from his vision. He heard a faint tone from it as his lifted the blade as though it sang to him. He looked at it as though remembering something from a dream.

Starring at it, he pondering the visions that still lingered in his mind and weighed in his thoughts. Eventually, he would write these things down in a book and it would become of great value. For now however, he would give this powerful gift a name.

"Dorlimere," he said softly. He held it in his hands feeling the cool metal. "Dorlimere-*Sisu*...A light in the darkness to overcome all evil."

*　　　　　　　*　　　　　　　*

When he returned to the city, Lorwin was waiting as

well as a small crowd of people who were about to begin a search for him. They first showed their relief as they recognized him, but then they noticed the sword which he carried and their eyes grew wide. Many others stopped their work and looked on with wonder as he passed by. Leánder strode with confidence, tall and strong with the sun rising brightly behind him. It then dawned on Lorwin that she was no longer looking on her husband but on the Light's anointed. Her king. She bowed to her knee.

Leánder moved to lift her up but then stopped short as he perceived the crowd. To his amazement, many others knelt just as Lorwin and one by one so did everyone else. He did not know what to say and stood there at a loss.

Suddenly, someone from in the crowd shouted, "Our King! Our King at last!"

Not knowing what else to do, Leánder raised Dorlimere high and the people, awe inspired, cheered and rose to their feet welcoming him back. Confidence and hope washed over their faces as they perceived their leader. No longer would they be lost and confused. Leánder would be their king, and they would follow him.

III

In Tenébris

Into the Darkness

He ran through the night, sweat pouring from his body. His muscles strained and tightened with every motion but his heart drove him on, ever on. He had lost count of the days he had traveled. Numbers held no meaning to him anymore. *Home*. Only the thought of home drove him onward, and the fear that he may be too late to warn them. He paused briefly against the side of an aged tree and stole a gaze at the moons. They were bright and brilliant, shining defiantly against the blackness of night, and their light gave him hope. A light in the darkness.

He had traveled many times in the dark before, but this night felt different. Someone, something behind him had been stalking him in the darkness. For more days and nights than he could count he had stolen away from its silent hunting and he felt that he had put some distance in between him and it in recent days. But now, though he could not explain how, he perceived that it had gained on him and was closing in.

Why did it not just finish me off earlier? Why now? Why?! He wished he could scream. He wished he could just shout and yell as loud as he could and break the silence that stole away his courage and filled him with fear. *It could have done as it wanted so many other times, why is it now that it closes in?* He closed his eyes and gripped the tree tightly as fear took over.

The winter cold had come and gone seven times since he left in glorious exodus with Ahriman and the others. The *others*. They used to have names, each one of them. Now they were just dimmed faces in the memories of the past. They were glorious when they set out those many years ago. Glorious and strong. Brave men with a purpose and a single driving will lead by a man they loved and respected. They were devoted to Ahriman, their brother and leader. It was his strength of resolve and determination which drove them on and inspired them. They had vowed to follow him to the uttermost ends of Alária, and they had. They journeyed farther than any of them had ever dreamed. Over land and sea, through deserts of sand and ice, through mountains and wilderness. They risked it all and spent their lives in pursuit of the nameless evil which filled their hearts and promised doom upon them through the vision of Ahriman. It was for the love of their families and for the good land given them by Light Enduring Himself that they set out. Not for adventure, not for glory, but to stave off the end of all things. If only they knew then what he knew now, how different things would have been. They would have stayed with Leánder.

"Leánder..." he whispered to himself. That name now sounded more beautiful than any other. He was the one who kept his wits about himself when everyone else was becoming drunk with fear. He was steadfast and level and he never wavered when he said that he would wait on the Light for guidance. What was that guidance? What was that wisdom that Leánder waited for? Did it even matter? Nothing could have been worse than what befell the men who left. Of those thousands who left at the onset, now only he remained. The odyssey was beyond imagining and the evil lying in wait was more than could be believed. Images flashed through his mind of that fateful day. One winter had passed and another was upon them when they had come to the misty shores Ahriman had seen in his vision. It was a land of coldness and shadows. Even the air smelled stale and lifeless and it had made the men restless. They pressed on with courage however, determined to finish what they had begun.

The days had grown shorter and shorter until finally one morning the sun didn't rise at all. The stars were darkened and the men were seized with fear. There was talk of turning around, of starting back to Everfall, but Ahriman wouldn't have it. He led them on into the cold ice. As they marched the sound of their footfalls echoed off the mountains and cliffs calling out to them in the darkness. It was then that evil surrounded them. Darkness and its bodiless underlings gathered on either side of Ahriman and his men and despite their spears and shields, despite the sharpness of their swords; nothing they had could have prevented evil's plan. For the demon hands and feet were not of this world, they were spirit and perceived by the eye only as shadow.

Ahriman led his men by torchlight. His beard had grown long and he glared out from underneath a weathered brow. There was a stirring. Just beyond the firelight, yes, *there*. He narrowed his eyes to see farther into the dark and he suddenly realized that all was still, not even the men behind him breathed. Just then, the darkness beyond the torchlight began to close in. He thought at first the torch was going out but the light just could not penetrate the closing shadows. The men made a great circle with their torches and backed into each other until there was nowhere left to go.

Out of the darkness there was a soul-penetrating screech and the men could endure no more. Someone cried out for their invisible foe to show himself and many who hadn't already drawn their swords did so then. Finally, just when the darkness was upon them their courage melted and gave place to rising fear. The men broke ranks and began to flee in every direction. Ahriman called and shouted for order, but his orders were overcome by the sound of screams and the terrified cries of horrified men. In the faint light which remained, he witnessed his friends being drug off into the black by formless shadows only for their screams to be suddenly silenced. All was fear and panic and in that moment fear was his only ally and he used it to run back the way they had come. A torch had fallen from a man when he was pulled away by one of the creatures and this he now picked up as he dashed away as quickly as his feet could carry him.

He ran through the dark and felt many forms pass him, heard their screeches as they tore at their victims, but none laid a hand on him. By some miracle he had slipped away. He made his way back to the shore and readied a small boat they had towed behind one of their beautiful schooners. They had built truly magnificent ships for their voyage on the shores of Lanália and he hated himself for what he had resolved to do. He feared whatever evil had befallen them may try to use them in their pursuit of him and so he took no chances. He left those shores with the flames of the burning ships rising high behind him. He had felt back then that something may have followed him from that dreadful place, but he had ignored it then knowing that he was on his way home. He could not ignore it now. As he opened his eyes he looked at his hands and saw them buried in thick moss growing on the side of the tree. This he had not seen since he had left Everfall. He must be getting close. It suddenly dawned on him the intention of his pursuer.

It means to find the location of Everfall, and it has used me all this time to lead it there! I'm tired of running...I'm so tired...

"Damn it to hell!" he shouted aloud. He stumbled back from the tree into the moonlight and drew his sword, the only thing he had kept throughout all his great odyssey. It would be here, his final stand. He could never allow the creature to enter Everfall and if he couldn't stop it he would die trying.

He was in a small clearing surrounded by thick woods, but at least here he hoped to see the creature's shadow in the moonlight. He buried the point of his sword into the dirt in front of him and drew his torch. He had gotten used to not using it at night as not to give away his position but now he dared fate and welcomed a fight. Just then, in between the trees, he saw a shadow move, a shadow darker than the darkest night. It moved quickly from place to place along the ground and moved closer and closer.

The old fear began to rise in his soul and the hairs on the back of his neck began to rise. He always knew it was there, just behind him...following. But now, seeing it, he could barely keep from trembling. He fought down his thoughts and steadied himself. He readied the torch and his flint. The creature now moved directly toward him, slowly at first, but then faster as though it were beginning to run. Just when it was about a spear's length away, he struck the flint and the torch blazed to life. The creature halted and the man drew up his sword.

"Fight me coward!!" he yelled.

A quiet and dry disembodied whisper came from the shadow, "Darkness will have his way with you, yes, even the ones that are most dear to you."

"We shall see," he replied.

With that the fiend leapt into the light and he thrust with his sword. He felt a sudden pain but he knew that he too did not come away empty. There was blood on his blade and he himself was bleeding under his left arm. He heard the creature screech long and loud, just as the one did on that fateful night so long ago and he shuddered. It leapt at him and he thrust again. This time, all went black and he knew no more.

*   *   *

Morning came. As he opened his eyes, he saw the clear blue sky above him and the trees blowing in the wind. He was laying back on a crude gurney being held by tall, strong men. Men! His kinsmen! He wanted to laugh and cry and sing and lament all at once but he found that he could not speak. He was so tired he could barely open his eyes. He tried to speak but nothing came. Another man walking beside them saw him stir.

"I am Hemley, servant of King Leánder," he said kindly laying a hand on his chest. "You shouldn't speak. Try to rest."

The man was carried as relief washed over him. "I am Jädus..." he managed to say finally. "I'm home..."

IV

Abductiō de Lárwin

The Kidnapping of Lárwin

The years of Ahriman's absence became long and happy ones, yet the people of that time, even as the people of now, appreciated little the time they were given until it was gone. This was the case of many in the country of Lanália.

In those years, during the time Ahriman was just setting sail for the shores of Gorgon, Leánder and Lorwin were blessed with their most beloved gift, a daughter; their first born. As last names were not yet common to them as a means of showing relation, she was named Lárwin, similar to her mother.

As the years passed, she grew more and more akin in appearance to her mother with her slender, delicate features, lighter skin and long hair. Indeed, as she grew older, the only difference between the two was the color of their hair. Lorwin's was long and light, colored as the rays of the sun in the evening and Lárwin's was deep brown and auburn like the color of the autumn leaves which always fell there.

This was during the days of the First Men, before age and death infiltrated the bodies of those led astray. It was the unbroken communion of their spirits with Light Enduring which gave life to them and kept them fair as the years waxed. Leánder and Lorwin ruled as the first King and Queen and Lárwin followed after them. Her character was a beautiful mix of the two for she had her mother's calmness and voice which she used to sing to invisible Light Enduring, and she had her father's strength of will and tenacity. She looked up to them and respected them with love and humility and sought ways to better their growing city.

From an early age, Leánder would wrestle with her and teach her sword play (which he himself was just learning), and her mother would teach her to sing and to appreciate the knowledge she could learn if she just opened her eyes to the world around her. Honor and integrity became her shield and skill and knowledge was her sword.

As Lárwin grew, her training with her father became increasingly tougher. He was a loving man but he was also fierce and he brought the same out of her. He himself grew in skill with a sword as he practiced with his servants (of course, *servants* in those days were much different than servants of today. The word 'servant' implied a place of honor and of high rank in the social chain). These same men later would become men of renown, his first generals and captains in the Evealian Army. They knew that one day the skills that they were learning might indeed be used against the very same evil which seduced their people years before, and they shuddered at the thought, yet it was ever present in their minds. They practiced and as they did so, they developed shields, armor, and many others devices of combat which they thought may be useful. All these things Lárwin also learned, and on her twenty-third birthday, Leánder and Lorwin presented her with a full set of armor, the first set wrought with a newly discovered skill in metallurgy. It was incredibly lightweight, slender and formfitting, flexible in all the right areas, yet hard as tempered iron or folded steel. It covered her from head to foot, and in it she was exquisite and terrible at the same time. At her side was an equally wrought double edged sword fashioned after the image of Dorlimere, though shorter and fitting for her size.

"It's so light!" exclaimed Lárwin.

"I call it VolFerrum," said Leánder. "It's stronger than iron, yet not a burden to the wearer." As he spoke she picked up a leaf embroidered gauntlet. It felt as though it had no weight at all and she held it out with an open palm. Slowly, and to her amazement, she took her hand out from underneath it and watched as it floated there, suspended momentarily in midair before beginning a slow descent to the floor. Even Lorwin could not hide her shock and she too took in a deep breath of awe. There was a small sound as it touched the stone floor at Lárwin's feet.

"*How* did you accomplish such a thing?" spoke Lárwin finally, picking up the gauntlet and admiring it anew.

"Your entire set of armor is made of the same material. It was not hard to make once we ran the lightning through it," replied Leánder casually.

"*Lightning*?" repeated Lorwin, raising her eyebrow.

"Yes...of course catching *that* was much harder," he replied shaking his head bashfully. Suddenly blurred memories came to mind of a drunken bet he had made with his friend Bularius over a drink in the tavern one night. Leánder had boldly accepted, slamming down his glass on the bar. Someone had then pointed out that it might rain that night and so the bet was on. He remembered dim images as they stood on a random mountain peak during a lightning storm. Thunder and lightning crashed all around them as they waived giant metal poles up into the onslaught of rain in the drunken hope of actually *catching* lighting. Waking up from his stupor the next morning he found he was in the smithy near the White Tower and it was nearly noon. He looked around and suddenly heard noises coming from above, and there on the ceiling was Bularius wearing Leánder's breastplate!

"It's about time you woke up!" he had shouted. "I've been up here half the night! Get me down from here!"

Leánder scratched his head and looked up. "Bularius?" He wondered then just how much he had drunk the night before. The more he looked though, the more he realized that his friend was just floating there, pinned to the roof by some invisible force. Their adventure ended when Leánder tied a one hundred pound bucket of ore to the breastplate and Bularius came crashing down. The night came back as slurred images as his stupor wore off and that day Leánder gave up alcohol entirely.

It took weeks for him to duplicate what they had done that night but when he did the results amazed him. By passing light through the crystal he named Zánic Stone, he could change light itself into hard physical matter and cast it onto any object like a painter might use paint. Using a prism he discovered that different shades of light could be made into many common elements and some not so common. With the Zánic Stone he was able to mix colors of light and create the wondrous VolFerrum metal his daughter now marveled at. Of course, he was thankful he and Bularius were indoors at the time of their discovery and he shuddered to think of what may have happened if they had been outside when they conducted their original 'experiment' with the breastplate. He felt lucky that Lorwin did not inquire further.

"This is amazing," said Lárwin again as she danced about her room light as a feather.

"There is more that I need to show you...Come," he said.

He led them through the city and down to where the stone met the shore and the Great Sea beyond. There in the harbor was a vast ship under construction, but not with the regular sails they had seen on other ships. Its design and rigging was much different as it's 'sails' extended outward from the sides of the hull and stretched out with long fingers on both sides with a shining, deep blue metal thinly stretched in between.

"They look more like *wings* than sails!" said his wife as she took in the sight of it.

Leánder nodded. "They are the VolNarri and I call this one *Sacred Wind*. Her wings are made entirely of VolFerrum, just like Lárwin's armor but with one difference."

Lárwin took a step toward it and was utterly captivated by its beauty as she caught hold of its purpose. "It can *fly,*" she whispered.

"Not yet, but yes. It will when it is finished," said Leánder proudly. "We'll be able to navigate the world with ships like these when they are done. Hopefully, this will be only the first of many."

"My husband..." said Lorwin with a crooked smile.

As they walked along admiring all that Leánder had accomplished his mood began to grow somber.

"I know when you worry," spoke Lorwin softly.

"Yes," he said after a pause. He stopped his walk and drew his wife and daughter in closely. "There is more that I must tell you...I fear that there may be an enemy among us, and what I confide in you must be kept hidden at all costs."

"I have felt it too," replied Lorwin. Ever since Jädus arrived and told us of Ahriman's fate, I have felt a presence in the city yet I know not from where it comes."

"I trust Jädus, though not even he with what I am about to tell you. When our brothers left, I remained behind to seek the Light and inquire of Him what should be done about the coming darkness. He showed me a star low on the horizon and explained to me that it was another world, like this one. One we could flee too and escape Alária's doom. He revealed to me a doorway between our two worlds which is opened only once every thousand years when our two worlds are closest... and then only for a short time. My fear is that the creature that consumed my brother Ahriman will learn of this door and seek to use it...and pollute another world with its evil. We cannot permit this to happen. If the passage is breached, then there would be no escape. Forgive me, my loves, but that is why I have concealed this from you. That others may not hear of it as we spoke or otherwise coerce you into revealing its location until the preparations were finished."

"What *preparations*?" asked Lárwin full of concern.

"I have secretly constructed a gate to guard the doorway. One which only a handful of people now know about. It is strong and only the bearer of Dorlimere may open it to protect it from Darkness."

"How will people escape through it though if it has such a gate? How will they find it?" asked Lorwin.

"I have hidden a signal fire on the summit of the mountain above the gate. When the doorway is opened it will shine out with the same fire that burns in the White Tower so that all will be able to see it and come. When they do, the bearer of *this* sword will be there to ensure no evil passes."

They continued their walk along the shore. Eventually, they turned to lighter matters and chose to forget about anything evil for a time. Leánder slowed and let his wife and daughter walk ahead as they talked together. Seeing them there, walking along the sand with the waves at their feet and the sun in their hair, he took a deep breath and drank in the sight of them. He was a happy man indeed.

*   *   *

Deep under the rocky crags of Gorgon, however, Ahriman and his brood were growing restless.

"How long my Lord? How long until the assault on these... *Men*...?" asked Teivel, bowing low before the throne of Ahriman and nearly choking on the name of Men.

"Soon Teivel...very soon," replied Ahriman in his deep and powerful voice. I have spent many long days reaching out into the world and observing the doing of Man. Soon we will strike."

"Forgive me my liege, but he has proven to be patient and may refuse to leave his city. A battle there would prove to be...difficult."

"Yes...that is why I will draw him out into the open," he said raising his massive hand and clenching his fist, "...and crush him in the darkness..."

*   *   *

In the twenty-sixth year after the departing of the Ahriman (referred thereafter as A.L., Ahriman's Leaving, which marked the beginning of the first calendar), Lárwin walked alone through the forest outside the city. As she grew older, she took on the fierceness of her father, yet she craved to walk among the trees and seek solitude the way her mother had long before. She walked amidst the sounds of running water and singing birds and nothing brought her more joy than to take in the sight of the sun glinting off wet leaves after a summer rain.

Taking a seat on a smooth stone, she sat beside a stream in the wood and watched as a bird alighted on a nearby rock. The stately cardinal strode toward her confidently and if this were not unusual enough, upon reaching the edge of the stone stretched forth its wings and bowed. Rising once more it looked at her with a curious look as if expecting a reply and in her mind she could sense the creatures fervency as it reached out to her. He was a beautiful bird, yet Lárwin's heart sensed alarm in his countenance and she quieted herself to understand its meaning. As she looked into its large black eyes, feelings and images came into her mind and an uneasy disquiet descended upon her soul as she perceived his thoughts.

At the edge of the forest in the west near the coast, the locusts have stopped their nightly song. In the east squirrels and mice refuse to reveal themselves after the setting of the sun for fear of the dark...Something evil stirs in the forest. There was a pause and she suddenly heard the sound of rushing wind through the trees like the sound of the ocean and she turned to see the trees bending and swaying with it. When she looked back the cardinal was gone, having flown off into the tangled woods.

Lárwin pondered this in her heart. *The only evil this world has ever known is the vision of Ahriman*, she thought to herself. *I wonder if that is what draws near?* She emerged from the thin paths of the wood near her escort and found them waiting with horse and carriage just where she had left them hours before. They had been warned by the king not to let her too far out of their sight, but like everyone of that time, they had no fear of evil and Lárwin had grown into a quite capable woman, so they let her have her leave. As she approached she had a rather troubled look about her.

"My Lady?" began one, noting her concern.

"Take me to the palace at once," she commanded shortly but not unkindly.

"Yes my Lady."

They traveled back into the city proper and through the smooth, white stone streets of Everfall. It never ceased to take her breath away. The White Tower was burning its silent light against the evening sky and the trees were ablaze with a colorful glow. The stone buildings bathed in their radiance.

When she arrived the vast doors to the palace opened from within as her servants saw her coming. She walked down a long arched hall to the Central Chamber, once known as the Hall of Meeting where her Leánder and Lorwin were facing each other, both in light armor and swords drawn. They appeared still as statues as they stood in the slanting sunlight which poured through the high glass windows. Suddenly Leánder leapt toward Lorwin with a shout and skillfully lunged with his blade. Lorwin was too quick, however, and with one fell swoop she parried his attack and with an elegant twist and hidden move of her foot, she tripped him as he stepped back and she brought her own sword down just short of his neck, resting her blade there on his collar bone as she raised a curious eyebrow at him.

"What was that 'new move' you wanted to show me again?" she said, smiling down at him.

"I'll show you when I'm ready," he said tartly.

The door shut and its sound made them turn. There was Lárwin, standing at the edge of the hall watching them humorously.

"She beat you again, eh Father?" she said, raising her eyebrow. When she did, she looked much like her mother save for the color of her hair.

"I can only take that look from *one* of you today," said Leánder, still lying on the floor. He stood and noted something else in her eye. "But there is more to that look than you lead on my daughter. Tell me, what troubles you?"

How he was so perceptive she never knew, but she couldn't hide anything from him and she never tried. "I was in the forest when a cardinal came to me. I could feel his thoughts and sensed his fear. Something approaches in the forest."

Leánder crossed the hall to where one of his servants was waiting with a basin of water and a glass. Taking a long drink, he looked levelly toward a window, though his thoughts seemed much, much farther away. Finally, he looked back at her.

"Yes…I know. Ahriman draws near, and he will not be alone." He looked at his wife. "We must prepare."

Her gaze narrowed with seriousness and she nodded in agreement.

"We must hold council. Ruthial," he called to one of the servants, "call a council gathering tonight. I must meet with the commanders."

"Yes my king," said Ruthial with a bow. And then he departed.

Leánder turned his gaze back toward the window and his thoughts reached out to some impossible distance once more. He had been warned by the Light years before that evil would present itself and he must be prepared to discern it and to be on guard. It was not long after this that Jädus returned and told of the fate of Ahriman and his company. Lorwin had cautioned him then that perhaps it was Jädus himself who may be harboring some hidden evil as something in her soul was disquieted whenever she was in his presence, yet Leánder took pity on him as the sole survivor of that hellish nightmare and placed him among his servants. Since then he had risen through the ranks and had proven to be both wise and skillful in strategy and Leánder placed his full confidence in him. Still, Lorwin had her doubts. She concealed them out of respect for her husband.

"I have thought of a new word," he said finally with a quiet voice as Lorwin and his daughter drew near to him. At its sound, the hairs on that back of Lárwin's neck stood on end.

"War."

        *   *   *

Deep in the shadows of Gorgon, Ahriman had perceived the seeming weakness of Men and it enraged and disgusted him to think that they were chosen to bear *The Image*. He had also seen in his mind the bestowing of Dorlimere-Sisu to Leánder and this troubled him. He feared the power that was within the sword for he knew not its strength nor what it could do, yet what he did know disturbed him. He understood that it was meant to destroy him and the evil work he had begun. Of course not everything could be undone. Lies and deceit need only a start and then Men do a wonderful job at perpetuating them on their own. That is how he was able to grow his ranks and flourish in Gorgon's desolate wastes. He had sent his underlings out into the world disguised as men with supernatural abilities of magic and strength. Through them he convinced many more who had spread throughout the country of Lanália and even the new-found Southland to forsake their homes and travel to Gorgon where he made slaves of them. Despite his pride, he found that he needed them for labor and to carry on the menial tasks of his plighted realm and he became intoxicated with the power he held over them.

Not all was as he planned however, as Darkness had felt a change upon entering the body of Ahriman. He found that the longer he inhabited this fragile container the more he was bound by it and he knew that it would be only through a great sacrifice of power that he would be able to be parted from it again. Therefore he had given orders to his dark officers not to be careless with themselves, for if death came to the bodies they were inhabiting, then their spirits would be greatly diminished. It would require more power from him to sustain them if this happened. Darkness himself now felt constrained as he inhabited this wretched carnal body, yet he wore it like a prize as one would wear a tailored suit. He smiled as he reminisced. *It has been too easy*, Darkness thought to himself. Ahriman, the brother of Leánder had marched his entire army into the Gorgon winter to face him in battle. He was proud and defiant and that made his possessing that much more satisfying. He had surrounded them in the dark and before they even knew danger was upon them their fates were sealed.

"The authority you were given is now mine," he had whispered quietly before giving the order to attack. His demons screeched loud and unleashed violence without mercy. As for Ahriman himself, that was *his* prize, to be his to display upon himself. Darkness had placed his hands on Ahriman's shoulders and spun him around for all to see. He reached back and plunged his shadowy right arm into Ahriman's right arm and then his left arm into Ahriman's left. He then stepped into his legs and filled his chest and face wearing his body like a puppet or a crude suit. Ahriman blinked. The terrified and screaming faces of his loyal friends were the last thing he saw before his spirit was overcome by Darkness.

"Take who you will my children!" shouted Darkness through the voice of Ahriman. Then the other shadow creatures plunged into the screaming multitude and did the same to the others. They pushed aside the frightened spirits of the men and wore their flesh as one would wear poorly fitting clothing.

"From the beginning of time, Light has been our destroyer!" he shouted raising an enormous fist. "But no longer! Thanks to these brave and courageous men, who so *graciously* volunteered themselves by coming here, we can now go forth even in cursed sunlight with all authority and destroy the Light which corrupted the dark!" At this, gruesome cheers erupted and hundreds of disjointed bodies raised their hands in victory. It was a joyous night.

But now Darkness turned his thoughts to Dorlimere once more and his lust and fear was ignited. He craved to have the sword, to wield its power for himself if he could, and to be rid of its threat. He went so far as to have a sword like it in appearance made for him, though it paled in comparison for it was made by human hands and was only metal. He named it DarMir-Itah (in their tongue meaning *blade of darkness*) which he carried with mocking pride and the fear of it fell on many because of he who carried it. It still did not satisfy him though, and he greatly desired a trophy he could put on display. Something he knew would taunt righteous Leánder and mock him. He felt the taking of Dorlimere would do just that. Ahriman was not ready for open war just yet, however. He fancied the idea of revealing himself at full strength, marching against good men with their own brothers in broad daylight, but he knew that the numbers of men had increased greatly since his first deception and that he would need a great many indeed to accomplish this task. For the taking of the sword, then, he organized a stealthy plan. Now that he was bound to the earth through the body he wore, he could not simply fly there on his shadowy wings as he once did, and so he chose to use a creature most in appearance to himself in his glory. He gathered a great many of his underlings for the capturing of this beast, for none of his slaves could stand against one of these in its full fury.

They had fashioned massive chains for this task and wove them into an enormous net, the weight of which none could measure; indeed it took over thirty of his strongest to carry it upon their shoulders to where the beast lay in her den. The beast herself was a massive dragon, the first of her kind, and many of her kindred lived among the arid climes of Gorgon as they enjoyed its shady mountains and fed on the numerous sea creatures which surfaced around the coasts. They grew large and were awesome to behold.

The dragon they now hunted stood more than four times the height of a man, and from tip to tail was nearly seven times as long. Her muscles outmatched any other creature and her bones were stronger than bronze. Her armored scales were knitted tightly together; they were tough, able to turn the blade of any spear. Her tail trailed behind like a cedar tree and could crush a man without effort and from her mouth she could pour forth unquenchable flames. Not every dragon was as large or strong as she, yet some in later generations were, and they never forgot the treachery Ahriman now set in motion; for Ahriman did not know that the offspring of dragons retained the memory of their forbearers, so even though their numbers had always been few, from generation to generation they never forgot a thing. Especially this.

Ahriman stationed his underlings atop the mouth of the cave which they crept upon with the massive metallic net. They had bound the net with thick cloth to keep it from rattling and awaking the dragon. Now they undid their burden and poised to spring the trap. Ahriman himself walked boldly to the mouth of the den. He feared no darkness, for he himself was Darkness and he could see the dragon sleeping peacefully far back in the cave, escaping the rays of the morning sun. What he did fear, however, was the destruction of his body without which he had no authority or means to channel his power. Therefore he had clad it with armor, a massive plated suit which covered him from head to foot and encased his precious body in hardened metal. Darkness within Ahriman contained power beyond imagining, yet he coveted his prized body and wished to protect his investment. Only his face was exposed, yet his helm had a hinged visor which he could pull down in case the dragon decided to unleash her fiery fury upon him. He stood at her door and called.

"Dragon! Your master calls you!" boomed his powerful and arrogant voice into the cave, instantly waking the sleeping dragon.

There was a long pause and the sound of stirring within the cave. Then a deep, angered voice thundered from within. "I know no master save one, and you are not He," and with that two flames ignited in the dark and burned like torches as her eyes caught fire with fury.

Ahriman produced Dar-Mere, the light glinted off its dark blade as he called again, "I say again, your master calls you!"

The sound of rushing air entered the cave as the dragon took in a massive breath. There was another pause, and then suddenly, to the shock of those who stood above, a fiery inferno erupted from the mouth of the cave and consumed the sight of Ahriman in flame. Those who hid nearby reeled back from the heat and fear arose that their leader may be in peril. Before the flames had reached him however, he held out his hand and the fire parted around him so that not one hair on his head was scorched.

When the flames ceased, there stood Ahriman, as bold as ever, standing in the midst of melted rock, smoking glass and blackened dirt which had split apart from the heat. All was burned and smoking save for a tight circle around where Ahriman stood. He stepped forward now in defiance, challenging the dragon once more.

Seeing that her fire was not enough for this intruder, the beast now stalked forward and prepared to bring down her full weight on him. Stronger than any fire were the jaws and muscles of her body and her rage had only increased. As she stalked forward, a tremor went through the rocks and startled the underlings waiting to spring the trap. For a fleeting moment, Ahriman thought that maybe their fear may spoil the entire trap, but they kept quiet as the beast advanced. Clearing the mouth of the cave, she drew herself up to her full height and unfurled her massive wings. So great was the sight of her that even Ahriman drew back a step. At a signal, the trap was sprung. Before the dragon could escape, the heavy, iron-laden net fell down on top of her pinning her to the ground beneath its tonnage. She struggled violently but to no avail. Ahriman's horde piled on chain after chain and pounded each one to the stony ground with metal stakes. For hours she struggled, even spewing flames about her at times. Finally when her great strength was spent, she looked loathingly at Ahriman who stood at a distance.

"Kill me then, if that is your desire!" she panted.

"Kill you?" Ahriman replied. "I have no desire to kill such a beautiful creature. You have a power greater than any that walk this world. I only wish that you use it in my service," he said eloquently.

"Then you must surely kill me, for no dragon will serve *you*. I know the darkness that is within you."

"Yes...I was afraid you may say that. That is why this trap was not laid for you." As he spoke, a dark shadow crossed over the sun and it was then that the beast realized that it was not her that he wanted, but her offspring, a large yet adolescent male dragon who may yet be swayed by evil words. Ahriman quickly ordered his troops to bind the mouth of the dragon so that she could not speak before the other arrived.

Seeing his mother chained to the ground surrounded by evil men, the younger dragon was enraged. He swooped to the ground landing heavily a little ways from where Ahriman stood. The dark blade in Ahriman's hand pointed down toward the chest of his mother. No other being would he have feared, but there was his mother, the strongest of dragons, bound by this man and he suddenly feared his blade. He stalked now furiously to the left and to the right, pacing quickly, never taking his eyes off of Ahriman.

"Do you understand what I say, dragon?" shouted Ahriman.

The dragon remained silent as he paced, and fire was rolling in his eyes.

"Do you understand *this*?" shouted Ahriman, shaking his downturned sword and digging its point into the scales of his mother.

"I understand you perfectly well arch-fiend!" boomed the dragon, ceasing his pace and squaring his fierce gaze upon Ahriman. Taking a step forward he continued, "I am Fanglóriun, Prince of Dragon's, and since the day you entered this realm I have not killed any of you for your bodies bear *The Image*, but that vow no longer stands and your life is forfeit."

"Is it my life or *hers*?" replied Ahriman, and with that he plunged his blade into the scales of his mother. Only his power and blade could have turned her scales and horror

filled Fanglóriun as he heard his mother growl in pain. Ahriman spoke quickly, "The wound is not fatal if it is treated quickly, and the only one who has the power to treat her is me. Do I have your attention Fanglóriun?"

"You have it," hissed Fanglóriun through clenched teeth.

"I require your willing obedience in my service for a short time. After which you may go as you please."

"What is it that you require of me?" he hissed.

"I need to be taken across the sea and back again in haste. I must retrieve something that belongs to me."

"Is that all?" growled Fanglóriun.

"That is all. When we return, your mother will be healed and you can go on your way. Do we have an accord?"

A dragon's word is his bond and Fanglóriun, young as he was, knew that he could not break an oath once his word was given. Looking at his dying mother the fire went out in his eyes and he slowly hung his head. Despite the foreboding evil he sensed was yet to come, he felt he had no choice.

At length, he finally spoke. "We are agreed."

"Good. We shall set out immediately. Tievel," he said turning to his second in command. "No one can lay hold of Leánder's sword except for me alone, therefore I must go. I give you full authority while I am away. Do not disappoint me."

"Yes my liege," said Tievel reverently, bowing low.

Fanglóriun struggled against his own will as he let Ahriman's armored body climb upon him like a parasite. They set out quickly to the west, both eager to return.

Lárwin stood at her window admiring the stars as they shone down on Everfall. It was an amazing thing how the starlight lit up the sky despite the glow from the city below and the fire burning from the white tower. The city had grown quickly and sprawled for miles in every direction. There had been a watch set around all the borders since the day the Cardinal spoke to her. News indeed had spread of kidnappings and abductions in the outer lands beyond the city and further out in the hill country. Something sinister was brewing and everyone could feel it.

It all seems so distant though, she thought to herself as she gazed out into the starry night. She was as at peace wondering why anyone would wish evil in such a beautiful world. She withdrew from the arched, stone window and let the night breeze follow her in. She loved to sleep with fresh air all about her and to wrap up in warm, soft blankets made by her mother. She pulled herself under them now as she lay down to sleep. Just before blowing out her candle she stole a look at her splendid armor displayed across the room. It was truly marvelous and she felt powerful just looking at it. No one, save perhaps her father and mother, truly felt the gravity of what lay before them. She blew out the candle and laid herself down to sleep which came upon her quickly.

Across the palace, King Leánder and Queen Lorwin were already fast asleep, lying close together in their starlit chamber. Dorlimere-Sisu and their own armor were also displayed at the far end of the room. Suddenly Dorlimere's blade began to shine with a blue flame from within its sheath. Its cool light burned slowly at first, casting a gentle blue glow into the dark room. Then, as though its anger were kindled, its flame erupted and engulfed the entire length of the blade and sheath. Though it burned silently, its wild light now illuminated all the room, stirring those who slept.

*   *   *

Ahriman rode through the night on the back of Fanglóriun toward the sleeping city of Everfall. No one here knew evil nor the devices he had contrived in his mind. His sole intention was to steal the very heart of their leader by taking his most beloved object, Dorlimere-Sisu, the hope of good men. He had perceived it from afar with his searching thoughts, and now he felt its presence stir as he approached. He would have to be quick. If his enemy were to awake before he could reach the sword, all may be lost. As he approached however, his far seeing eyes beheld a new thing he did not expect.

Through the dark miles that lay between, he could see through an open window a woman, pure and dignified, sleeping soundly. Her innocence pierced him and he felt a lust for her ignite in his black soul. *So this is the daughter of my enemy...* he thought to himself wickedly. *Perhaps, if the sword becomes out of reach, there is another thing worth taking which is just as valuable.* He smiled at this and imagined taking her anyway as a trophy and what a hurtful blow it would be. Fanglóriun also felt the presence of the sword, and now that he saw the brilliant city fast approaching, his heart sank further at being oath-bound.

*   *   *

Leánder was fast asleep and dreamed. He dreamt of a young boy having the courage to stand up against an unruly father. He felt connected to the boy somehow and in his dream he stood behind him in his armor holding his drawn sword. There was a terrifying expression on the face of the boy's father at the sight of him. He said something to the man, though he could not remember what, yet it felt incredibly real as though he were actually there. Before he could take a step or utter another word, a mist closed in about him and all was dark save for a pale blue light. Without warning, he heard a distant scream down the hall from a familiar voice. Then he awoke.

When he opened his eyes, he saw the entire room filled with the blue radiance of the burning sword.

"An enemy approaches..." he whispered into the silence. "*Ahriman!*" Leánder jumped from his bed and ran to the sword. He quickly gripped the handle and drew it from its sheath and its full brilliance illuminated the room, startling Lorwin. "Awake!" he said earnestly. "Our enemy approaches."

Lorwin said nothing as she wrapped her gown about her and reached for her own sword. Leánder had only enough time to buckle his sheath and lash his grieves when he heard a scream, the same scream he had heard in his dream. It was his daughter and something was in her chamber. They both ran as fast as they could. Forgetting all else they made for her room. They found the heavy oak door locked from within but that did not stop her father. Even without the power of the sword, he plowed his shoulder against the wood and it shattered before him like glass. They rushed in.

By the light of Dorlimere they could see there had been a struggle in the now empty room. Just then they heard movement outside the window on the terrace in the darkness. Being outside the light of Dorlimere, they could only see blackness stretching against the night as massive wings unfurled against the stars.

"Forgive me, *Image-Bearer,*" came a deep, sad voice. And with that the creature launched itself into the air, cracking the masonry and knocking down both Lorwin and Leánder with a powerful blast of air as its wings took flight.

They had never seen the likes of the creature that now bore away their daughter, but their anger and grief outweighed their amazement. The sword had awoken Leánder and warned him of Ahriman's coming. Yet despite this, he was able to steal one of the only other things Leánder held of value. Lorwin looked into the eyes of her husband as the light of Dorlimere faded to a glimmer.

*   *   *

There was much council held in the halls of Everfall that night. Bitter rage and torment sought to tear Leánder apart from the inside as he pondered on what his course of action should be. And there *would be* action. Despite his grief, Leánder encouraged himself with the words the Light had spoken to him and it gave him strength. Over the next several days word spread quickly from person to person through all the surrounding towns and villages as to what happened and the people readied themselves in expectation of the King's resolve.

V

Virtus et Venia

Of Courage and Grace

A gentle spring rain steadily fell from a cloudy, morning sky as the Evealian Army gathered behind Leánder's soaring banners. They stood at attention; solid, disciplined, ready to face the unknown...or so they believed. Their boldness was strengthened by their king's resolve and their own loyalty to rescue one of their own. The abduction of Lárwin sent shock and outrage throughout the land and thousands gathered to offer themselves in service to the king. There was not enough time to outfit everyone with VolFerrum armor and *Sacred Wind* was weeks from being completed. Leánder ordered they be clad in traditional armor much the same as Ahriman's army long before.

This was not just *his* fight, he realized soon after, for nearly everyone had fallen victim to this evil when their loved one's did not return with Ahriman years before. Now they sought to meet this enemy in battle. It had been a full seven days since Leánder witnessed his daughter being carried off into the night on the back of that fearsome beast, and he had slept little not knowing what dark plans Ahriman had in store for her.

"The men are ready," said Bularius walking up confidently behind his king.

Leánder stood arrow straight looking out from the city gate. He paused, then turned his head and spoke over his shoulder. "There are some that are not willing to leave the city unprotected," he said, turning and facing Bularius. "Ahriman himself had as many men and they never returned. We do not know the devices of the enemy, and so I hesitate to commit our full force and leave the city vulnerable."

"But we have something that Ahriman did not," replied Bularius, putting a hand on Leánder's shoulder. "We have Dorlimere-Sisu…and we have *you*."

"We have Light Enduring," replied Leánder, placing his own hand on his friends shoulder. "He is the one who holds the victory."

"Indeed sir. What are your orders?"

"We will only take five thousand to test the enemy's strength. The remaining force will stand guard at Everfall and await my instructions. We leave immediately."

"Yes sir!" replied Bularius boldly. He turned and marched to an awaiting company of officers to carry out the king's orders.

"Light Enduring," whispered Leánder quietly to himself. "I thank you that you are always with me and that your hand is always with those who trust You." He put his hand on the hilt of Dorlimere as he spoke. "May this sword of mine save and not destroy. May it mend and not tear. Let this blade heal those who have suffered, but crush and destroy those who rebel against you. You are my rock. You train my hands for war and my fingers for battle. You are my great love. My fortress. My shield in whom I take refuge."

Suddenly, as if waiting for that very moment, the glory of the morning sun broke out from behind the clouds and bathed them all in brilliant sunlight. It shone upon the faces of the soldiers, his friends, and sparkled against their armor as it dripped with the fresh rain. Just then, a long, loud blast from a battle horn rang out and signaled the beginning of the march. Leánder had no idea how long they would be on the march or how far Ahriman had carried his daughter, but he knew that dark things lurked in the forest beyond the Evealian Mountains and the plains which lay before the sea. He hoped that his force was large enough to draw his enemy out of hiding and into an open attack and perhaps learn from a captive where they had taken Lárwin. He took a step forward and began the long march with those behind following. As he passed the gate, there was Lorwin, shining in all her glory with many of the woman as they waved goodbye. She however, did not wave nor smile, and neither did he. She was standing tall and straight and as he passed their eyes met with a level gaze. In that moment it was written in their eyes all they wanted to say.

Goodbye my love.
Come back to me.
And with that he marched out of the city.

*   *   *

The scout returned, out of breath and cursing himself for taking this frail body long ago, and he knelt before his commander.

"Men are marching from the city my lord," he said.

"The only lord is Lord Ahriman!" replied Teivel, kicking the soldier to the ground. "How many and which direction?"

"Forgive me commander. Five thousand men and they march east along the road Lord Ahriman took," he picked himself up and continued. "They will be here within a day at their present speed."

"I see. I value your watchfulness Durn. It will not go unrewarded," spoke Teivel as he considered the report. *This will be my chance to prove to Lord Ahriman my skill and power in battle. Besides, since Lord Ahriman is resting on his throne in Gorgon, what is stopping me from taking the body of Leánder himself and casting off this wretched one I now possess?* He cut off this thought quickly though, for he knew that capturing Leánder alive was his lord's prize and would be deserving of a great reward back in Gorgon. He turned, and set his mind to drawing up a plan to ensnare these men. He hesitated to simply surround them in the darkness and overwhelm them the way they had Ahriman since now they inhabited physical bodies. Whoever let their body fall by the sword would have to report back to Lord Ahriman why they were deserving of another body since becoming separated from it meant a sacrifice in power from the spirit of Darkness, and *that* he would not lightly endure.

*   *   *

It was fast approaching evening on the third day of the march when Leánder ordered that the trumpet sound signaling them to stop and make camp. It had been a long three days and he was looking forward to a night of rest when up ahead he thought he noticed something. Behind him, his men were beginning to spread out and drop their heavy gear in the hope of much needed rest, but as he peered deeper into the forest he could not help but feel a presence, as though something, or someone, were looking back at him.

"Shall I post a guard sir?" asked one of his officers politely.

There was a long silence as Leánder stretched his senses out into the air trying to understand why he was feeling some inner alarm.

*   *   *

"Do you think he sees us?" whispered Durn as he peered through the dark trees at Leánder's forces.

"No," whispered Teivel. He had full confidence in his preparations as his own forces lay concealed in the dense shrubbery of the forest on either side of Leánder's men. He would wait until his men had made camp and were bedding down before he launched his attack. It would be quick, simple; an easy win. His master would be most pleased.

*   *   *

"Sir?" inquired the officer.

Leánder raised his right hand quickly to silence him as he listened. "Signal the men."

"I do not understand…" he said, but did not have enough time to finish his sentence before Leánder cut him off.

"Signal the men captain, tell them to arm themselves. Quickly!"

*　　　　　　　　*　　　　　　　　*

Durn shot a nervous glance at his commanding officer as he watched Leánder give a signal to one of his men. Suddenly a deafening blast from a battle horn awoke the quiet evening air and Leánder's army began rearming themselves. *Teivel's plan may not prove to be so easy,* he thought.

*　　　　　　　　*　　　　　　　　*

The men heard the battle horn ring out and they immediately rearmed themselves.

"Fall in line!" cried Bularius' strong voice above the din. He stood proudly with his chin up and shoulders back as he appraised their movements and hoped that his undaunted air would inspire them. He rested the palm of his hand on the hilt of his undrawn sword, Ténmei,' a uniquely curved blade whose name meant the will of God. He considered it for a moment. *May it ever be so,* he thought to himself, finding strength in his resolve.

As the men arranged themselves, they pointed their spears to either side of the road with Leánder in the middle. He had determined that whichever side the enemy showed he would take the lead, but for now, he watched and waited…

Suddenly, from the northern tree line there came a rushing sound like that of a flood as a multitude of warriors broke out from the shadows. Those men facing southward quickly turned their spears alongside their brothers. Their faces fell at what they saw. Through Jädus they all knew that an evil enemy had conquered the forces of Ahriman, but this was the first time that any of them had actually laid eyes on the demons and the sight was terrifying.

They had all suspected, but now they knew, that they would be fighting the bodies of their friends and kin as they were now possessed by some unspeakable evil. As they looked on with horror they heard the enemy's battle cry coming from the faces they once knew and loved so well. Some of the men's hands began to shake with dread.

"Steady men!" shouted Leánder as they rapidly approached. "Steady!" He shouted once more, unwilling to produce Dorlimere. "You are men of the Light! And these are *NOT* your brothers! Show them no mercy!"

Many of the men were encouraged by his words, but others were not so lucky. None of them had ever seen battle before and the courage of many melted in the face of it. Not so with Leánder. He strode to the head of the battle line and took the spear of a young man.

"Draw your sword, and stay behind me!" cried Leánder to the man.

Just then, the dark forces of Gorgon met the spears of Men in a resounding clash. For a brief moment the spears held and dug deep into the bodies of the frontline, but then more came, and still more. In the dim light of evening Leánder could see black mist erupt from each of the fallen attackers only to rush onward and possess the body of a next fearful victim and make his body fight his brothers.

Not so with those who stood boldly however, as their spirits were not so easily disposed and certainly not with Leánder, whose sword produced a much different result. As he drew Dorlimere a blue flame erupted from its sheath and the enemy drew back from its light. Had they not possessed the bodies of men, they would not have been able to stand against it, as they feared its power.

Leánder plunged his blade deep into an oncoming enemy who wore the face of an old friend. The body shrieked before falling before him. As it collapsed the evil spirit within rose up into the air and dispersed like smoke.

Abruptly both sides in the immediate area paused and looked with astonishment. The body which had fallen stirred. Amazingly, the man stood and looked at Leánder squarely showing no trace of a wound. He looked down at his hands in wonder, having control over his body once more.

"Give me a sword," said the man, now suddenly free of the evil which possessed him. Someone quickly produced a sword from a downed soldier and he fell in line behind Leánder. Fear and dread fell upon the enemy as they realized their own mortality and the power of Leánder's sword. It had the power to pierce the evil spirit within, yet leave the man held captive untouched. The moment was short-lived however, and new rage erupted from both sides. The attack pressed on and as it did Leánder struck blow after blow and Dorlimere never return unsatisfied. Those he felled rose again to fight alongside him. Tragically many of them fell to other swords from which there was no returning. With his sword in his right hand and his rounded shield on his left, he plunged into enemy after enemy, driving himself forward. He stepped over the bodies which fell before him and he felt the sweat of the men at his flanks. To his right and left there were six men; twelve in all pushing forward trying to keep up.

*　　　　　　*　　　　　　*

Standing just inside the tree line, Teivel reeled back when he saw one of his captains fall to the blade of Leánder. He felt a sense of his own mortality as he realized that death was not limited to men alone. Furthermore, his attack was not fairing as efficiently as he planned and Leánder's blade was not helping. "No matter," he muttered to himself, "it will be over soon enough." Now that all of Leánder's soldiers were engaged in a single direction he signaled to the second wave.

*　　　　　　*　　　　　　*

Darkness had now fallen and Leánder stole a look at his flanks and saw that his ranks were thinning rapidly despite his best efforts. Fear was his men's greatest enemy as it allowed the spirits to take them over and turn them. Many of his men had fallen, some had been turned, others had retreated. Over his shoulder he heard the sound of another wave of attack. Just as he had feared, the enemy had waited until all of his men were committed to the fight in a single direction only to launch an attack from behind.

In the confusion and panic, his men began to scatter. Leánder and those closest to him found themselves alone in a small circle of chaos held at bay by their shields and swords. Up to this point Leánder had been fighting with his own strength, but now something began to stir deep within him. It rose up out of his spirit and filled his body with light and strength. As he poured himself out into the fight his very sweat began to glow like a thousand shining diamonds falling from his skin and his eyes became a blue flame like that of Dorlimere. The enemy drew back as the light shining from within him pierced their eyes and blinded those nearest to him.

To his men, however, their courage renewed and their strength returned more than before, flowing through them as though by an invisible force. His light shone on them and they advanced, straightaway fearless of the vast numbers which surrounded them. They went to work…bodies without number fell before them and piled high on either side as Leánder led his men deep into their ranks.

They kept a tight, unbroken circle as they advanced slowly, step by step behind their king, their swords flashing wildly in the night. They found that the harder they fought, the more strength they had, as though Light Enduring was welling up inside their own bodies. After what seemed like mere moments though it had actually been hours, the tide began to turn. A loud signal was given and to their dismay, the vast army which had seemed so confident at first, broke off the attack and fled before Leánder and his men.

*   *   *

In the morning, those who survived came back only to strip the dead and bury their friends.

*   *   *

Leánder spoke to the twelve who had fought beside him; Bularius, Jädus and the young man from whom he had taken the spear being among them.

"My brothers," he began, "we have won a great victory today. When we return however, do not despise those who fled in fear, for they did not know what they could have done with the power of Light," and he looked levelly at each one of them. "It was not by our own strength that we won, but by Light Enduring alone. Forgive your brothers, and do not hold this against them. There will come other battles and you will see that they will not fail you." At that they each bowed their heads and solemnly agreed.

*   *   *

Lorwin stood on the city wall looking out at those returning from the battle. Many had filtered in slowly the day before, but then a great many more that morning. It had been days since Leánder led his men out from the city and the reports of those who returned frightened her. After seeing the downcast faces of many who had fled the battle, her hope at seeing her king began to wane. At midday however, his banner was seen far off and she rushed to the nearest balcony to see.

Leánder marched into the city followed closely by twelve men and the ranks he had reunited with along the way; nearly five hundred in all. There was a great celebration that night over their victory, but a bitter-sweet one. Each death was a great loss. Each one a friend. A brother. To Leánder and Lorwin there was still fear as they considered the fate of their daughter. They would not give up so easily.

VI

Inimicus

The Enemy

Deep underneath the mountains of Gorgon upon his dark iron throne, Ahriman brooded; the pale light of a faint fire flickering in his narrowed eyes. Teival's attack on Leánder and his men went...*poorly*. He had greatly underestimated the sword Dorlimere and the power wielded through it by their king. *A mistake not to be made again,* he thought coldly. The attack was not entirely without its benefits however, as his spy within Leánder's company now held his position without question and was a constant supply of information. His underling, Karawan, had done his job well during his pursuit of Jädus and followed his orders to the letter. He had followed him closely with patience through the long wilderness. Jädus was an unfortunate soul. So confident now. So devoted to his king.

Upon reaching the outskirts of Everfall, Karawan feigned an attack on the man, infiltrated his body, and in that moment inflicted a wound on the man with his own sword to make it look as though he had somehow won...then laid dormant in the recesses of the man's soul awaiting an opportune time to strike where it would hurt the most. In the meantime however, Karawan's dark spirit reached out to Ahriman and revealed the condition of his enemy.

As he mulled this over in his dark mind, his thoughts strayed to his most recent prize. He turned up the palm of his hand and curled his fingers summoning the fire before him to rise. As it did its tongues took on the image of Lárwin as she too sat brooding in her prison. Her dull, flickering image in the fire ignited his wicked imagination and he lusted for her, but he restrained himself, allowing not a hand to touch her. *Everything is within my power,* he thought proudly, and then with a sigh of discontent, *Except for this...*

Not long before he journeyed alone throughout the vastness of the void, proud and exalted in the emptiness, but now he felt a change within himself he did not understand. In the darkness of his heart, he was afraid. He had witnessed the affections shared between men and their kin and though he denied it and swore to destroy it he longed to experience it: the wonder of love. The thought repulsed him. It made his pale skin crawl and his anger flare, but yet it was there like an infection or a scourge. Perhaps it was some lingering notion from inhabiting this body, perhaps not. One thing was for sure, he desired Lárwin more than he had thought possible, but more than this, he desired her to choose him of her free will. *That would prove to be revenge indeed. The daughter of Leánder, the image of cursed Light Enduring, giving herself freely to Darkness...yes...* He held out his hand and took a portion of the flames forming the image of Lárwin and held it there before his eyes letting the flames dance in between his fingers, imagining.

*　　　　　　　　*　　　　　　　　*

Lárwin sat perched upon the edge of the magnificent bed in her room, her *prison*, and thought silently to herself. It had been nearly two weeks since she had been taken from Everfall and carried to this wretched place. She had learned much since her arrival, and it would avail her much if she ever escaped. *Escape,* she thought, *from this place? Is that even possible?* she stopped herself and broke off the thought before it could take root. *No, this will not be my fate. I am a child of Light and will not succumb to whatever wicked schemes Ahriman may contrive. Besides, I may have friends in unexpected places.*

She recalled her arrival in Gorgon. It had taken three days of long hard travel on the back of the giant beast. Though the words shared between her capture and the beast were few, they revealed much. She had come to know his kind as *Dragon*, for instance, and that his name was Fanglóriun. Apparently, he too was a victim of an unspoken crime by Ahriman and forced into this errand and she sensed that he would have otherwise been a friend if the situation were different. Upon their arrival she had wished greatly to speak with him but Ahriman would not have it and ushered her off under heavy guard as soon as they landed. As she was being bound however, she overheard the low, sad voice of the great creature.

"Forgive me," he had said. "I did not know..."

And with that he disappeared as she was taken into a deep cavern. Since then her treatment was most unexpected. She had been shown into a lavishly decorated room full of ornate furniture and tapestries. The designs which covered the walls and ceiling were of a nature she did not understand and the symbols which they swirled into and created she found troubling, though she did not know why. What was most disturbing however, were the faces of the guards which stood outside her door and escorted her to the limited places she was allowed to explore. They wore faces which looked very much like those of her own kin in Everfall, yet their eyes were filled with black voids and they were eerily silent, saying not a word.

Ahriman had also sent her many expensive gifts which, if it were not for her situation, she would have found to be most luxurious. Her room was laid with priceless diamond necklaces, gold rings, delicate crowns inlaid with sapphires and rubies, and silver hair dressings which sparkled even in this dim light. An incredible gift for each day she was there. But she would have none of them. She even refused the extravagant clothes which were brought to her and instead chose to remain in her own bed-dress which she wore on the day she was taken. She had pushed all of Ahriman's gifts into a corner and refused to look at them.

Unbeknownst to her, this angered Ahriman greatly as he had hoped to prepare her to accept him when next he planned to visit her, but he did not understand her nor could he grasp what was in her mind. Just as Darkness did not understand the Light during creation, he did not understand now, and this baited his anger. Her only desires were that of home, of her family, of the forest of Everfall, running water and sunlight. These things she longed for and held most dear and no diamond could ever be big enough or clothes extravagant enough to steal these desires or to quiet them. She contented herself with thoughts of home and of her rescue by her father which she believed was sure to come.

"Of course he will come. He will come for me...I know he will...

*   *   *

Ahriman's gaze still lingered upon Lárwin as he peered through the fire in his hand and he perceived the subtle movement of her lips.

"Home..." he said allowed, gleaning her thoughts from her whispers. His anger began to flare as his patience crumbled. Never before had he let such a trivial thing destroy his countenance but never before had he desired such a thing...and been utterly rejected by it. He threw the flame to the ground as he rose from his throne and its embers dashed against the stone floor. He stood and allowed his anger to well up inside of him, driving him, feeding him and he took great strides toward her chamber.

Lárwin jumped in surprise as the guards quickly threw open the double doors and posted themselves on either side facing one another and kneeling down beside their upturned spears. She knew they knelt for Ahriman. In the darkness beyond the threshold there was only blackness save for two small glowing flames, like that of candlelight, at a height where a man's eyes would be. It was his anger which she saw, burning visibly just behind the darkness of his eyes and she knew then that he had heard her whispers.

"You have rejected my unrelenting kindness and have forced my hand upon you," spoke Ahriman coolly.

"You forced your hand upon my people unprovoked long ago," replied Lárwin defiantly, gathering her confidence.

Lárwin drew back as Ahriman stepped into the room, his shimmering black cloak trailing behind like stardust in the night sky; the room suddenly became dimmer. Bending down and grasping the back of her hair he trapped her against the wall as he spoke. "Child, I was here long before this world corrupted the holy darkness...and now you will corrupt it no further." With that he pulled her by the hair and drug her forcefully from the room. Throwing her to her hands and knees at the feet of a large sentry, he commanded him to take her to the lowest dungeon. "Deprive her of the *Light* which she so preciously desires," he said violently turning again toward her. "And see if my face is not the last thing you will ever see in the light again."

VII

Invádo

Invasion

Wind swept through his long dark locks as he gripped tightly to the railing. For the moment, he let his cloak trail out behind him in the stiff breeze as he looked onward to the misty horizon. Soaring above the open sea, riding high on a ribbon of gray, Leánder could just make out his shadow through the corner of his watering eye as he flew through the empty air aboard *Sacred Wind*.

Sunlight glistened off silver vapor trails on either side, the wake of her sister ships. There were seven in all, each one laden with Evealian soldiers clad in full VolFerrum armor. They had set sail before many of the ships had been fully completed and much work had to be done along the way, but time was of the essence. Lárwin had been gone for far too long, nearly a month to the day, and Leánder refused to wait any longer. They had worked night and day to complete them, yet despite their haste better craftsmanship had never been seen. Each ship was strongly built and sturdy enough to withstand both wind and waves. Artisans had decorated each with intricate designs and fixed lavish banners to every mast declaring the strength and nobility of each captain. The day of their launching was truly a marvel and awesome in the eyes of all who gathered to see it. Nearly every man, woman and child in all Everfall and the surrounding lands had crowded the shores and tall buildings around the wide bay where the ships were docked to see them off. Over two thousand of Everfall's bravest men, and more than a few women, marched steadily to their assigned ships under the careful eye of their captains who stood proudly under their waving banners. As they passed, many in the crowd threw roses and petals along the way and a steady stream of colored ticker rained from every window as they waved goodbye to their loved ones. Upon reaching the shore, they split up into groups and gathered under their assigned banners before marching out and boarding their ships. Three hundred boarded each of the seven ships and many wondered if there would be room for them all. They were surprised to find the vast ships widely accommodating for both humans and supplies.

Once boarded, Leánder strode to the head of the crowd and publicly gave control of the city to the Council until his return. He also entrusted them with his writings, the book he had sealed containing the record Light Enduring had instructed him to keep. Taking the hand of Lorwin, they both boarded *Sacred Wind* and stood upon the bridge at the rear of the ship waving a long farewell to their people.

At Leánder's command, his captain ordered the sails be raised and hoisted into position. There in the early morning sun, the vast, blue-metal VolFerrum sails unfolded like the immense wings of a giant bird taking flight. Two main sails supported the weight amidships and smaller sails for steering and balance were mounted on the sides of the prow and stern. Once fully unfolded, sunlight glistened from each like a mirror and many had to turn away from their brightness. Everyone, including those aboard, marveled at the sight. Despite the circumstances of their mission, even Leánder was impressed and he laughed within himself as he saw the eyes of his captains grow wide at their deployment. The captain shouted another command and at his word the two main sails began to tilt slightly and rotate upon a massive hinge which ran starboard to port and supported the mighty wings. As the sails tilted, it appeared as though an invisible force were pushing against the thin metal and Lorwin gripped her husband's hand tightly as she felt the weight of the massive ship begin to move steadily forward. On either side she saw the other ships unfolding their own sails and moving into position behind *Sacred Wind*, three on each side forming a great V.

She looked behind and saw the shores of Everfall quickly falling behind as they gained speed. The ship began to rock forward and back as it gathered momentum over the waves and the spray of the sea broke upon its sturdy bow and its ornate figurehead of an angel pointing defiantly forward. The massive ship broke upon another wave, yet to her astonishment, the rocking stopped and all was suddenly smooth. Looking down, she let out a gasp as she saw the water falling away beneath her. To those on the shore looking onward, a great cheer went up as they witnessed the magnificent ships take flight for the first time. As they climbed higher and higher they appeared at first as seven giant stars illuminating the dawn; then continually smaller as they fled away. They watched with eyes full of wonder and fascination until finally they faded to a shimmering glimmer on the distant horizon...and then vanished completely.

To those on board however, the long uncertain journey had just begun and they were eager to see what lay ahead. They used a combination of flags and mirrors to signal to one another as they navigated the uncharted sky and they skillfully skirted around towering clouds and threatening storms. Upon reaching the coastline of Lanália, Leánder looked out from the bridge. On his left, peaking just above the clouds in the far distance were the white caps of the Snowy Mountains. To his right and just behind, lay the great mouth of the Andír River and the glistening waters of the White Falls. Ahead of him stretched the open sea. There he knew navigating would be much more difficult as none of them had ever ventured beyond the shore, save one.

Jädus told them of a long chain of islands which stretched from the ice of the Snowy Mountains to the northern tip of Gorgon, the land of his enemy. These islands Leánder had determined to follow at the word of Jädus. Looking out upon them now, he wondered to himself how anyone could have survived the journey alone, so far from home. *It must have been a miracle indeed.*

All went exceedingly well, and each ship performed wondrously as they plotted from island to island. Always traveling as fast as the wind in the day and very slowly and cautiously at night for fear of running into an unknown mountain peak or even each other. To avoid this, they lit great beacon fires on the prow and stern of each ship and the luminosity of the torches were magnified by the metal sails, lighting each one against the starry night sky. After several weeks of tedious travel, they arrived. There, *just there*, he could make out the distant shores of his enemy fast approaching.

Wrapping his cloak about himself he turned and strode from the prow toward the stern, making his way through the busy deck hands and rigging. Walking had been something of a challenge when they had first set sail from Everfall and many of the men had unexpectedly become motion sick. Lorwin had been among those who were most affected, yet after several days she had recovered and began to truly enjoy the sensation of sailing among the clouds. As they neared the shores of Gorgon however, the mood upon *Sacred Wind* had changed drastically as if an invisible, icy hand had reached out to lay hold of their hearts and challenge their courage. Leánder stood boldly against such notions and sought to encourage his men, though he proceeded with caution.

"Captain," he said, addressing the young man in his characteristically calm voice.

"Yes my king?"

Leánder stood beside him and looked out into the mist toward the dark horizon. "Double the watch and take us higher... I have a feeling it's going to get very dark soon."

"Yes sir," replied the captain in a curious tone.

"Also, signal the other ships. Bring them in closer so that we do not get separated in the mist."

"Right away."

*   *   *

Ahriman's dark eyes dimly reflected the firelight through narrow slits as he slowly lifted his head from long and deep meditation.

"The sword approaches," he whispered quietly to himself.

Karawan had proven a remarkable spy within the Evealian ranks, however his recent failure would cost him dearly. Dorlimere-Sisu had prevented his wondering mind from peering into the doings of Leánder and if it were not for Karawan reaching out to him in the night as he possessed Jädus' body while he slept, he would have no information at all. He learned that Leánder was planning an assault, a vain rescue attempt for his daughter, but nothing more. Their *king* had proven surprisingly secretive in the matter and apparently executed his plan before Karawan could report. His thoughts troubled him. *Why has he fallen silent these many weeks? How is it that Dorlimere approaches so quickly?* As he pondered these questions the answers slowly revealed themselves. *The VolFerrum, Leánder's* flying iron...*could it be that he succeeded in his foolish idea of a flying ship? If so, that would explain how he is able to approach so quickly. Jädus is one of Leánder's trusted men as well. If he is aboard and cannot escape the presence of Dorlimere, Karawan may not be able to report in without arousing the Sword and alerting its master...Perhaps Karawan has his reasons...*

Jädus awoke in his hammock below decks at the usual time for his shift as watchman. During the past few weeks aboard *Sacred Wind* he had been pleased to have been chosen for the position as it afforded him a unique opportunity. During mealtime or sometimes over a pitcher of ale, someone would ask him if he was afraid to return to Gorgon, after all, he was the sole survivor of a terrible tragedy. He never spoke much about it, but he had determined long ago that if he had the chance to exact revenge on those responsible for the slaying of his kin that he would not hesitate to take it. Leánder had been a good man before he had left with Ahriman, now he saw him as a good king and was proud to be in his service. As watchman of the ship he had the chance to spot the enemy first and be the first to alert his mates of any danger. He was satisfied with that thought as he donned his VolFerrum armor. *What incredible metal!* he thought. He continued to marvel at it though he had possessed it for some time now. Climbing the narrow stair above decks he emerged into what should have been the full light of day, but instead an unnatural mist had gathered about them and hid the sun from view. Seeing him, Leánder welcomed him warmly.

"My friend!" spoke Leánder with a smile brighter than the sun.

"I am at your service my king," replied Jädus, and they clasped arms firmly and with a smile.

Leánder's expression grew more serious as he spoke again. "We have crossed into the realm of Gorgon. I have given orders to double the watch so you will have company in your perch today."

"I understand. I have a feeling we will spot the enemy soon, despite this mist."

"Surely it is a trick of the enemy, and it parts with resistance before the prow, but as surely as the Light is with us, it will not last."

Jädus nodded in agreement and climbed to his perch to begin his duty as lookout.

*   *   *

"We cannot continue in this darkness my king," began the captain. "If it were only darkness or only mist we might venture further, yet in both is madness. It is supposed to be noontime. I could cast a stone to the ships at either flank and yet they are nearly impossible to see."

"Aye, right you are. We cannot continue like this. Signal the others to come to a full stop until I give the order."

"Yes sir."

Leánder went below decks to his quarters where Lorwin stood at a round window, waiting.

"We have come to a stop?" asked Lorwin curiously.

"Yes, we cannot navigate any further without risking the ship and her crew... I am at a loss."

"My dearest love," replied Lorwin, crossing the room with her stately stride, "we have all we need." She touched his face as he wrapped his arm around her waist. She looked up into his eyes letting her hand fall to the hilt of Dorlimere which rested in its sheath at his belt. In one fluid motion she drew out its full length and, stepping back, swung the blade up to Leánder's face and stopped mid-stroke right between his eyes. Silent blue fire reflected off Leánder's unwavering eyes as the cool blade just touched his skin. "Caught off guard were you?" asked Lorwin, raising a challenging eyebrow.

"Your beauty has always caught me off guard," he replied, taking hold of the sword and studying its radiance. "We are close."

Her expression softened. "Lárwin is near. I can feel her despite this darkness." She looked at the blade of Dorlimere shining brightly in the room. Suddenly, they looked at one another as the same thought struck them both. Leánder turned and left the room making his way to the bridge and leaving Lorwin behind as she donned her own VolFerrum Armor.

Summoning the captain, Leánder spoke. "Send word to the other ships. Make ready for battle."

"My Lord?" said the captain, his face displaying his bewilderment.

Drawing Dorlimere from its sheath, Leánder held out the blade for all to see. Seeing the pale blue flame emanating from the sword he nodded with understanding.

"We are approaching our enemy and a great light is coming," replied Leánder in a low tone.

"It shall be done as you say my king!" and with that he began issuing orders to the signalman and the lower officers to rouse the men. Leánder himself made his way to the prow and waited until he was confident that his orders had become known to the other ships. Then he looked forward into the misty darkness. It was a void of black, above and below, and it was a labor to breath.

"Not for long..." he whispered to himself as he kneeled to one knee and lifted Dorlimere high above his head, its blade pointing straight up into the clouds of darkness."Light Eternal!" he cried aloud into the abyss. "May your light shine for us now!"

*   *   *

Lárwin lay in a dreamless state somewhere between asleep and awake. How many days had it been? How many nights? Weeks perhaps? More? She did not know, nor have any way of knowing. The only way she had of marking any sense of time was when a silent servant came to feed her the crumbs which made up her daily meal. Fortunately, she was free to move about her miserable cell, small as it was, as the chains which hung from the wall made it all too apparent that her situation could be worse. It had taken her a long, long time to adjust to this near darkness, though she knew not from where the dismal light came from. She had gradually come to make out a small window atop her prison, though she could not see what lay outside and it saddened her. Only darkness met her. She missed the sun and the forest, her family and she had spilled many tears alone in that darkness...she wondered now, how many more tears would it take to wash away the rock and iron which kept her prisoner. How many more...

*   *   *

Ahriman's disgust over Leánder's unyielding quest was threatening to tear him apart from within. He had conjured the blackest veil of mist and enchanted darkness his power could summon from within this frail body and blanketed the whole of his realm within it, yet he could feel the sword nearing undeterred. Teival and the bulk of his forces had been dispatched to Lanália to waylay Leánder expecting a ground assault much the same as their first encounter, but the Evealian king had moved much too quickly and unexpectedly for any trap to be set before he had embarked on his journey to Gorgon. And now they were here. It was not Leánder himself, his men, nor any tactic they might employ which concerned him. It was only the sword. The blade forged for his undoing which possessed his thoughts. He roused himself from his black, iron throne and stood. *If Leánder cannot be kept from arriving, then let him come...What are he and his sword compared to Darkness...?* He reached out with his thoughts and summoned his Guard, all which remained in Gorgon, to come and make ready for battle.

"Lûctus Nöcturn, gather yourselves that you may feast on the meal to come," he said with a powerful voice which echoed clearly throughout the whole of his realm, "that you may have your fill of the glory which was meant for us! Let it be yours for all time!" Scarcely had he finished issuing these orders than a sudden pain gripped him like fire and he raised his hand to shield his eyes which he tightly shut in anguish.

Meanwhile, deep in the recesses of the fortress, a brilliant shaft of pure white light exploded in from the window of Lárwin's cell and pierced her eyes. The shock of its sudden resplendent brightness startled her. With closed eyes she held out her hand and felt its warmth. Stepping into it, blinking, she could feel it on her face and she knew that it was sunlight…and something more… Her father had come.

*　　　　　　　*　　　　　　　*

The seven glistening ships of Everfall descended rapidly through the gleaming shaft of sunlight which bore through the dark clouds like a spear. Leánder still knelt at the prow of *Sacred Wind* holding aloft Dorlimere and it shone with such magnificence it appeared as though it were its own star and no one could approach him because of the light of it. Just barely could Lorwin make out the shape of him as she stood upon the bridge and shielded her eyes from its radiance. His arms held up, lost in a ball of light, his face tilted down, and his cloak bellowing out behind. He was a sight to see and it emboldened his men. Aboard another vessel, Bularius had just received his signal to be ready for battle when through the darkness he witnessed a shaft of pale blue light streak up into the sky, into the very heavens themselves it seemed, and then suddenly widen to engulf the entire flagship, then every ship as the darkness and mist was rolled back for miles in every direction to reveal the bright blue sky above and then the sun which broke free and shone warmly upon them for the first time in many days. Far below they found themselves surrounded by a ring of black, jagged mountains in the middle of which they spotted a great crevasse in a rocky plain. Out of this poured creatures and men, the wicked subjects of Ahriman's dark design.

"Take us down," Lorwin ordered. "Set us upon the plain facing our enemy."

The captain ordered the landing skids lowered and to brace for landing. Lorwin expected the touchdown to be rather rough, though she was pleasantly surprised when *Sacred Wind* alighted atop the gravely plain and came to a gentle stop. Not so with many of the others which plowed their metal-reinforced keels forcefully into the ground erupting a spray of dirt and rocks and skidded to a hard stop. Notwithstanding, they each suddenly dropped their port and starboard boarding hatches and these in turn slammed into the ground with a great pounding followed immediately by heavy footfalls. Two thousand of Evealian's finest poured out from within. The invasion had begun.

Lorwin continued to stand on the bridge and watch as Leánder rose from the prow and walked steadily to the gangway. As he neared, she could see his serious expression and she knew his intentions. Following him down, light continued to pour from Dorlimere and its radiance poured from every opening as Leánder moved through the ship until he finally emerged with his troops on the ground. He and Lorwin moved to the head of the formation as the soldiers gathered themselves together under their respective banners and looked out toward the horizon, toward their enemy, beyond which lay Lárwin. There on the waving horizon Lorwin could see a thick cloud of dust rising high into the air and the ground began to tremble.

"Our enemy has been waiting and now approaches," spoke Leánder with a distant voice. He turned to address his men. "Men of the Light!" he began boldly, "this day we take back that which the enemy has stolen! We will not sit idle as our lands are razed and our daughters taken. Our families will know peace and we will return victorious or die trying! I assure you brave men, death is not the end for us, but even so, do not be careless with your lives that you may return home with the glory yours to claim! Our enemy stands between us and victory. May Light Enduring have mercy upon them because *we* will not!"

With that a roar erupted from among the shining ranks which stood before the shimmering sails of the Evealian ships. Leánder stole a look at Lorwin, glimmering in the light of the sun as she stood proudly in her armor, her hand resting on the hilt of her own magnificent sword as she looked back at him. He had no desire to put her into danger, but he knew that she would have it no other way. Besides that, she was marvelous with a blade and deadly in her tactics. Men and women alike respected her and obeyed her commands and it was thus determined early on that she would command the left flank, Bularius the right, and he himself would lead the center where the fighting would be the fiercest.

She nodded at him in understanding. He turned and stepped out toward the battlefield not knowing what evil may befall them, yet confident in the power of Dorlimere and his men. They began the march slow and cool, their spears tilted toward the front over their large shields. As they advanced, they maintained a tight, straight formation like a metal wall. As the enemy ate up the ground before them the ground began to shake all the more, yet Leánder's hand was steady as he led the way, standing a stone's throw away in front of the battle line so that all his men could see him and follow.

Ahead, the masses of the enemy gained momentum and seemingly impossible speed as their dark spirits gave them energy. The sunlight was a distraction, and if it were not for the shelter of their mortal bodies the battle would be most difficult. Leading the way was a huge, brutish figure, unnaturally enlarged by his dark power. He drew his heavy iron sword as he ran and brandished it behind his giant shield which he used to guard his eyes from the gleaming light of Dorlimere. Behind, his forces gathered together like a great spear with him at the tip, ready to tear through the thin wall of Evealian soldiers like an old cloth. He laughed within himself as he realized that his own company greatly outnumbered Leánder's. *I will enjoy this pleasantry.*

Leánder looked out from under his helmet and lost count of the vast numbers which swept down upon him. *How have they grown to be so many? I cannot bother with that now...*

He raised a closed fist. "Hold!" he shouted. Every man came to a complete stop in unison. "Arm!" he shouted over his shoulder, and at the command the butt of every spear along the front row was dug into the ground for bracing and those behind stuck out over the shoulders of those in front. They locked their shields together and braced for the impact which was sure to come.

As the titan closed distance with Leánder, he raised his dark sword high and brought it down with a crushing blow

which would have destroyed an ordinary man. But as he swung, Leánder dug his foot into the ground and launched himself to the side with blinding speed and let loose the fury of Dorlimere. The titan took another two steps and blinked as his shield and enormous sword fell neatly in two where Leánder's sword had passed. His tattered armor and clothing also bore a clean cut from one side to the other, front to back, yet the man himself was unharmed and he stood there, facing blankly the soldiers of Everfall as he recovered himself, free of the evil within.

Leánder continued to look on toward the oncoming rush of doom and moved steadily and purposefully toward his next target. He knew those who met the swords of his fellow men would not be so lucky and he pitied them. The feeling soon passed however, as he engaged his next opponent. As for the titan, the man now freed from his inner prison, he stood there and let his former comrades rush from behind him to crash into the wall of Evealian soldiers. He looked down, seeing his broken sword cleft in two he reached down and lifted its hilt and broken blade with both hands like a club. Turning, he swung the blade in a great arc and halved the nearest oncoming enemy at the waist. With renewed strength, he fell in behind Leánder and let loose his pent up rage and fury. Behind him the sound of a great crash erupted in a maelstrom of violence as shield and spear met at the battle line. The bodies of the Lûctus Nöcturn smashed into what seemed like an immovable wall of steel as the hard VolFerrum armor turned away nearly every point, protecting all that it covered. Exposed flesh however, was another matter.

As the first impact subsided and the battle set in, the soldiers of Everfall began to move steadily forward. As they progressed, Lorwin sent word throughout the flanks to close the gap in their rear and so create a great circle of men to prevent the enemy from maneuvering behind and gaining an advantage. They were well-equipped but greatly outnumbered. Leánder himself remained always just in front, breaking all who came before him as they crashed into his shield or met the fury of Dorlimere.

The battle raged on. From noon 'til dusk the next day they fought until finally the assault reached a crescendo. All organization seemed lost in the fray. The light of Dorlimere-Sisu had illuminated the battlefield throughout the night and as the stars passed overhead and on into the next day its power flowed out into the combat and strengthened Leánder and his men to impossible feats.

They had come to the very doorstep of their enemy, a vast fortress built upon a steep ledge leading down into a dark, jagged, crescent-shaped valley. The fortress itself was built into the valley and extended from the uppermost cliffs to the uttermost recesses of the valley floor. As the turrets of the fortress loomed darkly overhead victory seemed near, and as the sun began to wane on the second day Leánder lifted his sword, letting out a long battle cry and rallying his men to him.

In every direction the broken bodies of good and valiant men laid beside their fallen enemies. The fighting had been so fierce here that he could scarcely see the ground through the bodies, broken swords and shields. Amidst the dead however, he found one still living who was thrown down during the fight. His battered armor bore the crest of an Evealian soldier and seemed oddly familiar, yet his rounded ears and the rest of his appearance seemed strange. Blood flowed from beneath his left arm and the rest of his body bore grievous wounds as though he had taken the brunt of the fighting himself. No doubt he was brave, but hidden in his eyes Leánder could see his struggle with defeat. Even so, he knelt down and extended his hand.

"Can you stand boy?" he asked.

The man lifted his hand weakly and nodded. They clasped wrists and Leánder pulled him to his feet with a strong pull.

"Victory is not to the strong, but to those who trust in the Light! Be strengthened!" he said.

Looking into his eyes Leánder could see his strength renewing and it struck him that he had somehow seen this man before; perhaps in a dream.

"My king!" cried one of the captains pointing with his sword.

Leánder turned to look.

"The enemy approaches!"

Leánder turned back to the man he had helped but there was no one there and his hand hung empty in the air. It puzzled him greatly and he stole a glance around but there was no time to pursue the matter. A greater thing was calling his attention.

Just then the great enemy stepped out from the shadows. His own men, and not a few Evealian soldiers, gave way before him as he towered over the battlefield. Standing nearly three feet above the tallest man and drawing his own dark sword, DarMere-Itah, Ahriman was a terror to behold. He swung his blade in wide arcs sweeping away men and even his own soldiers. None could stand before him and live.

Seeing this, Lorwin sent for Leánder and boldly approached Ahriman in his fury. Producing a curved dagger, she flung it skillfully towards him. It dug deep into his neck just between his helmet and breastplate. Ahriman paused and drew off his bloodstained helmet. Reaching up with his left hand, he pulled out the length of the dagger from his bleeding neck. To the amazement of all, the gaping wound closed immediately to leave only a dark scar. He tossed away the blade scowling, and advanced toward her as she braced herself. He lifted DarMere high and brought it down with his full force as she lifted her own sword in a vain attempt to parry the blow.

The unstoppable force of his sword suddenly stopped and shattered like glass as it broke upon Dorlimere like a wave upon a rock. Its pieces washed over Lorwin who hid her eyes, but not before seeing Leánder standing there, guarding her from the fury of Ahriman. Leánder looked up into the face of his brother's body with a defiant look and, though Ahriman's eyes were as black as pitch, he could sense the carefully hidden fear behind them.

Catching sight of his king from across the battlefield, Jädus cried out to Bularius. "Our king faces the enemy! Come brother; let us aid him if we can!" And with that Jädus valiantly ran through the maelstrom of battle cutting down all who stood in his path as he closed the distance between him and the king he loved. Just behind, Bularius struggled to keep up. Having taken a blow to the face the night before, he looked out from his bloodied left eye and could just make out the massive frame of Ahriman retreat from the flame of Dorlimere. The king he could not see through the torrent of fighting, but he knew that Leánder was beneath that flame and he longed to fight beside him.

Meanwhile, Leánder rose to his full height and stepped boldly toward Ahriman who had begun to retreated and order back his remaining forces. Beyond him, the dark fortress rose up from the cliffs of the ravine it was perched upon. Somewhere within was Lárwin and he could not let this monster retreat to where she was lest a worse thing befall her.

Taking his shield and raising it high with his left arm he brought his full weight down upon it and struck the ground with a terrible force. In front of him and stretching out past Ahriman toward the fortress, the ground began to tremble and split. A fissure opened and cracked the very foundations of the bedrock the stone walls and ramparts were built upon. Far down below, unbeknownst to him, the bars of Lárwin's cell buckled and gave way to the crumbling walls. Ahriman himself had fallen from the earthquake during his retreat and now the king approached unhindered with an intimidating look of finality.

Just then Jädus emerged out of the carnage as he parried the charge of an enemy with his shield, the broken body rolling off Jädus' back. Leánder turned and his expression softened as their eyes met. "Come Jädus! Victory is near!" he cried.

Jädus...Karawan! thought Ahriman suddenly.

Leánder stood over Ahriman and looked into the eyes of Darkness. "This body does not belong to you," he said quietly, his eyes aflame.

Leánder held up Dorlimere for the finishing blow, its flame burning hotly and shining out with blinding light. As Ahriman raised his arm in defense he cried out, "Karawan! Serve your master now!"

Jädus' expression suddenly changed as Karawan took control of him. Coming upon Leánder, he lunged forward with his spear, piercing the king's side beneath the armor just as he was bringing down his sword upon Ahriman. In sudden pain, Leánder cried out and missed his mark, grazing instead Ahriman's leg. The light of Dorlimere dimmed as it fell from his hand. Ahriman, seizing the moment, reached out for the king's sword. Laying his hand on it however, he was suddenly gripped with searing pain and his flesh burned upon it.

Bularius had caught up to the scene just in time to witness Jädus run through his king and suddenly all around was much darker as the light of Dorlimere flickered out. Bularius screamed in a blind rage and tossed aside his shield. He charged behind Jädus and with a fell swoop, cut him down with his sword. Jädus' face twisted in anguish as the spirit Karawan departed, his mission complete. He died there, heartbreak and lament fading in his eyes as his life flowed out of him.

Bularius now looked down upon Ahriman who was beginning to rise, cradling his burned hand. At his feet was his king with his sword close beside.. Gripped with anguish Bularius cast away his own sword and picked up Dorlimere, and though it did not burn with a flame as when the king had wielded it, it was intimidating none the less. It dawned upon Ahriman that the sword had a will of its own and chose to be handled by this *man* instead of himself. Retreat was now his only option and he turned to flee with Bularius just behind, but as Bularius began the pursuit, he heard a familiar voice call out to him above the melee.

"Bularius!" cried Lorwin through tears as she cradled Leánder in her arms.

"Lorwin…" he replied.

"The king lives!"

"My king!" he exclaimed, his eyes growing wide. He ran to Leánder and removed his helmet as he knelt. "Forgive me my king, I did not know. I thought you had died," he said grievously and placed Dorlimere into his hand once more.

Blood streamed down from his side where Jädus' spear had pierced him, and he spoke with a weak and distant voice. "My friend," he began and attempted a weak smile. "Help me stand." And with that Bularius and Lorwin placed his arms upon their shoulders and helped him up. From across the battlefield he could just make out the ravaged fortress and the soldiers of the Lûctus Nöcturn retreating into its crumbling gate. Suddenly, emerging from the darkness within, he saw an impossible sight and his eyes grew wide. Out from the confusion, he could just make out a young girl in an embroidered gown, holding a sword with both hands and wielding it wildly and cutting down all before her.

Lárwin had escaped! *She will be safe,* he thought to himself. Turning his face in the direction Ahriman had fled; he gathered his strength and stood upright, gently pushing aside the loving hands of his wife and most trusted friend. He spoke then, with a steady and resolute tone.

"Pull the men back. Tell them not to pursue," he said, his gaze upon the fortress unwavering.

"But sir, we have them…" began Bularius but was suddenly cut off as Leánder's sword burst into a raging blue flame once more, and he understood. This was Leánder's final move.

"Ahriman!" roared Leánder into the fray and walked slowly forward. "Ahriman!" he thundered again, the ground beneath him splintering as waves of energy began to pulsate from Dorlimere and swirl around him tossing back his hair and cloak.

Ahriman was nearing the safety of his fortress. If only he could get there he could find refuge in its endless tunnels and darkness and escape the fearsome light of Leánder's cursed sword. That's when he heard his name, the name of the body he wore, being called out by the King of Men and he cursed the day he had taken possession of it. If only he were somehow free of it, the power he could unleash. But now, being trapped within, his dark heart trembled with fear.

"Ahriman!" cried Leánder the third and final time. "Embrace your darkness!" and as the last of his soldiers fell back Leánder drove Dorlimere's blade deep into the ground and it split with a terrible crack which echoed off into the furthest reaches of the world. In a straight line extending out to his left and his right the ground split and began to give way as deep tremors shook the foundations of the land and steadily, up from the deep fissures, red searing light erupted as burning sulfur and brimstone erupted from the heart of Alária.

Bularius looked on from beside Lorwin with wide eyes as the landscape in front of his king transformed into a hellish scene. He alone, surrounded in wild blue flame, was the only thing untouched by the chaos and complete devastation. The fissures had reached out and split many of the nearby mountains causing unimaginable landslides and liquefied rock to come pouring into the plains below trapping it all as if in a giant bowl.

"Get the men to the ships!" Bularius commanded loudly to his nearest captain, suppressing his fear. Of course most, if not all, were already in an all-out sprint to board the vessels and needed no such order.

He looked into Lorwin's face and saw her fear for her husband and decided to take it upon himself to retrieve him if he could. Sheathing his sword, he began to sprint back to where Leánder knelt at the heart of the burning light. As he approached, however, he had to shield his eyes from the light and strain against wave after wave of energy as it poured from Dorlimere. Finally, he was close enough that he reached out to lay a hand on Leánder's shoulder but as he did so, at the faintest touch, a shockwave blasted out and blew him backward and he landed hard on his back.

His own sword, Ténmei', was loosed from its sheath but for the moment he had no thought of it. He roused himself with effort and approached Leánder again, this time, grabbing him firmly by the armor around his collar and wrenching him backward with all of his might. He knew that no force of his own could separate Leánder's hand from Dorlimere, but gave it his all anyway and as they both fell to the ground the roaring light suddenly vanished. Bularius knew that Leánder had finally let go.

They both lay there for what seemed like a long, long time as the scenery around them engulfed itself in flames and ash. They looked up into the sky and watched as thick smoke rose high into the air and drifted along with the wind. They rested. The battle was over.

Through his one, dirt-covered eye, Bularius caught a glint of sunlight being reflected off something in the sky against the smoke. And then several more as they rose higher and higher like stars in the daytime. They looked so beautiful. Just then there was the sound of a large crash behind them, but he was too tired to look. Instead, he closed his eyes and let come what may.

It was the sound of a boarding plank hitting the ground followed by hasty footfalls. He strained to open his eyes. When he did, he looked to where his king lay and there above him knelt Lorwin cradling her love, behind her, the polished sails of *Sacred Wind* stood proud against the gloomy sky. He felt strong hands lift him up and they were about to carry him when he saw Ténmei' lying in the dirt, its blade buried in rocks.

"Wait," he managed to say and motioned to where his sword lay. Another soldier lifted his sword from the ground and handed it to him, but when he did so he paused for a brief moment as he noticed that the blade now glowed faintly, as though power from Dorlimere had somehow flowed into it and now radiated out. What mystery it meant was lost upon Bularius for the time being however. He quickly faded out of consciousness.

Now aboard *Sacred Wind*, Lorwin sat beside Leánder and prayed. His body still bore the grievous wound dealt by Jädus and the bleeding had slowed, but not stopped. Her tears fell like slow rain at his bedside as she wept for him and their daughter.

He could not have known, she thought sorrowfully. *No one knew...oh Lárwin...* They had both witnessed Lárwin escape from Ahriman's fortress, and accompanied by Evealian soldiers, had assumed she fell back to the ships with the rest of the men. But when the ships were gathered together a count had been made and she was not among them. Leánder was lost in a dreamless state for days and during that time they had searched through the carnage and smoke for any sign of her, but in the end, Lorwin was pierced just as deeply as her husband at the loss of their daughter. With deep sorrow, they began the long journey home.

VIII

Ceciderunt Fortes

The Mighty Fallen

The sky was ablaze with the colors of the sunset. Bright pink and deep purple illuminated the clouds and cast a soft glow upon all those aboard *Sacred Wind*, flying high upon a magnificent sky. The king's crest waved proudly upon the mast. Had it been under different circumstances, Lorwin would have believed it was the most breathtaking sunset she had ever seen. She lowered her eyes from the window. As it was, she looked upon the face of her husband and fought to hide her grief. He had been pierced too deeply to recover and she knew that his end was near. She gripped his hand tightly.

"Do not grieve for me," he said quietly. "I go to the house of Light, our Father's house, in whose mighty company I will stand renewed."

"I know that my love," replied Lorwin softly, a hot tear escaping her eye. "But I dread the thought of you going where I cannot follow…"

He reached up and wiped her tears with a loving hand. "All things have their end. This body will fade with the fading of the sun, but there will come another after me who will finish the fight and put an end to the evil which we've only delayed. You will see him with your own eyes, and when you do, you must give him this." Slowly, and with great effort, he brought Lorwin's hand to the hilt of Dorlimere. "Only he who the Light has chosen can wield it, and he will come to you in a time of great need at the end of all things."

With that he called for his men, his mighty companions in battle, his friends, and they led him out into the fading sun.

"I can stand," said Leánder, steadying himself against the ship's railing. He looked out and took in the sight of Lanália unfolding across the horizon. He longed to see his fair city one last time, yet there in that company of mighty brothers and his wife, he realized what he wanted more than anything was right next to him.

"Captain!" bellowed Leánder with a surprisingly strong voice.

"Yes my lord," replied the captain standing abreast of the steersman.

"What mountains are those which lie beyond the shore?" he said, pointing at the grand peaks on the horizon.

"Those are the White Mountains of the northeastern coast which lay beside the Andír River of Lanália"

"That will do," he said quietly, looking into Lorwin's beautiful eyes. She understood his meaning and she nodded solemnly. "Bularius," he said, motioning him to step closer and placing his hand upon his shoulder. "There is coming a time when the light of Dorlimere will not shine. I have seen the glow of Ténmei' at your side and know that it now holds some of the power bestowed by

Light Enduring himself. Guard it carefully. May it ever remain in your family as a witness to all that has happened in these days."

Bularius' lower lip trembled as he tried to think of his last words to his great friend. "I will…" he managed to say.

The sun was nearly gone and he gave each of his men a long, loving look. Then he turned his gaze back upon Lorwin. He embraced her and held her face in his hands as the last of the sunlight faded.

"There is one more thing I wish to tell you..." he said softly as he ran his fingers through her long hair. "Lárwin lives. Though I do not know how, I have seen it. And you will yet see her with your own eyes… and I as well, though from a distance."

She cradled his hand against her face as she felt hope for her daughter return, yet grief and doubt remained. "This is a mystery to me…How can these things be?"

"I have only seen it in a dream. But I know it to be true. Have faith my love. And hold on to that faith though all the world challenges it...I will see you again...My wife...My love..."

He kissed her, and with that his body glowed and then faded into a million yellow points of light, each one like a small flame carried along with the wind until finally all was gone.

Lorwin let a single tear fall for herself, and then straightened. She ordered the captain to make for the White Falls which pour out their mighty waters at the feet of the mountains, the place Leánder had pointed to. When they arrived, she instructed the men to build a small acropolis upon the summit of a small mountain called Windermere wherein she may hide the sword Dorlimere-Sisu until a worthy bearer claim it.

It took time to build, but they crafted it with skill and great labor. In it they laid a great stone table and behind it, against the wall, they fixed an intricate glass mirror, one of the great signaling mirrors from *Sacred Wind*, now to be used for a much different purpose. When it was completed, Lorwin dressed herself in a simple yet magnificent gown and ordered the sword and Leánder's book be brought to her. Carefully and thoughtfully, she wrote something within its pages before giving it to Bularius for safe keeping. She then sent away everyone save for Leánder's friends, his trusted mighty men, and explained to them the secret of what she was to do.

"Go now my friends. Guard this place throughout the generations to come that only he who is worthy may find it."

They each knelt to their knees and swore on solemn oath to do so, and with that she turned and retreated inside. Laying a seemingly delicate hand on one of the stone pillars, she spoke to the walls.

"May you be found just as you are by the chosen one of the Light." When she finished, she laid herself down gently on the stone table and drew up the sword to her chest. Quietly, in that still place, Lorwin, wife of King Leánder, disappeared. Only her reflection in the glass gave away her resting body as she clasped the sword.

Part II

IX.

In Amet Temporis

The Tides of Time

Some things, once began, cannot be undone. Evil had been birthed into the world and as it grew, its cold and icy grip laid hold of the fiery hearts of Men in the very heat of life, the dawn of their prime. Like a flame in the cold of winter, with the passing of time the agents of Darkness slowly stole their fervency and raging passion bringing low the mighty ambitions of greatness and reducing their glorious triumphs to dust and ashes. Their shining cities with their lofty spires and sky-bound towers lay across the landscapes of Alária in great ruins from horizon to horizon leaving the stories of those who lived and died smashed beneath the rubble, lost to the pages of history. Those who remained were left to wonder at the tales of the past and what great and terrible things transpired there.

Everfall had flourished following the destruction of the First War and its borders had sprawled along the entire western coast of Lanália. From there, many mighty men ventured out into the world fearlessly and charted the world, flying high in the VolNari ships left to them by the first king. Over many hundreds of years they grew into shimmering realms and cities, like pearls fallen from the greatness of Everfall and they grew up to rival it in beauty and stature. Yet as Men cast their eyes toward heaven and reached out to accomplish feats thought unimaginable, shadows lurked in the corners watching... Plotting...Waiting...

In the fall of the throne of Man's great enemy much of his dark army was also fallen or trapped, concealed by the power of the king to a tomb of stone and cold far beneath the surface of Gorgon...but not all. Those who remained of his ranks drifted through the world cut off from his mind and will yet craving his passion for evil as they were made in his likeness. It would take a long time for them to accomplish their task, but as a cancer first begins undetected and works in secret until ruin and death is all that remain, they would corrupt the hearts of Men and bring low their lofty stature. Diming the great light in their eyes until they fed upon their very lives. It took a long time, but as the turning of the tide, as the slow dimming of a light, they eroded the souls of men unaware and wore them down like water upon a stone. The clarity of their eyes clouded, their shoulders slumped beneath their labor, and the span of their years declined. What once was meant to endure through the ages diminished to a span of only a few hundred years...and then two hundred...and finally men thought themselves fortunate to reach the young age of a hundred before their lives slipped away and death overtook their ruined bodies.

Such was the decline of the beauty of Man. As they slipped further and further from the Light their shimmering cities of crystal and stone also became polluted with the ramparts of manipulation and deceit. The children of Everfall grew to resent its power and authority and rose to cut themselves free of its perceived tyranny. It was not too long after that those entrusted to its protection failed in securing peace.

Good men within and without abandoned forgiveness and diplomacy and rose once more to war. The fighting engulfed the known world and the skies were filled with violence and the seas with the blood of brothers. The strength of allied cities matched the might of Everfall man for man, ship for ship, VolNari for VolNari, and for entire generations there was no end to the slaughter. Everfall held firm against the tides of destruction in a war which lasted for nearly a thousand years. It held strong, and may have held out indefinitely...if it were not eroded from the inside by jealousy and resentment incited by a lust for power and orchestrated by the agents of Darkness.

It was on one single day, in the heartbeat of a man, in a moment of weakness, the Evealian strength waned and fell to the victors. Great was its fall. At the tumbling of their walls the ground shook and the night sky blazed with the burning of their homes and grand halls. Dark ash rained down for an entire phase of the moons and the stars were concealed behind the blackened sky for an entire season. Such was the destruction and rain of black that many works of old perished or became lost to memory; even the summit above the great doorway, the passage to safety constructed by the Light across the stars passed from all knowledge. Only the inner capital remained, being carefully concealed just before the end by the Bularians in an enchanted mist hidden against the smoke of destruction by the power of Ténmei. There it lay in secret and saved against the marching passage of time within the fog. Outside, generations of men came and went like wheat in its season and withered away in the heat of the summer sun.

After the destruction of Everfall, the agents of Darkness were free to bring into isolation the habitations of Men and aroused suspicion and jealousy with ease. Their great works declined. Their glory faded. And the thirst for knowledge which once drove them to the heights of accomplishment parched and finally ceased, being replaced with superstition and mystery. Isolationism gripped the world and its icy fingers tightened as the centuries passed.

It was then, as the endless flow of time slowly wore away the binding spell of the king, the bonds of Darkness began to loosen and he was once again able to reach out from the depths of his long imprisonment and call to those of his kind, though he himself still lay entrapped in the body he possessed. It would take another age before he could surface again and bring a final destruction to those he hated, but he had learned patience in his dark prison. He had reasoned that hatred and patience after all, can prove to be a useful ally. During this time he gathered together those men he might sway in dreams and visions to rebuild and establish an empire upon the very ground he now dwelt beneath. Through his evil knowledge and twisted wisdom, the new Gorgonian Empire established itself as the new capital of the world and sought to bring low every other nation and realm until all were subjected to its iron rule. Soon, only a few isolated realms in the southlands and small cities scattered throughout Lanália stood between the shadows of Gorgon and world domination.

All the while, the white beacon, the signal fire above the soaring cliffs in the west which should have revealed the Millennia Gate and called Men to refuge, shined out in all its brilliance beneath the ashes four times…Four times it blazed with fury to summon those who would escape the doom cast upon them by Darkness. Four times it was lit and four times it silently faded away with no one to see it.

Another thousand years would pass before it would steadily glow to life again signaling the opening of the door hidden behind the massive stone gate Leánder had placed upon it. But in that time many things had changed.

A new star appeared in the night sky, dimly, but grew brighter as time passed. As its yellow light grew brighter in the years which followed, many began to suspect that it was the fulfillment of a great prophecy, though none now lived who knew its nature or meaning. No one remembered. No one knew. Yet high in the mountains an unseasonably long rain washed away many years of dirt and stone and when the sky cleared in the weeks that followed, the summit of a lonely and long forgotten mountain stood out against the sun washed anew, waiting for the four brothers of Alária to align themselves one last time.

X

Relicto Domum

Leaving Home

The autumn sky was cool and clear with a strong northerly breeze on the day he was born and his father looked down on him with a stern face as he was laid in his mother's arms. The room they were in was a part of a much greater hall made of stone, the only stone hall in their small village south of the city of Deiriador. Here, things had carried on much the same as it always had for as long as anyone could remember. As the ages of men came and went, the people of the Southlands carried on quietly working their fields and tending their livestock. They were a people of farmers and had a liking to keep things according to tradition, yet often forgetting from where such traditions came from.

For generations, spanning from the time Deiriador was first settled by folk from the north, people spread out into the Southlands and settled the open plains and forests to make farms and villages all across the middle of the continent from the east coast to the west, and for the most part they lived content, happy lives despite their labor. That is of course, until recent years, when rumor of dark things stirring in the night and in the depths of the forests came to the ears of those in the villages from those living in more sparsely populated areas.

Travelers would come with embellished stories of death and the disappearance of whole families, vanishing without a trace even while they sat in their homes. They were only rumor, for no one actually saw any of the monsters that supposedly carried off young maidens or haunted the hunters in the woods. They were fantastic tales used by parents to keep their children in line and not to be believed. For the Lanálian family, they had a monster of their own that was far more dangerous than any evil tale could match up to.

They were in the House of Healing where all came who were sick or suffering from an injury. Today, however, the largest room was reserved for the delivery of the son of Kamaguil Lanálian and his wife Merial. Their four other sons, Jahor, Makïa, Aarondil and Eldïr waited impatiently outside the door, playing idly on a wooden bench or chasing each other up and down the hall. With a sharp glance from their father through the arched doorway all play stopped instantly and they quickly sat unmoving on the bench. Even at such a young age they knew all too well what would await them if they misbehaved in sight of their father. Jahor, the oldest, still held a scar on his chest from the belt used.

Earlier in the spring Jahor had forgotten to clean out the stall of their only horse and answered for it with an unusually harsh beating in front of his brothers as an example. He was only eight, but his father was drunk again and in an evil mood. During one of the swings of his father's belt, the swing went wide and the buckle swung around his side and caught him square in the chest, leaving a nasty cut. He had held his tears until then, but that was unbearable and he let out a cry of pain and anguish. His three brothers began to cry out loud and begged their father to stop. At that he slapped Jahor hard across the face, knocking him to the ground and turned to the other three.

"Stop your crying!" he had shouted. "If I hear one more cry out of any of you..." he said lifting up his belt, red anger pulsing through his contorted face, "I'll make you regret it!" His voice dropped to a mocking tone, "I don't even know why I bother. Half of you probably aren't even my blood knowing that whore you call a mother."

"She's not a whore!" shouted Aarondil, the second youngest yet bravest of the four, clenching his tiny fists. He was six.

Dark wrath and furry flooded their father's eyes as he turned hotly toward him. Fear filled Aarondil and his little fists dropped limply at his sides and he looked down at the ground hoping his father's anger would pass him by. For the children, time seemed to slow as their father let the belt uncurl from his hand and the heavy iron buckle fell and thudded on the wooden floor like the sound of doom. He began to step forward toward Aarondil who stood trembling, waiting for the blows to come.

"Kam stop!" came a weak and fearful voice from across the room. It was their mother, Merial, who until then had hid in their bedroom sobbing. She almost never spoke against the will of her husband, whether he was drunk or sober, especially when he was in a wrathful mood as then.

Her body still carried the scars from the times she had, yet she couldn't let what was happening continue to her babies. She knew if she spoke she would answer for it harshly, but she did so now despite the consequence.

He turned toward her unexpected voice. Hot tears still streamed from her eyes and stained her face as she stood meekly in the doorway. His rage increased as he faced her. Her apparent lack of respect for his authority was to him much more offensive than anything the children had done, and now he had a new target. A look of disgust filled his face and he looked back at his children.

"You're just a bunch of crows anyway. Worthless brats!" he said, spitting on Aarondil's face. He strode hotly to their mother, belt still in hand.

"Go play outside," she managed to say before he grabbed the back of her hair.

Pulling her by the hair he whispered into her ear with an evil voice, "I have something much worse in store for you," and he slammed the door to their bedroom. Jahor, Makïa, Aarondil and Eldïr hurried out of the house before they had to endure the sound of the muffled cries. Such was the conception of their newest brother, nine months later.

Kamaguil looked down at his wife and the baby with contempt as the midwife wrapped another blanket around them. Merial refused to even look up at her husband as she knew all too well the evil look she would see and she did not want this moment taken from her. She held him gently and cooed to him as he lay against her, his eyes sparkling as he looked at the small silver leaf which hung from a frail chain about his mother's neck.

"You have a healthy new son," said the midwife to Kamaguil. "What will you name him?"

Up until now he had not thought much about naming it. He didn't even like to think of him as a person as all he felt was that he was just going to be another mouth to feed and they already could barely feed themselves as it was. To him, this was just going to be number five and he loathed himself, not to mention this unruly wife of his, for making him.

Finally, with a terse tone and a disgusted look he replied "Call him *Quinn*, because he's the fifth mouth I have to feed."

The once happy smile fell from the midwife's face as she looked at him and she quickly looked back at Merial. "That is a fine name, a fine name indeed," she said, shrugging off the father's negative tone.

"Quinn," repeated Merial softly to the baby in her arms. Whispering lower than her husband could hear, she went on, "That name means far more than he says. I know you have a great destiny before you...Don't ever forget that..."

Luckily for Merial and the children a fair summer had brought forth a great harvest and Kamaguil worked long in the wheat fields with the other men of the village, and for long weeks a blessed peace filled the house as her husband worked too long to go out to the pub and came home too tired for beating the family. Throughout the rest of the winter, the other four brothers kept quiet around their father and Merial was extra cautious to tend to his every need and desire as best she could that he be appeased during Quinn's infant months. Even into early spring things appeared well, yet despite their best efforts, when the grain of last year's crops had finally fermented, alcohol again became plentiful and so did the sorrow of Quinn's family. This was the cycle of their lives until Aarondil's thirteenth birthday.

*   *   *

Quinn, a strong and growing boy of nine, was becoming increasingly dissatisfied with their father's treatment.

Quinn sighed deeply and looked up from his wooden plate of old rice and beans. It was more than just the food, he was truly grateful for it and for his mother's hard work around the house, yet looking around the table at the sad and gloomy looks, he had had quite enough.

"He's going to be home soon, isn't he?" asked Quinn looking around the miserable table.

"You know he is dear," spoke his mother, not looking up. Though he did not see her eyes, Quinn knew that she tried to hide her fear of his father.

"You deserve better than this," spoke Quinn directly at his mother's downcast face.

"Shut your mouth!" snapped Jahor, now nearly sixteen. "We cannot change our fate so why make things worse by complaining?"

"Why can't we change? Why do we need him anyway? All he does is bring nothing but misery and today is Aarondil's birthday. Everyone else celebrates birthday's but we don't because we're always afraid Father will get mad... I'm just tired of it."

"Eat your food honey," said Merial quietly.

Quinn was quiet for the rest of the meal and then excused himself with his older brothers to go outside. While the others began to play in an open field Quinn sat at the foot of a great willow tree beside a nearby stream. His mind had been turning in new and unexpected directions for some months now, and as he sat he tried to make sense of it. All of his young life he had been quiet, even quieter than Aarondil, and never complained or even got angry despite his father's injustice. But recently, he noticed that his patience was growing thin with their father and even with the way his brothers continually put up with it even though they were old enough to stand up to him if they wanted. But he realized that they were beaten with fear and had endured many unspeakable hardships even before his was born, so he didn't say anything. He was finding it harder and harder to simply bite his lip and hold his words back though. He knew that someday soon he would let his mouth slip and unexpected things would come flying out at his father if he didn't do something about it. He leaned back against the tree and let his mind drift as he stared at his brother's playing field.

The sun was setting low in the west and the tall grass was ablaze with a bright orange. No wind blew, and despite the arrival of early summer, the evening air was cool. He was at peace. Without knowing it he was asleep and soon, strange images drifted into the mists of his imagination as he dreamed.

He dreamed of an old castle, slowly falling apart in a deep forest, of riding a dragon, the kind he and his brothers made stories about. Of a fierce warrior riding courageously into a battle he had no hope of winning, and of a beautiful woman sleeping with her arms folded about the hilt of a shining sword. The images were faint at first, yet as they became clearer it seemed as though he were actually there, watching from an invisible vantage point all that was happening.

He could make out the bricks and old arches in the castle walls and noted the vines that crept along its stone heights. He could feel the power of the dragon as it heaved its massive wings and hurled them both high into the clouds toward some unknown destination. He heard the distant cry of the warrior as he spurred his horse on toward certain doom, leading thousands as they followed close behind. And then he could see the gentle curves and delicate features of a royal woman clothed in white asleep on a table of stone, holding to her breast a long, shining sword. There his mind seemed to settle, and he looked at her, admiring her. All was quiet and undisturbed, when suddenly she moved her head and looked at him. Quinn was caught off guard and was beginning to feel quite embarrassed, but as he looked at her he was suddenly lost in her blue eyes and noble face. All else was lost to him, and then she spoke. Her voice was strong and deep and in a language he had never heard, though he could understand.

"Your heart is not bound to the fate of your father," she said. Her voice pierced him like an arrow. "You carry a great light within you, and many will follow it, even into bitter darkness."

He tried to take a step toward her and suddenly felt his body was much larger than a boy of only nine. All at once the image began to fade and he strained against it as his waking mind struggled for control.

"Father's home Quinn," shouted Makïa as he and his other brothers made their way back to their little home.

Quinn awoke with a strange sense of destiny. For the first time he felt as though he had some purpose, something larger than himself stirring the gears of fate and tempting him to become something greater. *I'm only nine*, he thought to himself. *What difference could I make?* Yet there it was. And that feeling, as well as the images he saw in his dream haunted him.

He walked slowly toward his home where he knew his family would be waiting. Already he could hear Father's voice yelling and complaining about something his mother or brothers either did or did not do to his liking. Luckily however, it did not sound as though things had escalated to the point to physical abuse yet and for that he was glad. *Glad. What a miserable thing to be glad over.*

His feelings quickly turned to something unexpected and his mind grappled for control before he did something he might regret, but it was too late. Just before he walked into the house, he saw through the open door his father's hand slap Aarondil across the face.

"How's that for your birthday!" he shouted in a drunken stupor. "You probably thought I would forget didn't you? Well that'll teach ya!" he said taking another pull from his bottle.

Something beyond anger sprang up like a fire inside of Quinn. For the first time he felt rage and this time he didn't hold it back. Quinn stepped in through the door behind his father and saw all of his family crying and his mother holding the bleeding face of Aarondil. His other brothers were standing helplessly at their bedroom door. Suddenly they all turned their eyes to Quinn who had just walked in.

Before his father could turn around Quinn planted his foot in his father's back side and kicked him off balance sending him stumbling across the room and dropping his bottle. Perhaps if he had not been drunk, Kamaguil might have been able to react faster. As he caught himself bewilderment flooded his face. Never once had any of his children stood against him, *never*. Oh how he would teach this one a lesson. As he stood to turn around, red anger flooded his face and the rest of the family braced themselves for what they expected to come next, yet instead, something quite different happened.

Quinn stepped in through the door letting his rage guide him. He was never going to let his father lay another hand on his family again for as long as he lived. With that resolve he reached down and grabbed the broken neck of the shattered bottle and placed himself between Aarondil and his father. He stood firm as his father turned toward him slowly, though inside he was trembling. He could feel the eyes of his brothers growing wide. Kamaguil faced his son but through his stupor he did not recognize him, and before he could turn away terror gripped his soul.

Before him stood not the boy he expected but a fierce nobleman in glorious armor, taller than himself and holding a great sword burning with blue flame. Upon his forehead lay a jeweled crown of light and a white flame blazed in his eyes. Kamaguil reeled back in sudden fear and he screamed aloud. To his mother and brothers they only saw Quinn standing there with a broken bottleneck and they marveled as Kamaguil screamed out loud.

"Please... Please don't kill me!" he pleaded in terror.

The image of the ancient king stepped forward, though no one else could see it. "Leave here. Never return and I will spare you."

Kamaguil nodded quickly, grateful to be leaving with his life and he ran for the door, knocking over a chair and nearly busting the door off its hinges. It was the last they ever saw of him.

There in the dim light of late evening, Quinn's mother and brothers stared at him dumbfounded. Quinn dropped the bottle neck and turned toward them, now quite composed as the adrenaline passed, but they continued to marvel.

"Well someone had to do it!" he said, noting their continued bewilderment.

There was a pause..."But," began his mother. "What do I do now?" she sobbed, suddenly feeling lost.

For longer than she could remember, her life had been all about her husband and she had somehow let herself believe that his abuse was normal and the lie that she even perhaps deserved it. But now he was gone and she felt that he would never return. As these thoughts flooded her mind, other emotions, so deep and buried in long forgotten parts of her soul began to surface as well. She didn't deserve the treatment she had been given and neither did her children. She knew it was wrong and evil yet she had always been too weak and afraid to do anything about it. She buried these emotions for years and years until she forgot she ever felt that way and simply accepted the lot she had been given. And now here was her son, her nine year old son standing up to the man she could not. *And how he backed down to him!* she thought to herself. *Who would have thought that he was simply a toothless lion this whole time!* Her prison of fear was now broken, and though it would take a long time before she would ever feel comfortable with that reality again, she knew she was now free, her and her children, and it felt good.

They cleaned up the house, sweeping away the broken glass and rearranging the scant furniture. They all gathered together around their mother in her bedroom. As they lay there letting the night enfold them, Eldïr, the second youngest, looked around their dim house and noted their very few possessions.

"Our house is so empty," he said quietly. "We don't have anything. How are we going to live?"

Merial arose from the blankets and produced a small candle from a drawer. Lighting it with a match she filled the room with its warm radiance.

"This house is full of light," she replied tenderly, looking upon the faces of her children. "And we have each other."

"Jahor, Makïa and Aarondil are already working in the fields. We should make enough to make ends meets," spoke Quinn softly.

"That's right," spoke Jahor quickly, now speaking up and trying to look tough. "Don't worry mother, we'll do just fine. Besides, with him gone all of our money won't be wasted at the pub anymore and so we should have plenty left over." They all shared a light laugh at this as the thought of having excess money had never occurred to any of them. They fell asleep there, all of them together, and for the first time since any of them could remember they all enjoyed a deep, peaceful, and unbroken night of rest. When the sun arose the next day, they found no trace of their father, neither outside their home, nor anywhere in the village.

Quinn rose early to see his brothers off to work and as he stood in the threshold of the door he saw his elderly neighbor Mrs. Ripkin tending her garden outside and decided to ask if she may have seen or heard any of their commotion last night. She had always been more than gracious to him and his brothers and pitied his mother's situation. She often wondered what she could do to get Kamaguil to leave his family alone, but she figured that was futile thinking and so nothing came of it. Still, she longed for the day when someone, or the boys themselves, would finally stand up to him.

"Good morning Mrs. Ripkin, Have you seen anyone about this morning?" he asked.

Looking up from her vegetables Mrs. Ripkin replied, "No dear. I don't think so anyway." She paused. "Come to think about it, I did hear something come run'n by the back door last night. Gave me an awful fright. It almost sounded like some wild animal the way it was hoot'n and holler'n. Must've been scared to death whatever it was. But I didn't hear a peep after that and today's been noth'n but peace and quiet."

"Alright, thanks," replied Quinn, and he noticed a peculiar look on her face as she returned to her garden. Perhaps she somehow knew what had happened, perhaps she knew in full the way nearby neighbors always do, or perhaps only in part, but either way, Quinn and the rest of his family were happy and he wanted the whole world to know. Many other things were soon to change, but for now, all was well and that was all he cared about.

XI.

Quinn Conversus Occidentem
Quinn Turns West

Quinn stood at his post tall and erect and looked out across the eastern plains toward the sea with clear, bright eyes. His hands were steady on the shaft of his spear and his strong back felt the weight of his round shield as it lay strapped across his left shoulder. It had been nearly twelve years since the day he had stood up to his father and now, as a young man of twenty-two, he was facing a world that had changed. The rumors he had heard as a boy of people disappearing in the woods and evil things that lurked in the shadows had turned out to be more than the ramblings of exhausted travelers or the tales of those looking for attention at the bar over a drink.

All had ignored it and pretended that nothing was happening despite the mounting threat, and like one who walks in the night fearing to look behind, everyone carried on until it was too late. Finally, on a fateful day in winter when Quinn was thirteen a rider from Deiriador came to his village with terrible news. The entire village of Yellowgrass had been found emptied of its people, a thousand in all. They had vanished without a trace, leaving no clue as to what had happened. Meals were left half eaten, doors left open swinging on their hinges, tools left in the shops and fields as though dropped suddenly as a fear descended upon them. Upon hearing about this, the King of Deiriador, King Durogan the Second, ordered everyone who would come to gather in and around the city of Deiriador for protection. The city battalion, which had been simply a small group of city guards for more than three centuries, had suddenly grown as villagers and townsfolk alike sought comfort in protection of arms.

That is how Quinn and his brothers found themselves in the Deiriadorian Battalion, better known as the Dorian Army. It had grown from a small group of old men to over two thousand in only a period of months, and those in charge were finding it difficult to manage the new recruits as leadership was sorely lacking. That is how Quinn, as well as his brothers, advanced in rank quickly as they were tougher than many others and had already been through personal trials of their own.

Jahor and Makïa had been promoted to captains as they both showed skill in training others and planning strategy exercises. Aarondil and Eldïr became lieutenants in the archery division as they had grown into excellent bowmen and skilled at long range defense. Quinn however, was too young to join a fighting branch of the service when they moved into the city but instead enlisted as a messenger carrying transcripts from the city to the outlying towns. This excited Quinn because in a way it was much more dangerous than any other task as he was often traveling alone for many days away from the protection of the city. Shortly after joining he was given a horse which he had named Namír, meaning *swift*, and he quickly gained a reputation as being trustworthy and reliable. When he was not delivering messages his duty was guardsman and lookout upon the city wall, which surrounded the inner city.

This is what he was doing now as he looked eastward, wondering if perhaps the nameless fear they had all prepared for was from somewhere over the middle sea. He could not see much of the sea, even from his vantage, except for a long blue ribbon dividing the sky and the ground. Usually, the only way he could tell it was even there was on clear, early mornings during the sunrise when he could see the faint shimmer of yellow sunlight playing off distant waves. Every now and again though, an easterly breeze would bring to his nose the smell of water and he would imagine himself sailing off into the unknown like the legend of Thordul and other brave adventurers.

He was more or less content, however, and thought often of the present circumstances. Many reports had come in over the months confirming that those who had disappeared over the years did not just vanish into thin air but were carried off toward the coast by an armed force which was increasingly showing itself in the open. No one knew from where they had come, but it was clear that they were a strong, warring race, like men but different. Many were taller and darker, pierced with strange adornment, tattoos and ancient armor.

Widespread attacks had been few, but when they happened, they left a deadly wake and only a few lived to tell about it. Now, with most of the people of Mid-Southland gathered in one place, they were feeling safer and more confident. Through leaders like Quinn's brothers, the Dorian Army was stronger, more regimented and disciplined. Many soldiers and bowman boasted their skill and rightly so, for no one in an age had been as skillful as these, and it gave them a sense of strength. Only in one other town, Vitoria, was there another outpost of soldiers liken to those in Deiriador. Vitoria was much smaller, however, since most flocked to the high walls of Deiriador and because that was where the vast majority of soldiers encamped in defense of the king.

The soldiers of Vitoria were originally part of the Dorian Army at the first gathering of people when it was clear that defense was necessary. The people there also had no intention of leaving their homes to ruin. It was also clear to the king that Vitoria held significant strategic value as well since it stretched across both banks of the winding river. If Vitoria fell, then a seafaring enemy would have unrestricted access through all of Mid-Southland, as the winding river stretched all the way from the Middle Sea, through the continental interior and the lake of Clearwater, to the shores of the Great Sea on the western banks. It was originally reinforced with one thousand soldiers, however that number grew significantly as villagers emigrated in from the outlands looking for work and finding it in the service. Regular patrols were sent back and forth between the two cities as well as the surrounding outlands and it was felt that if anything abnormal crossed into their borders they would be able to respond quickly.

Quinn thought about all this as he stood guard over the wall looking outward. He felt proud to serve in the army, even if he wasn't in a combat division, and he thought he looked rather handsome in his uniform. He did not wear a complete set of armor like the foot soldiers or a simple tunic and leather like the archers, his was somewhere in between with brown leggings and steel greaves, a dark blue tunic with a breastplate bearing the city's crest of dual maple leaves and plain steel vambraces over his forearms. His spear and shield seemed strictly ceremonial, yet they made him feel strong and fierce. Of course, he was not the only one who thought so.   Standing there at his post, he felt the slender fingers of a warm hand cover his eyes from behind.

"Guess who," said Nora in her charming, musical voice. She was seventeen and the daughter of his Captain, Captain Toring. Toring Bastille was an impressive man. A farmer before the gathering, he lived a hard life but won respect and honor through his discipline and attention to detail. He expected no less from those under him, and Quinn kept a wary eye out when he was around his daughter. But Nora was chaste and as honorable as her father, though her affections for Quinn were hardly a secret. She had grown up in Deiriador, and had noticed Quinn before he enlisted. It was actually she who had insisted that he join the messenger service when he discovered he was too young for a combat position. She was attracted to his confidence and his good nature and he would be remiss if he said he did not feel similar toward her.

Suddenly jolted out of his daydream, Quinn turned around to see her standing there in her white summer gown, her long sandy hair swaying in the breeze and her dark eyes taking in the sight of him.

"How can you be a look out for the city if you can't even hear a clumsy girl sneaking up behind you?" she asked playfully raising an eyebrow.

"The inner guard down below is supposed to alert me of any danger from *inside* the city, my lady," he jested back. "Though you are a grander sight than anything else I have seen on my long watch today," he added, taking her hand in his and kissing it gently.

"The inner guard knows my father," she responded, "and there are perks to being his daughter."

"And danger," said Quinn playfully, yet somewhat serious as he cast his eyes up to the Command Tower where he knew his captain sat surveying the land.

"I've been looking for you all day," she continued. "There's to be a festival tomorrow to celebrate the first harvest and I wanted to know if you would be able to escort me."

From high up in the adjacent tower, Captain Toring looked down and saw Quinn holding the hand of his daughter. He liked Quinn, he was trustworthy and capable. *He will make a fine captain himself or even more when he is older,* he thought. He even rather enjoyed the idea of him courting his daughter as he knew Quinn would treat her better than any other in Deiriador, though he shuddered to think of ever letting Quinn know this.

"The enemy's out there soldier!" he shouted from the tower window.

Quinn jumped and his face flushed red with embarrassment.

"Yes sir!" he shouted back with a quick salute. Stealing a quick glance back at Nora he added quietly, "I'll be there," and he turned back to his watch.

At this Nora smiled but then frowned as she looked up at her father still starring angrily down at her. When he had finally turned around she childishly stuck out her tongue at him and walked away stubbornly, though she was delighted at the prospect of spending time with Quinn tomorrow.

When Captain Toring had turned around he chuckled to himself and spoke to his first lieutenant.

"See to it that that girl isn't up on the wall again."

"Yes sir," replied the lieutenant.

"And lieutenant," he added more seriously, "see to it that the guard down below gets an extra detail tonight."

"Yes sir."

The rest of Quinn's long shift on the wall was uneventful, but as he made his way home that evening he was filled with excitement at seeing Nora tomorrow, even if he had to endure his brothers' jesting for getting caught with her on the wall today. The city was large, but word spread quickly and they were sure to know.

"So Quinn's officially becoming a man!" said Aarondil as soon as Quinn walked in through the door. Aarondil and Eldïr were already sitting at the table with their mother waiting for Quinn to come home. Jahor and Makïa had wives and homes of their own, and so now it was just the four of them. Merial had also undergone drastic changes. Since the departure of Kamaguil, she had begun to laugh again and there was a light in her eyes Quinn had never seen before. In the absence of violence and persecution, she had grown happier than she had ever been before and Quinn was glad. Seeing them now he walked in and took his place among them.

The next day, Quinn expected to prepare for the Harvest Festival for he was not supposed to be on duty again for another day and a half. He was in deep thought as he pondered his work and what future it may lead to. He loved his position, yet disquiet followed his soul as he thought of the uncertain future. Upon the wall he had much time to reflect on his life and those around him and he decided to take a rare moment that evening to pour his heart out onto a page and became lost for a short time as he wrote his thoughts.

The King Within

Is this a cold February morning I see?
And snow gently falling from a dark sky?
Is this the work that lies before me,
And these the men who share the burden?
Are these the hands and these the tools that earn
My daily bread,
And will tomorrow prove another day as yesterday,
Each one a copy of the same mold?

I close my eyes and this I see:
A sword at my side and a cloak on my shoulders.
I breathe the scented perfume of falling petals
From the castle walls and walk with confidence and

Strength as I enter my kingdom, to rule and to serve.
To live according to the grace and wisdom of Light,
And fight with valiance and bravery the armies
That threaten my realm.

Yet when I open my eyes, I am as I was,
Frail, a coward and wanting to be
Something so much more than a boy
Looking up at thee.

Will I ever change, my Father in Heaven?
Will I ever find the strength to stand naked
Before men and answer with bravery?
Will I ever find my Love and make her my queen,
And will she want to be with me, even though
I see myself a failure and may never be
The man I see when my eyes are closed,
Who I'm truly meant to be?

I love you Lord, and I trust in you,
Because you have made the boy and made the king
Who both live in this heart of mine.
If I trust and if I believe,
I know someday through the course of time,
You'll teach this boy to be the man I see
Not just when I close my eyes,
But also when my Queen awakes to a brand new day,
And sees her king lying close beside.

He concluded and leaned back in his chair and sighed. Little did he know that this would be the last time he would enjoy such heartfelt expression for a long time. There was a heavy knock on the door. He quickly folded the paper and placed it in his pocket. Everyone else had gone to work, including his mother who was now managing a nearby inn, he was puzzled as he answered the door.

When he had opened the big wooden door, there before him was Captain Toring with a serious look on his chiseled face.

"Sir I apologize for Nora being on the wall yesterday..." stammered Quinn, but Captain Toring cut him off before he could continue.

"This has nothing to do with Nora, Quinn," he began, and it was only then that Quinn noticed the leather pouch slung across his shoulder. "I have an urgent dispatch from the king that must be delivered to Vitoria with all speed. The enemy has been spotted just twenty miles south of here and we may be in need of reinforcements."

Quinn was young, but his sense of duty was strong, especially at hearing such news. "Yes sir, I'll be ready in just a moment," he replied feeling the gravity of the situation. "Please come in."

"I mustn't tarry, preparations must be made and others need to be alerted," said Toring, handing Quinn the leather pouch.

Pausing briefly, Quinn remembered his promise to Nora to escort her to the festival. "Sir, can you tell Nora-"

"I'll tell her," he said shortly but kindly. "Now go. I must be off as well. May the Light be with you!"

"And with you," said Quinn as Captain Toring turned and quickly left.

Quinn redressed himself in his uniform and light armor and darted across the street to the stables where the horses of the guard were kept. There waited Namír who was surprised and happy to see her master. Namír was tall and black, perhaps the fastest horse in the city. Quinn was issued her after a year of foot-running messages and she had grown much taller and stronger since then. Namír's back now stood at eye level with Quinn and her flanks rippled with muscle, toned for running quickly over great distances. Quinn had taken good care of her while they grew up together, and now she was the envy of every other rider in the service.

Quinn gathered her saddle and bridle and soon they were charging from the city out into the open plains with their urgent message.

The tower guard saw him early and ordered the gate open quickly when he noted the speed at which Quinn was riding. *It must be an urgent message indeed, the way he is riding.* The gate swung wide and Quinn plunged through without breaking his stride and they were off, out into the open plains and soon northbound on the road to Vitoria.

He chose the most direct route possible since there was no report of any evil along the main road. It led him through many winding valleys and over many grassy hills until the halfway mark which turned to thick forest. At his fastest speed, Quinn gathered that it would take nearly three days to reach Vitoria, even with the power and speed of Namír. He rode hard and long that first day and camped by the roadside at an empty guardhouse well after sunset.

The next day he set off early, at the very break of daylight before the sun ever rose. He rode for hours through the open country until the sun was high in the sky and framed with vanilla colored clouds. His armor, light as it was, was stifling and the leather strap of his shield dug into his shoulder as it thudded against his back with the beat of Namír's steady stride. He was grateful when he reached the Vitorian Forest. There in the cool shade of the woods he found shelter from the grueling heat of summer.

Through the thick trees he could not see the smoke rising from Vitoria nor smell the burning of the houses. In his haste he did not notice how quiet and still the forest was, as though it was hiding from an unseen menace lurking somewhere in the shadows. He pushed every thought aside as he raced toward his goal. When he camped that evening and lay down on his bed roll, Namír seemed restless and at one point neighed wildly as he was just beginning to fall asleep.

"Easy girl, easy," he said. "We're ok and there's nothing to worry about," he reassured. It was strange, but when he spoke to Namír, he felt as though she could actually understand what he was saying and she calmed down quickly. He returned to his bed roll and closed his eyes.

When all was still and the fire had burned low to only a few smoldering embers, Quinn noticed, even in his sleeping mind, how eerily quiet the forest seemed. He slept lightly and uneasily. It was still dark when his eyes opened at what he thought was the beating of drums. He laid there, quiet and still, feeling the air. *Something* had caused him to awake. As he looked around in the dark forest, only pale shafts of silver moonlight met his eyes. He closed them once more and fell back into an uneasy sleep until morning.

At dawn the next day, a heavy mist lay on the woods and Quinn was forced to travel slower, though still at a good pace. He expected to meet people along the way traveling to and from the city the closer he got, but instead he was greeted only with emptiness and quiet. As he emerged from the forest into a clearing surrounding the city, Quinn's fear arose as he saw black smoke rising from within. He dug his heels into the sides of Namír and they jolted toward the gate of the city. The city walls around Vitoria were nothing compared to Deiriador. Deiriador's were erected many generations ago when there was a fear of evil things from ages long past; yet Vitoria was much younger and for hundreds of years had no wall at all until recently when the locals built a hastily constructed wooden stockade and garrisoned it with soldiers.

Now, the gate hung loosely from its last hinge and swayed lonely in the quiet, smoky air. As Quinn entered through the gate his breath was taken away at the sight he saw. The entire city had been burned and its people slaughtered. Soldiers and civilians alike lay lifeless in the streets and carrion fowl circled high overhead. All at once the stench hit him in the face and he and Namír both reeled back in shock and horror.

The days of people and towns simply disappearing were over. Open war had now come, and the enemy was not afraid to make their presence known. Whatever purpose they had to carry off those before had obviously been fulfilled and now they didn't need any more left alive.

Quinn produced a cloth and covered his mouth and nose as he regained his composure. Mastering his fear, he slowly walked through the streets surveying the horror. It was his duty to report whatever happened here to the king. In the square he found the worst of it. In the town square and in front of the worship hall were charred remains of at least two hundred fallen Vitorian soldiers. Behind them was the hall, and within Quinn could barely make out the bodies of countless victims who had barricaded themselves inside. The soldiers outside were obviously a brave last stand to defend the civilians inside, but to no avail. The soldiers outside lay bloodied and cleaved, and those inside burned alive. Quinn had seen enough. He felt his stomach rising in his throat and he had just enough time to dismount before falling shakily to his knees and throwing up.

With his head down nearly to the ground, he heard the deafening quiet of the town and it tortured him. Valiant men lay with mouths open in mid-scream yet no sound came. Swords and spears were held ready to strike in cold, unmoving hands that never had a chance. Their lifeless eyes were caught in various stages of grief and pain and they starred openly at him from the ground. He was surrounded by thousands, yet he was the only one. He closed his eyes. Suddenly, he heard the sound of anguished weeping in the distance and he jumped at the sound.

He grabbed the reins of Namír and led her toward the sound not knowing what to expect. Coming around the corner of a once busy street, he saw in the clearing mist an old woman with a fallen soldier in her arms. She wept bitterly as she looked down at his face. Looking up through her tears, she saw him, yet her eyes were glazed with grief and immeasurable sadness.

"They spared no one, not even my husband," she said through the tears and gripped the body tight.

"What happened here?" Quinn asked, controlling his voice.

"They came out of the night before the morning yesterday," she said with an eerie, disconnected voice. "They killed everyone, even the babies!" her voice swelled with sadness at the last part and fresh tears flooded her eyes.

"How many were there? Which way did they go?" Quinn probed, trying to get anything useful out of her he could take back to the king.

"I don't know, I don't know," she said, looking back down at her dead husband.

Quinn touched her shoulder gently and looked at her, "Please, tell me which way they went," he said softly.

"I heard them marching off down the Old South Road. I heard their drums as I hid in the field outside the city."

Quinn's stomach dropped as his heart filled with terror. The Old South Road was a less traveled road that wound through the roughest parts of the forest between Vitoria and Deiriador. Not many people use that way anymore since the making of the Main Road. That's when he remembered the sound of drums as he slept the night before. But they were much too far away to be coming from Vitoria. They must have passed on quickly toward Deiriador in the night. Quinn mounted Namír and dug his heals hard into her side. Fear filled his heart and all his mind as he tore through the dead city and out onto the Main Road. He had to get back to Deiriador before it was too late...if it wasn't already...

Quinn drove Namír hard, harder than ever in both their lives, in the race back to Deiriador. Sensing her master's haste and fear, she strove to keep up with his demands. When darkness came, they only slowed their pace and stopped only when it was too black to continue.

A few short hours later they were on their way again, pushing hard against the wind that seemed to refuse to part fast enough before them. Namír's hooves pounded the dirt and ate up the ground at a frenzied pace. As they entered the borders of Deiriador, Namír spent her last strength in the final push to the city and hurled Quinn faster than he had ever gone toward his goal, yet that wasn't nearly fast enough for Quinn whose sole thought was to warn his king and family.

Toward evening of the second day, as he came galloping over the last of the hills into the plain before the city walls, Quinn let out a painful cry at what he saw. Terror gripped both him and his horse, both reeling back. Quinn was thrown from his saddle. He landed hard on the trail and his breath was knocked out of him. Namír also had fallen next to him, and she lay there panting hard, muscles burning after the long run from Vitoria. Quinn looked up from where he lay and took in the sight of the fallen walls, disbarred gate and faint smoke rising from within. Fair and noble knights lay strewn in the fields and large black vultures gathered near the fallen.

All within and throughout him went numb as shock set in and he felt nothing...only cold. He stood, shaking, and walked slowly with wide eyes toward his fallen home. He passed the bodies outside the walls and burned fields and entered through the ruins of what was once the main gate, the one he had ridden through with haste toward Vitoria just five days prior. He took in the desolation which lay all about him. It seemed not one building was left on its foundations. Not one home left unburned or unsullied. Even the king's keep and the watchtower where Captain Toring commanded were in utter ruins. *Captain Toring. Nora.* His thoughts flashed back to the image of the town square of Vitoria and what he had found there. He suddenly broke into a run through the desolated streets toward the square.

When he rounded the corner, his worst fears were realized. Here was much the same as what he had witnessed in Vitoria. The uniforms of the Dorian soldiers were a different color than those of Vitoria, but their dashed bodies and fallen arms told the same story as they lay outside the Worship Hall. What lay within haunted Quinn for many years, and his life was altered forever.

Stepping carefully over of the fallen with great care and respect, Quinn walked slowly toward the burned remains of what used to be the entrance to a tall arched doorway leading into the Hall of Worship. The sun was sinking low in the west and a light breeze stirred the ashes as he climbed the stone steps to the entrance. Looking within he saw a wide shaft of red sunlight slanting in through the bare timbers of the fallen ceiling. There in the hall, huddled together in the middle were the remains of a mass of charred skeletons clutching each other in fear and confusion as their world choked with smoke.

Quinn marked what was left of their small bodies and knew that most were women and children. The brave men of Deiriador had defended it to the last man, but it was not enough. Quinn stood only a short distance from where the huddled mass lay when a sparkle of sunlight caught his eye. He stepped forward and looked down into the ashes. What he saw pierced through his numbness and he fell to his knees with a shout of bitter anguish.

There in the ashes were two objects, side by side in the black ruin. The first, an embroidered silver bracelet he had given to Nora on the day he had met her. The other was a small, silver oak leaf, the pendant which once hung from a delicate chain from the neck of his mother. Quinn clutched the two pieces in his shaking fists and buried his face in them letting out a long and terrifying scream. He could see what happened there as clearly as though he was there.

The enemy in the south was a decoy and misled the troops as an unexpected attack came from the north. The archers and soldiers held the wall for as long as they could, but when the wall and the gate collapsed and the keep was beyond saving, the survivors took refuge in the next strongest stone building, the worship hall. It was here, at this very spot where Quinn now knelt in uncontrollable anguish, that Nora and his mother clung to each other as the soldiers outside died and the building was set on fire.

He did not know how long he knelt there or how many tears poured out of his eyes, but when he finally stood, something within him had changed.

"Quinn!" came a distant cry from a wounded voice. It took him a moment, but it was familiar to him.

"Quinn... my brother!" it said again. Finally, Quinn looked up from where he now stood and saw the bloodied and stained body of his brother Eldïr standing before him just outside the threshold. Quinn walked quickly to him and embraced him. There in that desolate place they wept bitterly for a long time.

They walked together outside the city as the sun was setting and Quinn found that Eldïr was wounded badly, though not mortally. He confirmed what Quinn had thought about the enemy in the south being only a decoy.

"They came out of nowhere," said Eldïr. "They were like demons, and they were silent as they approached. It was on the second night after you left when the attack began, and we had no idea until the first boulder slammed into the watch tower. They brought in wheeled trebuchets and surrounded us from a distance all around. All at once we heard the sound of deafening drums coming from all directions and yet they lit no torches and carried no light with them and so it was impossible for us to count how many there were. Panic spread. Captain Toring and some of the other commanders though, they held it together. They stood strong and rallied everyone to their positions. As the blows began to come, the wall shook but it held tight. Then there was a pause and I heard a loud cry from the enemy, some command but I could not tell what it was. Then I heard the trebuchets launching once more, but when the rocks collided with the wall, they erupted with thunder and light. I had never seen anything like it before. The wall began to shatter and come apart like wood. When the gate fell, I was just inside and barely missed being crushed by falling stone. It was then that the enemy rushed in.

"They appeared to be men at first, and I felt my fear diminish. Men I could understand. Men I had a chance to defend against. But as the first wave burst through the outer defenses, I shot an arrow through the heart of one of the intruders. It was a clean shot, straight through the breast of his unarmored chest. His body fell as he entered the gate, but..." Eldïr paused as if making sure he was remembering properly.

"As I prepared another shot, I..." horror crossed his face as he replayed the images in his mind. "I saw a black shadow rise from his body...I couldn't believe it. It was like his soul was visible to me. It was black and horrible, impossibly bigger than the body it had come from. As I watched, it quickly entered into the body of another man who had come up from behind. It was as though it was using men's bodies. As they fell and died it would discard them and move on to the next one." He shuddered. "That was the last I remember seeing. Another thunderous rock struck nearby and its sound was the last thing I heard. When I awoke, it was the end of the next day and a villager was pulling me out of a pile of bodies which had fallen on top of me. Stragglers from the outlands came in after the battle and we've been trying to pull ourselves together ever since. But there are few of us...and no one to lead..." he ended quietly, bowing his head with sadness. Quinn placed his hand on his brother's shoulder and they both wept. Namír found them there and walked humbly to her master with her head hung low. Quinn turned, stroked her nose and back and untied the saddle. There they camped and spent a sleepless night.

Over the next two days the gruesome work of burial occupied the survivors. Each one was a dear friend or relative and the task was beyond heartbreaking. When it was finished, countless graves marked the fields beginning about a mile out from the city and covering the hills beyond. Many were too butchered or burned to be recognized or named.

Quinn stood over Nora's grave which was next to his mother's, his other brothers he never found. His tears had run dry and now he stood with quiet resolve as he hung Nora's bracelet on a chain about her gravestone, his mother's silver leaf pendant however, he wore about his own neck. He turned and walked away. He was on his way to his horse when he passed Eldïr who stood nearby.

"Where are you going?" asked Eldïr.

"The enemy went west..." spoke Quinn coolly.

Eldïr gave him an odd look.

"That is my road," he said, mounting Namír. It was only then that Eldïr noticed the supplies Quinn had fitted onto his saddle.

"You're only *one* man!" exclaimed Eldïr, his eyes widening. "There is a whole army out there and who knows how many more!"

"I'm not asking you to come with me brother," said Quinn, looking down at his older brother with compassion. "But some things *must* be done."

Looking up into the eyes of his brother, Eldïr felt a sense of leadership rising up in Quinn and his spirit longed to follow it. In him were resolve and action, and Eldïr wanted to be a part of it.

"Then I will come with you," he said.

Quinn nodded. He waited patiently with Namír until Eldïr gathered what was left of his belongings. He then outfitted one of the remaining guard horses.

Together, they set off into the west.

XII

Venator et Praedam

Hunter and Prey

Soaring at an incredible height, Whitefeather hunted for his daily supper. His keen eyes carefully searched the dry plains below noting every moving shadow in the charred fields and every blade of burnt gray grass. An increasingly common sight indeed. Food itself was becoming harder to find in these days and even the smallest scrap was not taken for granted. *I remember when I used to be picky*, he thought as his stomach rumbled and his wings caught another updraft.

He was large and hardy for a hawk, with wings which stretched the length of a man. They were shimmering black, yet when he was born his mother marked one white feather on his left wing for which he was named. It had been many years since he last saw the wings of his kin or heard their cry on the wind as they hunted the Thordul Plains together. Indeed many other fond creatures had all but disappeared as the days darkened. He had been forced to venture further and further north of even the Amanduil, the Gorgon Mountains in the human tongue, in search of food as even the smallest creatures left their happy homes in the once tall, yellow grass of the plains and kept now to the rocky crags of the foothills to avoid preying eyes. Not the eyes of birds of prey however, but far more sinister hunters which killed for sport rather than food. Whitefeather shuddered at the thought for he had seen many evil things during his lonely flights above the northern plains.

Suddenly his sharp eyes perceived movement against the shadows below and he threw himself into a swift dive headlong toward his prey. Before the tiny creature even knew what was happening he was upon it, his powerful wings scooping up the air as his talons pinned the furry thing to the ground. He looked down at the mouse he had found and decided that his hunger couldn't wait to carry the thing away. This was as good a place as any for dinner. He opened his yellow beak and reached for the rodent when he heard an unexpected voice.

"Wait!" screamed the mouse, finally able to catch his breath.

Whitefeather stopped short and closed his beak with surprise. Of all his years hunting he had never caught a mouse with courage enough to confront him during a strike.

The mouse coughed beneath the weight of the claws which held him to the ground. "Before you strike," he began with a frail voice, "I need to tell my story."

"Your *story*?" started Whitefeather with his commanding voice. "What story could a mouse tell that would keep me from having dinner for the third night in a row?" he asked eyeing the mouse closely.

"I assure you sir; my story is worth the hearing. I beg

your patience, for if my story does not shake you to your soul or demand something greater of yourself than you may have your dinner," said the mouse, sounding surprisingly confident for being under the hawk's talon, though weakness was in his voice.

Looking down at the mouse, Whitefeather's stomach rumbled and his eyes flashed with hunger. He was not given to rashness, however, and his curiosity at this brave rodent was getting the better of him; besides, the mouse stood no chance of escape.

"I have looked far and wide these days for food and found only you. Believe me when I tell you that if this is an attempt at escape my eyes can spot a flea a mile away at night and I will be looking only for you," said Whitefeather darkly, and with that he removed his talons and stepped back from the small creature, yet marked his every move lest he be deceived.

"Thank you sir," replied the mouse regaining his breath.

Whitefeather noticed how weak the little mouse seemed and it appeared to him that he was not the only one in need of food.

The mouse picked himself up with an effort and brushed himself off. First his big, pink ears and then his grey-brown fur. He walked lightly over to the bemused hawk and pulled up a small stone to sit on. "My name is Tavi Quicktail," he began after a deep breath, "and the story I am about to tell you should not be taken lightly," he said looking defiantly up at the hawk.

Whitefeather would have laughed long and loud at any other mouse desiring his audience, yet the serious expression on Tavi's face and the haunting look in his large black eyes gave him pause.

"I am from the mouse village of Brownfield some miles south of here, which lies under a large rocky overhang. Well, large for mice-folk anyway. It was a day like any other back then. A warm summer day it was with a fresh breeze blowing down from the mountains across the plain." His eyes closed in remembrance. "It was the day of the Summer Festival when we would celebrate the year's seed gathering in preparation for winter. All the mice of the village would turn out and we would feast ourselves on the best of the land in order to pack on a few extra grams for winter." He chuckled at this as he patted his now thin and empty stomach.

"My wife and I lived on the far end of town and were running late because we were busy with our young ones. We headed out and were happy then." Whitefeather noticed a small warm smile form on his lips as he remembered. "There was suddenly smoke in the air," he said, his smile quickly fading. "Thick grass-smoke and it became inescapable. We heard screams from the village and shortly after everyone came running for dear life as flames kicked up behind them. In the confusion I lost my family as I was forced to run from the flames with the rest. We ran and ran as far as we could until we came upon a large rock which I climbed upon to see if I could spot my wife and children but the smoke was too thick. Just then, I felt a hand grab me and force me into a small box. 'She'll like this one,' I heard an evil man's voice say. I was kept in that box for hours and hours, days even, being fed only dry crumbs of stale bread. I had no idea if it was night or day and I began to realize that as I was being carried away, my family was not missing, it was me! I was missing and I had to get back to them. Finally, after what seemed like an eternity had passed, the box opened and I found myself in a large glass box looking at the tail end of a gigantic green and black snake with a golden stripe down its back. My purpose there was clear and time was short. Before it noticed me I was able to grab a twig from among the debris on the floor of the cage and I bit off the end of it to make it into a sharp point. Thus being armed, I felt rage building within me. I was angry for what happened to my home, angry for being lost to my family, angry for being carried away into the dark and I would be damned if I was going to be food for a witless and arrogant snake!" His anger grew to a crescendo.

"I wanted him to face me and get whatever end I was to meet over with so I poked his backside to get his attention. He quickly turned to me with surprise and stared down at me with cold, penetrating eyes. Thinking back on it now, it was probably not the brightest move, but in my frenzy I shouted loud and said, 'If you're gonna eat me than let's have it you snake!' Before I knew it he lunged right for me, but they don't call my family Quicktail for nothing, and as he came down on me I pierced his eye with my twig spear. He jumped back coiling in pain and surprise. So great was his thrashing about that he knocked the whole glass cage off its pedestal and when it shattered on the floor I was able to escape into a small hole in the wall of the room. None too soon either, as I heard footsteps rushing in right after. I heard one swear and another yell. They were both trying to grab the snake which was loose and furious amidst the broken glass.

"Accompanied by the various noises I heard one wretched man say, 'first we get back late from the field-burning and miss chow and now this! In the name of Ahriman-' to which the other voice cut him off mid-sentence. 'Ahriman's name is not to be used lightly' said the other sinister voice. 'He'll be runn'n the whole joint before too long and you best watch your tongue before *you're* fed to a snake. Where's that mouse got off to any ways? That there was all we could find for poor Tulip here.' 'Probably off 'n some hole somewheres. We'll never find 'em now anyway. Let's get this glass 'ere cleaned up before the master gets in.'

"What became of *Tulip* or the two ruffians I don't know, but I waited there in that crevasse for a long time wondering what I should do when I felt a dark presence and heard their master return, swearing about his two idiot servants. He was with another person of apparent importance I learned as they began talking to each other, and this is where you need to pay attention Mr. Hawk," said Tavi leaning forward and placing his front paws on his furry knees.

"You may call me Whitefeather," said the hawk cordially, trying to hide his obvious interest in Tavi's story. "Please continue."

Tavi's voice was cold and haunting as he returned to his story. "They began to speak of evil things, some things which I will never utter as long as I live, but I tell you in truth that they spoke of an end of all that we know. This *Ahriman* is apparently an ancient dark lord and is right now preparing an assault upon everything that is green and good in this world. This is why all but his servant's fields have been burnt, why all the animals are missing here and why the days grow darker. They laughed of kidnapped families forced into servitude and made slaves to demons of darkness and how Ahriman will reward them for their service. I was terrified and at my wit's end when I heard them speak of Men far away in the northwest in a place called Everfall which pose their only threat. Hope! I thought to myself. They spoke of a shimmering army stationed there with high banners and gleaming shields ready for the defense of the west. 'Everfall was abandoned long ago,' said the one. 'But it was ever a place beyond understanding and not to be underestimated,' said the other. 'Safety in secrecy is what I always say,' said the first, 'and there is yet none who could even guess our plans until it is too late.' At this they shared a hardy laugh and I shrank in utter hopelessness there in my hole. But while I was there, I thought of the once green field of my village and my wife and daughter out there and how they would be harmed if these fiends have their way. I gathered what courage I could and when all seemed quiet and still I made my escape.

"For days I crept through holes and tiny opening in the walls and ate what wretched crumbs I could find. I climbed higher and higher through that stone labyrinth following my nose toward sweeter air. What I saw and the things that happened along the way amazed me."

*   *   *

Tavi emerged into yet another room after taking a route he thought would lead him toward the palace entrance but instead found it to be just another wrong turn. Days before he had found what he thought was the main entrance into the vast fortress, as he saw in the dimness soldiers going back and forth through a massive gate and what he thought may be distant sunlight on the other side. His heart had leapt for joy at the thought that he may actually be able to escape, but he dared not venture closer than he already had as troops were continually moving back and forth through the gate and he may be crushed. He then ventured back into the main palace where he supposed their leader took residence (as his was the fanciest palace in all the ugliness of that subterranean world) and thought that perhaps there may be another means of escape unknown to the common troops.

Upon finding his way in, however, Tavi quickly realized that this abode was more tightly shut and harbored more secrets than any other place he had seen in the dark city. It had many twists and turns and for a time, Tavi was frightful that he may not be able to find his way out. That is how he found himself in the room he was in now.

He had come out on an upper ledge midway up the ceiling through an ancient crack in the stonework and had a good view of everything in the room. It was strikingly different from the others, however, as it was brighter than the rest, being lit by many candles and torches perched high on the walls which were filled with all manner of priceless artifacts and weapons. Countless swords, decorated spears and golden shields lined the walls and shined in the firelight. Standing tall against the sides of the room were enormous coats of armor, the defenses of valiant but unfortunate men. They now starred through empty helmets put on display as though they were some prized kill. Tavi realized that this was indeed a trophy room and these must be the master's most prized possessions. In the center of the room, across from a plush, throne-like seat, Tavi saw a statue which he did not expect as it did not match the others and did not seem to belong. It was a young woman, beautiful indeed even to a mouse, yet with a fearsome expression as if she was poised to attack. She held a double edged sword with both hands out in front of her as though in mid-swing. Her stance was strong and defiant and her face was filled with nobility and virtue. Such was the sight of this statue that Tavi had to have a closer look.

Climbing down an embroidered rope which hung from one of the torches, he made his way to the smooth stone floor and stood at the foot of it. The statue looked so lifelike, down to the smallest detail, but now that he stood closer he was puzzled all the more as he could see that the entire statue was covered in a thin coat of clear ice. From the tip of the sword to her long auburn hair which seemed to swing over her shoulder, to the soles of her feet; all was encased in ice. Tavi stood and marveled at it for a long time. He then understood what the throne-like seat was for. He could imagine the master of this dismal place sitting on it for hours, like a king admiring his most prized trophy, mesmerized by her. *She looks so fierce,* thought Tavi. *He must think about* that *too...*

Suddenly, footsteps and shuffling from outside the vaulted door stole his attention. He crept quietly toward the door and found that he could just sneak underneath the bottom of it and see what was happening on the other side.

Just on the other side of the door stood a heavily armored guard at his post and beside him a chair with a cup of water on it. On his belt were fastened a brass ring of keys and in one hand he held an intimidating spear. From around the corner came dim torchlight which Tavi could just make out as the stranger emerged from a massive hall. He was a strongly built, yet hunched-over man, ancient looking and with an evil expression.

"Falling asleep again are we?!" he began.

"No sir!" replied the guard, hastily snapping to attention.

"You lie as bad as you guard your post! Look at that stain there on the floor by were you sat. In your haste to get up you nearly spilled that cup, which you aren't supposed to have anyway. Especially here. You men from the outside have no manners at all do you? You don't even know what it is that you guard."

"No sir! I mean yes sir! I mean, I know it's important sir," stuttered the guard.

"Maybe so, but you don't know the danger of what lies within, nor the danger of that water there. If so much as a drop were to enter that room the master would have your head! Now hand it over."

The guard sheepishly handed over the cup of water which the other took carefully. "Now, other than this, you have seemed like a good lad and I've come to tell you that you'll be training a new recruit eager to come in from the labor of the master's fields. Your shift is over shortly, and when it is you're to go top-side and fetch him. His name is Angburt and he is from your old field so you may know him. See to it! And let me not catch you again with any water here or I'll send you back to the fields myself."

His superior turned to leave but the guard stopped him.

"Captain, Sir," he began, and the other stopped short but did not turn.

"Yes?" spoke the captain tiredly, wanting to be free from the guard.

"What could a little water do to anything in that room?" asked the guard hesitantly.

The captain turned but not all the way as he took a deep breath and sighed heavily. Speaking over his shoulder in a low tone he said, "Only a few know, and certainly not me, but I've heard the Ancients speak of a witch the Master trapped long ago and kept as a prize. They say she nearly killed him once, and that water is the only thing which could set her free again. Beware the water." With that he turned again and left, leaving the guard to his post. Tavi heard him mumble something under his breath when he knew he was alone again, and he produced a small flask, obviously filled with more water.

"*Ha!*" muttered the guard quietly. "I don't believe in such nonsense, and they can send me back to the fields anyway, at least then I'll see the sun again." He took a long pull from the flask.

Tavi returned to the room and thought about what he had heard. He looked at the statue of the young woman again and then it struck him. She was no statue at all. She was someone trying to kill this *master* and nearly succeeded. That is why she was standing the way she was, with her eyes and blade tilted slightly up toward a taller opponent. She must have been frozen in that icy spell before her death-blow could strike and here she remains, to be trophy for a madman. As Tavi thought, another idea came to him. The guard is due to leave any moment to the surface. The guard has water. And here was perhaps the only other person who probably wanted to be free just as much as he did, though she did not know it. His course was then resolved and his objective clear, though he did not know how he was going to do it or even if it would work. Still he had to try.

He crept silently back out to where the guard sat, dozing off again in his chair, his flask hanging precariously from his loose fingers as his hand swinging limply from his side. Tavi walked over and stood at his foot thinking about what to do. He noticed that the guard was obviously underpaid as his low shoes barely covered his feet and were probably a size or two too small.

Looking at his exposed ankle, Tavi said to himself, "Well, here goes nothing," and with that he opened his mouth wide and sunk his teeth into the smelly flesh of the guard's foot.

The guard screamed in pain and jumped up, nearly crushing Tavi and dropping his flask. He saw the mouse almost instantly and his first thought was to kill him, forgetting all about the water which now spewed from his open flask underneath the door. Tavi quickly jumped aside from the guard's pounding feet and dove underneath the door; out of reach.

The guard reached down and rubbed his ankle and it was then that he saw his near empty flask at the foot of the door. Inside, the water was steadily making its way to the middle of the chamber. Horror filled the guard as he fumbled for the keys. He had never been inside the room before, but he had to stop the water before something terrible happened. Tavi watched as the water crept closer to the statue. Just then, the guard burst in through the door and for Tavi time seemed to slow as the guard saw how far the water had gone. It was nearly at the foot of the icy figure when he went into an all-out run to stop it.

His face twisted into astonishment as he reached for the leading edge of the water and began to mouth the word "Nooooo!!" but he was too late. The water touched the ice. Without warning, as though a million tiny shards of crystal suddenly exploded into the air, the ice shattered. Lárwin's blade, which had hung mid-swing for five thousand long years, came howling through the air finishing its course...a thin strip of red blood slung onto the wall and the guard stood there, blinking silently. Then his head rolled smoothly off his shoulders as his body slumped to the floor.

Lárwin stood there breathless and in cold confusion. Where was she? How did this happen? Where was Ahriman and the battle? She looked around in fear and confusion, wondering where she was, not even noticing the melting ice which clung to her skin and lay at her feet.

"I...I don't understand..." she said weakly as she looked around the room.

"Miss?" spoke Tavi shyly after a moment's pause.

Startled at the sound, Lárwin raised her sword once more and faced the voice, though she knew not who spoke it.

"Who's there?" she asked as defiantly as possible, though struggling to control her fear.

"I'm... I'm down here my lady!"

Lárwin looked down and saw the tiny creature which had climbed onto the back of the fallen guard. She was at first astonished that he spoke with audible words unlike the cardinal from long ago, but then abandoned the thought as she recognized him as a friendly creature. So happy was she at seeing a friendly face and confused at her surroundings that she could not contain herself. She spoke shakily through hot tears which began to well up in her eyes.

"Oh mouse, please tell me what has happened! Where is my father and what news of the battle? Where am I?" She scooped him up in her hands and sat him on her knee as she poured out her questions and sat on the plush seat.

"I am sorry my lady," began Tavi shyly, folding back his ears and looking down. "I know nothing of battles gone by, though I have heard of one yet to come. As far as I know, we are in an evil palace far underground and we must escape, and soon, for our opportunity is passing."

"Then...yes...I know where we are," she said sitting upright and wiping away her tears. "Forgive me mouse, I am usually more polite than this."

"It is no matter my lady. I am Tavi, Tavi Quicktail. And forgive *me*, for I know not who you are, save for an enemy of my enemy."

"My name is Lárwin, Daughter of Leánder, first of Men, and I am the enemy of Ahriman the deceiver. It was him I was trying to kill when..." she looked down at the body of the guard, "...when *this* happened."

"Ahriman must have stood before you a very long time ago my dear," said Tavi softly. "But there will be time to talk about such things later. We must first be away if we hope to escape."

"Yes...tell me what you know."

Tavi quickly explained the situation with the guard and how he was to go topside to fetch someone from a field and how it was to happen sometime soon. Lárwin quickly undressed the guard and stripped him of his armor. There was no sense in hiding the body since the door was always locked, so they left him where he lay and she donned his uniform. Since he was much fatter than she, she pulled down some of the tapestries to fill the spaces underneath the armor so that it didn't hang so loosely from her thin frame. She cleaned out his helmet which stunk with his perspiration and tied up her auburn hair. She needed something to carry Tavi in and spotted a small leather pouch which hung from one of the suits of armor displayed against a wall.

She crossed the room in the awkward suit of armor and began to untie it from the belt it hung from when she realized something horrible. This suit of armor had belonged to one of her dear friends. A kind, affectionate man who she knew fought alongside her father. This was Ruthial's armor, and his battered breastplate still held the marks of the fatal wound that brought his end. She touched it lovingly and sadly, and another tear escaped from her eye as she tied the leather pouch to her side and closed the visor of the helm. Tavi found his place, uncomfortable as it was, and they made their way back out into the hall and locked the door behind them. She had just finished locking the door and had picked up the guard's spear and flask when she heard the sound of someone approaching. She stood still and erect, the way she thought a guard should stand as he approached.

It was a man dressed just like the guard she slew, in full dress armor and carrying a single spear. She trembled underneath her armor wondering if the ruse would be convincing. The other guard took his place on the other side of the door and stood tall and erect, just as she was. There was an awkward silence. The other guard coarsely cleared his throat as though signaling for something, but continued to look straight ahead. Lárwin continued to stand still not knowing what to do.

Finally, the other guard turned his helmet toward her and whispered quietly through his visor   "Did   you bring the water?"

Lárwin couldn't believe it. He was asking for the flask of water which was apparently handed from guard to guard underneath the nose of their superiors. She knew it was nearly empty, but she awkwardly handed it to him anyway. He took it eagerly and opened his visor to take a swig.

Finding only a small sip remaining, he looked down at the flask in anger. "Must be Durn from first shift. Curse him. Always thinking of himself," he said with a sigh. "Have a good one Bill," he said, closing his visor once more.

Lárwin gave a little wave and walked silently off around the corner and down the empty hall, feeling relieved that her ruse succeeded. Tavi climbed from the pouch as she walked and scurried up onto her shoulder, hiding among the folds of armor near her helmet so they could whisper together.

"That was a close one!" he said.

"I know," said Lárwin in disbelief. "Can you believe that guy?"

"Do you know your way out my lady?"

"I used to, but things may have changed. Guide me if you see me take a wrong turn."

Together they navigated the winding halls and out into the main city street before the gate. Lárwin noticed that the original gate had apparently fallen during the battle in the past and it was now replaced with a smaller one which led to a long tunnel immediately past its threshold. She marked with pleasure the wholesale destruction her father had wrought on the city as it was now only a glimmer of what it used to be.

Massive stones the size of towers still lay where they had fallen amid crumbled ruins. Indeed, only half the city stuck out from a rock wall which once was liquid lava meant to destroy all within. She relived one of her last memories (which to her was only hours before) as she approached the gate and saw where she once stood defiantly against Ahriman as he retreated into his fortress. During the confusion of the battle she had managed to break free and get as far as the old Main Gate. The tunnel leading to it had been blown apart by some earth-shattering force which she knew came from her father's sword. It was then she picked up the sword of a fallen soldier, turned and led the advancing troops in an all-out attack on the fleeing survivors of Ahriman's army.

She had no armor then, only her sword and embroidered gown, yet body after body fell before her in her fury. Tall, strong men in full armor fled in fear as they saw her cut down their comrades with ease. She had plunged far into their ranks ahead of her following soldiers who struggled to keep up. It was then that she saw

Ahriman, fleeing and wounded, desperately trying to pull back from Leánder, though she could not see him. Suddenly there was a massive tremor and a great quaking coming from the earth. All were terrified not knowing what to expect, even she. As she looked she saw red lava and liquid rock flowing down from the top of the ravine just behind Ahriman as he desperately ran.

Many who followed behind him burned alive in the cataclysm and it separated her from her own following soldiers. It poured down like a red and vaporous waterfall; so thick that she could not see through it. The sunlight which had shone in so abruptly was just as suddenly gone, replace with burning fire and smoke. Ahriman stole a glance behind him at the total destruction as he limped toward his fortress and that was the moment Lárwin stepped out toward him, poised to strike. She raised her sword defiantly and aimed for the neck with all of her skill and ferocity. Ahriman had just turned to see her then, and that was the last she remembered…until the unsuspecting guard slumped to her feet from a stroke that was never intended for him...

Now she walked in disguise past that very spot and had seen how half the city was now encased in frozen lava and solid rock; the rest miraculously spared through the dark power of Ahriman. Her father had obviously intended to destroy all within with whatever power he had unleashed, but instead some had survived and were entombed underground for a long, long time. She wondered if her father knew she was there. He must have. That was why he had come. Wasn't it? To save her? *No.* A voice in her heart reminded her. Leánder meant to vanquish evil. That was his course and intention. There must have been something else that drove him to leave her there. But she had no time to think of that now. She was approaching the gate.

"Steady now," whispered Tavi quietly.

She nodded nervously.

They could both now just make out the dim sunlight far down the tunnel on the other side of the gate and she wanted so badly to break out into a run. Her heart beat faster as she neared the enormous guards at either side of the gate. They wore the ancient armor she had seen in battle and she knew that they must be some of Ahriman's oldest subjects though now bound to the bodies of men. She kept an even gait and followed others who were dressed in similar attire. Apparently, she was not the only one who was changing shift. She stepped over the threshold and into the tunnel. It was not long before they were out in the open and though the air of Gorgon was dry and bitter, it smelled sweet and fragrant to any free soul leaving that place.

Sunlight hit Tavi full in the face and he puffed his lunges full of fresh air. Lárwin wished desperately to throw off the helmet and do the same, but she kept calm and walked coolly through the ranks of her enemy. They found the main road leading north through the encircling mountains and she followed it for as long as she could bear. At first the going had been fairly easy as she hid among the soldiers traveling in the same direction. Soon, however, their numbers became fewer and fewer as they dropped out to their respective posts and duties and it became harder for her to go about undetected. Thankfully days were short in the mountains of Gorgon and the sun had already begun to sink.

At dusk she split off down a small trail that seemed little used and when she felt she was far enough away, shed her armor and broke out into a sprint through the dense forest. All she carried with her was Tavi and the sword strapped to her side. She was used to running through the lush Lanálian forest of her home so she covered a great distance that night. When exhaustion finally overwhelmed her it was nearly dawn. Carefully concealing herself, she laid down to sleep.

*   *   *

"After dodging and hiding in the shadows for what seemed like an eternity, we climbed out of that valley and headed north toward the mountains and the plains beyond." Tavi paused and anger burned behind his beady eyes as he looked squarely at the hawk's face. "This all began three long months ago and Lárwin and I escaped the pits of that wretched fortress just last week. Ever since, our progress has been slow. During the day it is my duty to scout ahead and see what little food I may find here in the wilderness. Lárwin now lies asleep some distance away," he pointed northward. "And now, after having gone through what we have, if you intend on eating me..." he paused and narrowed his eyes, "you would be truly *evil* indeed."

"Well I..." stammered Whitefeather, suddenly feeling rather embarrassed.

"Our course is clear Mr. Whitefeather," continued Tavi

with an intimidating look. "If I am ever to be safe with my family again we have to get to this Everfall and warn them of this enemy before it's too late and no dark lord, mountain, ocean or hawk is going to stop us," he said taking a step forward.

Stepping back from this fearsome little mouse, Whitefeather was quite beside himself. Tavi's big black eyes were on fire fearing nothing; his little fists balled up ready for a fight. It was clear to Whitefeather now that he was not going to be eating this mouse. Under normal circumstances he would have never believed such a story, yet never before had he met a mouse, or anyone for that matter, so bold and courageous in the face of death. Whitefeather turned aside and looked up at the grey sky. The sun almost never showed itself these days and what was left of it was fading fast in the western sky. He looked out across the northern plains with his farsighted vision and saw only grey and mist. It occurred to him that he, Tavi Quicktail and this Lárwin person may indeed be the only free souls left in this part of the world. His proud shoulders slumped and his face fell.

"I have not seen nor heard the cry of any of my kin for many years now," began Whitefeather with a heavy heart, "and all that I knew is either gone or fading and there is nothing that I can do to stop it."

"But there is!" roared Tavi with a voice larger than his body. "Come with us. We are going to Everfall and if there are good men to find there that will fight against this darkness then perhaps the world will be bright and green again."

"Everfall..." repeated Whitefeather, considering. "I

have heard of many things far and wide but I have never heard of *that* place before." He lifted his eyes to the horizon and thought for a long moment. "It must be outside the realm of Gorgon...Beyond the Middle Sea..."

"Then we shall find it together," replied Tavi with rising hope.

"Together?" laughed Whitefeather. The thought of traveling with a mouse, no matter how courageous, seemed ridiculous. Not to mention the least bit embarrassing. No normal, self-respecting hawk would ever travel with his food as a companion. Yet these were not normal times, nor was this a normal mouse, nor in times to come would he find himself to be a normal hawk.

"That is some tale you have. No pun intended, of course," began Whitefeather jestingly. "And it is worth the telling to greater kind than us."

"Then we are agreed; you will come with us to Everfall?" asked Tavi, hopeful to have another companion during the journey.

"Agreed," replied Whitefeather.

With that, Tavi began walking north toward where Lárwin lay in hiding with a confident mousy stride. He stopped short and looked back at Whitefeather who hadn't moved an inch.

"Well? Are you coming or not?" asked Tavi.

Whitefeather couldn't help but laugh. He didn't mean to offend his new-found companion but it escaped him before he controlled it.

"What are you laughing at?"

"You expect to spot enemies and find your route through Gorgon and across the Middle Sea by walking?

You are brave indeed friend," said Whitefeather regaining his composure.

"We are determined!" replied Tavi with boldness.

"I see that you are. Now let me show you a better way," said Whitefeather as he extended and lowered his left wing toward Tavi.

Suddenly Tavi caught his meaning and a broad, bright smile crossed his round face as the idea dawned on him. Saying nothing more he climbed aboard the wing and mounted between powerful shoulders; heart racing.

"Are you ready?" asked Whitefeather over his shoulder when he felt Tavi nestle in.

"Born ready."

"Then point the way toward this Lárwin for I am eager to meet her before the night." With a mighty thrust Whitefeather launched himself into the air with Tavi hanging on for dear life. They soared high into the twilight sky with the setting sun on their left and as they crested the mountain peaks, Tavi saw the last red shafts of sunlight piercing the underside of the dark grey clouds. He took a daring look down and marked with astonishment the vast distance he had intended to cross on foot and suddenly understood why Whitefeather had laughed. He chuckled to himself now as he imagined what they must look like, hawk and mouse, soaring swiftly together into the evening sky.

XIII.

Cum Dominus Apparebit

When the Master Appears

Quinn rode slowly down the trail with his head down and eyes only half seeing as the world went drifting by. His body was strong and healthy, ready for a fight, but inside...Inside he was tired. More tired than he had ever been. He looked down at his hands and noted how much bigger, stronger and more scarred they were than five years ago. Winter had come and gone twice since Eldïr fell to the sword and he had drifted on alone ever since. Five years. Had it been so long?

As he looked, a purple rain drop landed on his hand. He expected it to be cold but it was warm and it was soon followed by another and another. The colored rains had always been a mystery to him when the winds were strong enough to bring them down from the north. Here it seemed such a thing was common.

A gentle rain began to patter on the leaves and ground around him as he and Namír made their way to who-knew-where. The rain played a sad song which harmonized with the thoughts of Quinn's heart as he remembered memories he had buried for so long. He couldn't help it. The gathering mist smelled so much like the scent of his mother's hair. He also remembered a day when Nora had asked him to dance with her out in the rain during a lightning storm. Her funny smile made him smile even now and he sat up in his saddle, taking a deep breath of air as he let the memory play in his mind. She was so innocent and had such bright eyes and youthful laughter. He saw her standing there outside his doorway, clothes soaked to her skin and her just looking at him, holding her hand out for him to join her. She had a way of drawing him out of himself and taught him how to laugh even in the middle of a storm. Quinn closed his eyes and lifted his face to the sky, letting the rain wash away his tears as they fell. He felt the gentle weight of the silver leaf he wore about his neck under his tunic and beaten breastplate and instantly he was with his mother, watching her cleaning the kitchen and smiling up at him. Suddenly the joy of remembering became too painful as hurt returned.

Namír continued her slow walk through the drizzle, Quinn kept his face turned up to the rain...but it wasn't enough to mask the hot tears which streamed from his eyes as his heart tightened with longing and sadness. Every happy memory seemed tied to one more painful. He began to wonder why he even bothered to let himself remember at all anymore. All it did was bring him pain. He let his face fall and squeezed his eyes tightly shut, opening them only slightly and he saw both the purple rain and his own tears fall together from his eyelashes. *Such beauty and sadness. Could one ever stand alone without the other? Perhaps...Perhaps not.*

He finished the bitter thought and looked straight ahead down the path. Slowly, he let his heart rise again as he felt the warm, colored rain soak through his clothes. Wiping his long hair back from his face, he stretched his arms open wide and embraced the falling rain, pushing aside the sad thoughts. Nora would have wanted him to enjoy this moment, and he carried her happiness in his heart like a lamp no rain could ever put out.

As they trudged along, he realized that he had never been in this part of the world before and that few probably ever had. The road itself was terribly overgrown and sometimes not even there. Often the only way he could tell he was on a road at all was by the embankment on either side and the levelness of the ground. Whoever had built this road was skillful indeed, yet for all their skill there was none to travel it or maintain it. Quinn figured that they must have disappeared long ago and suspected that this derelict road was all that remained of a once glorious past, now long forgotten.

The Northlands were said to be shrouded in mystery and few who ever ventured into its borders ever found their way back again. It was a land veiled in mist and haunting visions. Even the few locals Quinn had met many days before warned him of unspeakable danger but where else was he to go? He had spilled more blood in the past five years in the defense of Deiriador than he could measure...and lost. To his knowledge, he was the last survivor of his realm, so he welcomed the mists of the north as an eternal respite to his weary soul.

That is how he came to this valley, guarded on either side by soaring cliffs and mountains clothed in pink and purple trees. Sakurra Trees, he was told, and they stretched out before him like a road guiding him to a nameless destination. As he ventured further, he felt as though eyes were upon him, yet he was unafraid and emboldened as he felt a stirring within himself to see where this road would lead him. At length, as the rain quieted and the sun broke free of the clouds he heard the sound of running water somewhere in the shadows of the forest.

Eventually, they came to rest near a small stream which poured out from a hidden source among the dense foliage and spilled into a dark crevasse toward the mountains. Here he allowed himself and Namír to replenish themselves. As Namír drank heartily, he felt a presence. Then heard a stirring among the brush not far into the trees as though some great animal were hunting them. Unlashing his shield from Namír's saddle and drawing his sword, Quinn stood silently feeling the air and listening intently.

A breeze blew through the tops of the trees filling the air with small pink fronds. He thought he saw movement to his left when suddenly out from his right sprang an enormous white beast. Quinn had seen it just in time to ward off its claws and fangs with his shield but it knocked him to the ground and startled Namír who ran into the woods in a fright. It was a giant, white tiger that fixed its gaze upon Quinn, pondering how best to attack this armored prey.

Quinn realized that his sword hand was now empty, the blade now lying evenly between himself and the beast. Fixing his own gaze upon the eyes of the tiger, he breathed slowly and tried to read his opponent for the attack which was sure to come. The tiger paused and dug its claws into the dirt and lowered himself preparing to pounce. It was going to be fast and Quinn knew his timing had to be perfect. If he leapt for the sword too soon the tiger would see and counter. If he was too late his life would end here among these beautiful trees. *It would be a good death...*

The tiger sprang and at the same moment so did Quinn who skillfully dove underneath its fearsome claws and recovered his sword only to have the beast whirl and leap upon him once more and its entire weight bore down upon him. It let out a long and painful cry which echoed from the mountains as his steel blade thrust through its heart and erupted from its back with a spray of blood. Quinn heaved the beast aside and rolled out from underneath it gathering himself and stealing a glance around lest the beast was not alone. When he was satisfied the danger was over he sheathed his sword. He took a deep breath and sighed. Now he had to find his horse.

In her panic she had run in the direction of the stream and followed it into a shadowy crevasse which disappeared behind great boulders. As Quinn passed beyond the rocks and into the shadows he saw how the moss clung to the ancient stone as though it had not been disturbed in a long, long time. Venturing further in, the stream quietly disappeared into some unseen chasm and he realized that all had become eerily quiet.

He paused and listened for any sound of Namír but only the sound of his own breathing met his ears. As he walked along the stony ground the narrow, rocky crevasse opened and allowed a few faint shafts of sunlight to fall upon the ground and a great rock wall which lay at the base of the mountain. A dead end.

He took a deep breath and was about to continue his search for his beloved horse when something upon the rocky wall caught his attention. There upon the rock some kind of words or ancient inscription were etched into the stone but it was so worn by age and wear that he nearly missed it. He brushed away some of the thick moss but what time hadn't worn away was written in a language Quinn had never seen before. It was obviously ancient and he wondered if there were any alive who *could* read it.

Pulling away still more of the aged moss another thing was revealed which needed no translation and as he took in the sight of it he stood there with wide-eyed astonishment. A large sheet of moss had fallen to reveal an ancient carving etched into the stone of a man, a warrior engaged in combat against a great white tiger and above them was an arc of five small stars. Quinn looked down at his tunic and right hand still freshly stained with the tiger's bright red blood and scowled. The image he found troubling, but its meaning was lost to him.

Either this kind of thing happens regularly here...or someone knew this was to happen...

Looking back to the image with a precarious glance he wondered. Just then, an unmistakable sound drew away his attention. Namír was not too far off somewhere out of sight neighing. He found her quickly and gave her a good look-over to make sure she was not injured in the attack. Finding nothing, he pulled her head close to him and ran his fingers through her mane.

He stood next to her and pulled on her reins slightly to get her attention. "What happened?" he asked with a hint of sarcasm. "After everything we've been through you're gonna let a little *cat* scare you? Come on." And together they walked back to the road.

As they emerged from the crevasse Quinn was startled to see a man dressed in a dark cloak kneeling down beside the body of the great tiger. His back was toward Quinn who could see him running his hands slowly over its thick fur and magnificent coat. He thought at first that this man must have happened upon the scene and was interested in the pelt, yet that notion quickly fled as the man leaned over the enormous face of the tiger and cradled it lovingly in his hands. He spoke softly into the air. He could not hear what the man was saying, but Quinn had seen enough death that he could tell that he had a special connection with the beast and he mourned as one would lament over a dear friend fallen in battle. Namír let out a sudden breath which caught the man's attention and he paused, lifting slightly his cloaked head, though did not turn from his fallen companion.

Quinn's hand fell to the hilt of his sword.

"That be not necessary lad," said the man in a deep, gruff voice.

"And who might you be stranger?"

"You'll bear witness to stranger things than I in times to come my boy," he said without turning. Producing a magnificent sword from his cloak he brandished it high overhead with his right hand and with his left he rested on the fallen tiger. With a long sweeping motion he brought down his blade over the ground yet the blade never struck.

Instead, his form and the tiger's turned to a sudden mist which faded in the gentle breeze.

Quinn stood confounded. He looked into the trees to see if it had been some kind of trick but there was nothing. No foot prints. No sound. Nothing. He spoke quietly to Namír. "We are indeed in a strange place…"

That night they made camp, and in the morning they continued. They did not travel far when the morning rays of dawn revealed a rider up ahead along the winding trail. It was the cloaked figure he had seen the day before, yet this time his face was unhidden and his ancient features were cast toward the golden sun. His short beard glistened like the snow along the mountain peaks and his eyes burned with the light of the morning. Looking toward Quinn, he trotted forward and raised his right hand in greeting, yet his countenance stayed serious and unreadable.

Quinn returned the gesture and continued cautiously forward. As he approached, he felt the man's eyes upon him; studying him, watching his every move as though he could see into his very soul. He stopped within a short distance, yet outside the reach of any blade lest his acquaintance prove to be less than noble.

The man finally let down his hand slowly and sighed. "I be a long time count'n the days which would bring our paths to cross'n. An'now though I be filled with the grief o' a lost dear friend, I stand filled with the hope o' meet'n 'nother."

"The tiger." Replied Quinn remembering how the man had cherished his fallen body.

"Aye...an' much more...He be a companion like no other and stick closer than kin that one. Longer 'an the lives o' men we roamed these peaks an tarried 'mong the blessed Sakurra blossoms. Yet when the eve o' life was still upon me and I was but a lad, it was revealed to my soul that I would cast me eyes upon the king at the death of me faithful friend. An' the sign of the white tiger would announce our meet'n." He paused and looked again toward the sun. "An'now here ye be...An the new star beckons yer call."

Quinn looked in the same direction toward the sun. Sure enough, he was referring to the new light which had appeared over the skies of Aláría. When he was younger it had only been visible at night just before sunrise, yet now it could be seen even in the daytime shimmering in the clear blue sky. Many folks had made up stories about its meaning and many wondered, yet with the darkness which descended upon his land such hearsay was lost and he had abandoned his thinking toward it a long time ago. Now however, he thought of the ancient engraving he had uncovered beneath the moss in the ravine. The star and the tiger. He wondered about its significance yet kept it to himself, wondering what sense this old man was trying to make. He obviously felt conviction in what he was saying, yet he hesitated. He didn't even know this man's name.

"Kôdaï be the name give'n me," he said as if in response to his thoughts.

Quinn gave him a puzzled look and wondered if he somehow knew what he was thinking.

Kôdaï gave a short laugh. "When ye live to be as old as I my son, you'll read the face of yer mate and know what he be think'n. Tell m'now, where does yer travels take thee and thy friend?" he asked, looking at Namír and nodding.

Quinn thought for a moment, considering whether or not he should share his course. Thinking it over, he relented since he had no particular destination in mind. As long as his course carried him away from the war-torn Southlands. That's all that mattered.

"North," he said finally.

"Aye..." replied Kôdaï, some deep thought forming behind his grey eyes. "If ye journey a thousand miles south and upon reach'n that great distance realize ye need to turn 'round, in that one step the other way, ye be go'n north." He paused. "North be not a destination lad. It be a *way*..."

Quinn raised an eyebrow and considered what the old man was getting at.

"Yer compass there," he continued, gesturing toward the small, brass case hanging loosely from one of Quinn's saddlebags, "that there point ye north does it?"

"Mostly," replied Quinn with a curious tone.

"Tell ye of the mountains and streams ye be cross'n? Or perhaps the heat 'o the day or the cold 'o the night ye are to be face'n? Of animals ye will be fight'n." His voice softened. "...Or of friends ye be lose'n?"

Quinn felt him hint at his past, one that he should not be knowing about, or speaking of.

"What are you getting at?" he asked cooly.

Kôdaï lowered his tone as a serious expression crossed his face. "That the unknown dangers which lie ahead changes not that north is north, and that it be yer destined path."

A puzzled look came over Quinn as he wondered at the old man's riddle.

"In times to come, I show ye 'nother kind of compass. One not need'n a brass box to point yer way." He suddenly straightened and a lighter mood came about him. "Come 'long now," he said. "There be much to share with ye," and with that he pulled the reins of his steed and made to leave.

Quinn pondered on whether or not he should follow, yet something in his heart compelled him. Where else was he to go?

"Come 'long now," said Kôdaï again over his shoulder.

Without prompting Namír began to follow and Quinn yielded to see what this mystery would reveal.

As they traveled along toward a nameless destination Quinn contented himself with listening to the old man speak as he spun a tale only a fool would believe. He spoke of a kingdom long laid waste and of an ancient evil reawakened. Of a city hidden in a mist and a line of descendants protecting its secrets. He explained how he himself was the fifth generation of a lineage called the Bularians, the guardians of a sword called Ténmei whose power was nearly uncontrollable and so must be chained to the bearer lest it be inadvertently flung to the farthest corner of the world.

As he explained Quinn's eyes drifted to the silver chain Kôdaï loosely concealed beneath his cloak which linked his belt to his sword and he wondered if there was any truth to this tale. As the words and stories continued to wash over him his mind began to daydream. In his thoughts came the dim image of a king long dead standing alone against enemies innumerable and a tragic sense of loss and betrayal.

"Even in me own lifetime I've bore witness to the rise o' the kingdom o' the dark ones. Their sails be terrible indeed which drift along on a cursed wind from the land o' Gorgonia where their dark lord sits upon a dark throne consumed in evil."

"The Gorgonian Empire was raised nearly eight hundred years ago. Everyone knows that. How could you have seen its beginning?"

"Aye right you are. T'was eight hundred and twenty seven years ago when the first o' their black banners began to wave amongst the first o' their prideful towers. I know, for I was there. I be a lad o' only one hundred and seventy two accompanying me father on a pilgrimage to the ol' battlegrounds o' the first great war. It was then we knew the end drew neigh and yet a little while longer an' as sure as the day is light here come the cursed star to seal our fate."

Quinn tried to hide his expression of doubt at the man's supposition of age but something belied his thoughts.

"Aye," he said softly. "I be fast approach'n the end o' a thousand years, an'now they seem to me but a day... Bularius be a blessed man they say. An' me fathers before gave faith to such fact as he was the first to draw the blade Ténmei after it had taken on the shadow of the powers of a vastly greater enchantment. Into his flesh and bone its might empowered him, and as the years o' man waned with sin an' death the corrupted world fell away 'round him 'til all which remained o' the former glory was he alone. He seen e'en the features o' man bowed low with shame an' remorse to where they no longer looked toward the blessed Light an' cast their faces to the ground. Their proud shoulders slumped as years of bitterness wore away their splendor and rounded their features as the wind and water do the mountains. Those ancient souls o' long ago appeared much different than those a'now, even in me own line." With that he ran his old fingers though his hair to reveal his ears. Not much different from any other, but slightly narrower and nearly pointed at the end. He continued.

'When ten lifetimes o' men he walked this world he uncovered the last o' the VolNari ships an' sailed yon wild sky alone in hopes of awakening his queen in vain ambition to restore his beloved city. Ne'er had the man Bularius returned. Yet prior to his abandoning this life, he pass'd on his most sacred treasure to his eldest son, laid hands 'pon him an' blessed him with life supernatural. Such been the case from father to son as tradition in me family e'er since. 'Pon reach'n his millennial anniversary he passes on the gift to 'nother worthy soul in the line o' Bularius. That is 'course, 'til me.

"At the raising o' the dark banners in the east it was known that the end was neigh and that I would witness the end o' all things. Much which was has been lost my son. An' much which might have been ne'er will be upon Alária. Yet hope remains for as long as the Light endures, an' He endures forever."

After a long silence Quinn finally spoke. "You speak in many riddles. And I do not presume to understand them all. You speak of a history and times which I have never heard nor dare understand, yet you speak with conviction and by your countenance you believe this to be truth. But even if what you say is truth, it is lost to a simple one such as myself."

"Truth. Truth calls to truth, an' recognizes a friend e'en in bitter darkness. Yet I carry on today no further. We've 'rrived."

"Arrived?" replied Quinn perplexed. For the longest time they had been riding along slowly through a misty Sakurra forest which led into a much older looking wood filled with towering maples and oaks. He hadn't noticed, but now looking around as if for the first time since the old man began telling his stories, he realized that it seemed to suddenly be autumn in the forest with great golden and purple leaves fluttering all around in a fragrant array. Ahead, he could just make out a gated wall through the trees.

"Everfall my lad. City o' the king. Much o' the former glory is long past, and those o' us which abode here do so in utmost concealment. The mist 'round us protects us an' what remains o' the city. Lest ye've a guide to lead ya, you may wonder 'bout till starvation or thirst overtake ye."

All along the watchtower noble looking men kept sentry while below men and women came and went behind the wall. Outside in the cold distance the wind which once was still began to howl and the sound of a wild cat echoed through the forest as the two riders approached.

Quinn's eyes beheld the once great city, now strewn about in great ruins with toppled monuments leading up to the soaring gate. Around the capital a wall had been erected from the rubble and sturdy ramparts and buttresses made for an impressive defense. At a wave from Kôdaï the gate parted and they entered.

The evening sun shone brightly upon the thatched roofs of the houses and monoliths which lined the street and the mist which concealed them seemed to hold its place outside the wall bringing a since of relief as he entered into the open air. Here the stonework and masonry appeared of ancient design and its intricacies and beauty astounded him. Within, he found the people to be more than inviting and many shared smiles of welcome and acceptance. These were a friendly, humble people living under the shadow of an unimaginable former glory.

"If you be will'n, I've prepared a place for ya 'neath the White Tower."

"Have you?" wondered Quinn. *Where else am I to go?*

He hesitated to leave Namír, yet the stables and servants seemed well kept so he stabled his mare and was shown to his quarters. It seemed to have been a once luxurious room, fallen now but repaired as evidenced by the stucco and plaster which lined much of the walls and ceiling. Despite its condition, it was warm and inviting. A fire had already been prepared in the fireplace and long purple draperies hung in front of a large arched window blocking the night air. Beyond, ancient trees glowed with a faint light he did not understand. As he surveyed the room his eyes fell on a wall which was seemingly untouched by any repair work, yet bore a grievous crack in the stone. Looking closer, he understood why.

There was yet remaining the faintest artwork upon the wall which the repairers obviously wanted to preserve. It was hard to make out at first, but as his eyes adjusted to the firelight he began to make out the image. It was a young woman with long reddish-brown hair standing nobly in a suite of armor looking over her shoulder as if to look toward a loved one. Her delicate features yet obvious boldness moved him unexpectedly and he felt a stirring in his heart as though he shared an affinity with her. As he gazed into the eyes of the faded painting it seemed as though she were looking at him from across the vast expanse of time which separated them, and he longed to know who she was.

"Discover one o' the ancient pasts treasured beauties have ye?" spoke Kôdaï softly, yet it was enough to make Quinn nearly jump out of his skin.

After he had recovered himself he let out the question, "Who was she?"

"That there be the princess o' the Lanálians. Lárwin she was called. Fallen in battle dur'n the first war 'gainst Darkness... 'Tis shame such a one lost..."

Looking back to the faded image Quinn too felt a sense of loss. In his short life, he had seen enough beauty, goodness and youth destroyed and he thought to himself why it shouldn't have been any different back then. He wanted to look away in disappointment, but his gaze held on.

"Get ye rest now tonight, for the morrow brings 'bout weightier matters," and with that he turned and left. What he meant by 'weightier matters' was lost to Quinn. He was simply grateful to be in a warm room with a sturdy roof and have a warm bed.

The mystery of this fateful turn of events will reveal itself in its own time...If fate indeed has anything to do with it. And with that, he lay himself down to sleep.

XIV.

Viam Draco

The Way of a Dragon

The three of them traveled together cautiously for many days after their escape from the Gorgon capital. It had been slow going as they avoided the main roads and navigated their way through desolate and uninhabited terrain. Without the aid of Whitefeather, it would have been impossible. They had been approaching the northern shores of the continent when Lárwin had sent them to explore the way of the sea to tell if there was any hope of crossing it without becoming lost to the waves.

In recent days she felt her return was all the more urgent for in the sky she had finally beheld an ominous star low on the horizon and it troubled her to think that it may be the doom foretold long ago. It had been a clear day when they had set out, a rare event for that part of the world that they hoped to exploit in their scouting.

It was morning when the hawk and mouse set off and they soon struck out over the open water to see what lay ahead for their female companion, a noble woman they had both become devoted to. Tavi and Whitefeather had become fast friends as well and there was nothing hidden from their gaze when they were together. Whitefeather had begun riding high upon thermals which lofted them higher than Tavi had ever imagined and Whitefeather himself seemed to be greatly enjoying the effortless gain in altitude which would certainly make their job easier. Already, only a few miles out from shore they had spotted what seemed to be a loose chain of small islands which stretched out toward the horizon and lazily curved to the west. That would be their desired direction to Everfall according to Lárwin. They had been able to travel much further than they had expected, and with the new information they were eager to return to their princess with the good news when things took a turn for the worse.

At first it started as a feeling Whitefeather had and soon Tavi too. The clear day had begun to produce a few scattered clouds far down below which at first seemed harmless enough. But almost without warning the entire landscape disappeared in a thick veil of white mist. Whitefeather had already turned to begin the long journey back, but the unexpected weather continued to worsen and as the clouds rose higher and higher they threatened to engulf them entirely.

Whitefeather was a powerful hawk and one of the strongest of his kind, yet even he knew his limitations. If he were to become lost in a cloud, it may very well spell doom for them both. Despite his rising concern, he hid his feelings well so as not to alarm Tavi who could only trust in his mighty companion's skills to navigate safely. Whitefeather had at first been confident in his navigating back to the shore by using the sun as a reference as well as his own aviary intuition, but as clouds formed overhead the sun was quickly blotted out and his every effort was spent on simply fighting the wind and the ever increasing tumult of the sky.

Darkness had enveloped them and Tavi did what he could to hold on tight. As they flew in and out of heavy rain he realized their peril and sought with all his might to see a way down. Lightning began to flash far in the distance between the cloud layers and Tavi could feel the alarm growing in Whitefeather as the air beat against his wings. Already, he had flown longer and further than any other bird and he knew that he could not keep this up for much longer. As the lightning increased, something suddenly caught Tavi's eye.

There, just there, he thought to himself. Another flash of lightning illuminated the sky.

"Yes!" he exclaimed out loud.

Whitefeather didn't have the energy to acknowledge his friend's shout.

"Toward your left wing!" shouted Tavi just barely above the wind and rain. "A mountain top!"

Whitefeather summoned all of his remaining strength and turned against the wind and sure enough, there in the dim light he could just make out the summit of a mountain rising from the clouds. He had thought they were much higher than they were and at first he was confused to see that they had descended unaware, but with the wind and the rain anything was possible. He didn't have the strength to worry about that now anyway.

Landing upon a mountain top was dangerous sure enough, but at least this was a mountain top he could see and if they were indeed lower than he had imagined, there may very well be many mountain tops he might crash into if he were to be caught in a cloud again. He beat his wings against the wind. As they steadily drew closer to the summit Whitefeather was nearing complete exhaustion and fought to keep his wings from giving out. In between the lightning flashes there was now total darkness but he had no choice but to fly blindly toward his goal.

Suddenly a great bolt of light illuminated the sky. It struck so close they could feel its heat and were deafened by the rolling thunder. In that moment, Whitefeather had seen a clearing atop the summit, an unexpected smooth surface on which to land. He made for it and with a final push of his massive wings he hurled them to the ground. They hit hard and tumbled. Tavi was flung into thick brush, Whitefeather fell headlong and was carried some distance with the wind into the shadows.

Recovering himself, Tavi crawled out and checked himself for damage.

I guess being small has its advantages, he thought as he wiped down his fur in the continuing rain. It felt odd to be suddenly on solid ground after such an experience and he began to wonder where he was. The rain continued to fall heavily; in the darkness he could not see where to go for shelter. As he looked around he became increasingly worried for his friend as well.

In the light of a distance flash he made out where Whitefeather had tumbled. It was a strange thing which caught Tavi off guard in the dim light; he could just make out the shape of large stone pillars supporting a heavy marble roof. Beneath was an open doorway leading to an inner chamber. It was there that Whitefeather had fallen.

Tavi ran along the side of the large stone stairway which led to the acropolis. The rain threatened to wash him away, but finally he made it. As he crossed the threshold he left the rain behind and began a cautious search for his companion. There in dim, stormy light, Tavi beheld a crumpled mass of feathers and water. As he placed his little paws upon the beak of his friend he could feel breathing. The hawk's eyes were closed and he didn't stir. There was little Tavi could do to move the weight of him, but at least he was out of the rain.

He quickly got to work searching the inside of the dwelling for anything that may bring comfort to Whitefeather as he rested. Thankfully, many leaves had drifted into the corners and remained dry and these he used to keep him off the cold stone. Venturing in once more, he found an old, tattered piece of cloth crumpled on the floor, the remnant of some ancient drapery, and he painstakingly drug it atop his friend to keep him warm. He himself nestled into the leaves beneath one of his wings and despite the storm raging outside, fell quickly asleep from exhaustion.

The morning brought new wonders. Tavi awoke to blessed sunlight pouring in through the arched doorway and it felt warm on his whiskers. He roused himself and looked at Whitefeather who hadn't moved since the night before but at least seemed to be resting peacefully. He decided to explore the rest of the building to see what else he may find to aid his friend. As he crawled out from beneath his wing he lifted his eyes and was suddenly taken aback by a startling sight.

The skeleton of a man lay resting against the inside wall, his empty eyes turned toward the back of the chamber. In his boney arms he gripped a tattered leather bag and the rest of him lay in unremarkable decay. He must have missed it in the darkness the night before and he was thankful he did as he wouldn't have had a moment's sleep knowing it was there. He shivered at the sight of it but soon shook it off. As he surveyed the rest of the room, he found it to be largely empty save for a large stone table in the center onto which the morning sun poured its radiance. The entire structure seemed to be in a state of decay and crumbling but here and there were traces of something extraordinary at work.

Remnants of stone pillars which had crumbled ages ago still hung loosely in the air supported by an invisible force. Pieces of the stone table also floated steadfast above the floor where they should have fallen. Something was preserving this place, but what he did not know. As he came around the table to the back of the chamber he discovered a gigantic silver mirror, once beautiful, but now barely reflecting a dim image. In it he could see the sunlight pouring in upon the table like an alter but there was something more. He wiped away some of the grime with his paw and looked again. What met his eyes was a surprise still more astonishing. Upon the table he could just make out the glowing reflection of a woman. From his stature, he could only make out but a small part of her, but what he could tell was that she was much different than the poor soul who lay by the door. He could see her brilliant white gown rising and falling with shallow breath. She also clasped something in her hands but what, he could not make out.

He decided that he would climb up and take a look for himself. If he could wake her, she may even be willing to aid Whitefeather. He carefully picked his way up through the great cracks in the stone table and made his way around some of the peculiar floating rocks until he finally crawled upon the top. When he got there though, he looked around in amazement. The table was empty save for the sunlight. He looked back to the mirror and sure enough, in the dim reflection he could still see her laying there asleep and basking in the sun and himself standing there beside her resting body. Her face was illuminated with oddly familiar nobility and upon her chest she clasped the hilt of a long sword laid with intricate work upon the pommel. Beyond that, he could tell nothing. He looked down at the face of the skeleton laying against the opposite wall by the doorway and it dawned on him why his face was turned the way it was. Looking back to the mirror he could see that the man had died with his eyes fixed upon the woman who lay here.

Looking upon her delicate features and peculiar ears a thought occurred to him. "She looks like Lárwin," he said aloud without knowing it.

"What did you say?" came a weak voice from below.

"Whitefeather!" exclaimed Tavi, and he raced down to the side of his friend. "How are you? Can you move?"

"My body aches, but yes, I think I may be able to," and as he tried to rise he let out a loud and painful groan. "My wing. I think it's broken." He tried with a great effort to raise his right wing, but sure enough, he could only raise it half way before the pain was too great. A serious looked crossed his face as he realized the gravity of his situation. Tavi may very well be able to survive on seeds and vegetables, but he required much more. To a hawk, a broken wing spelled death. "Leave me. I may very well die here, but you must return to Lárwin and tell her what we saw along the sea. That there is a way across. She must know if she is to make it back to Everfall."

There was a long pause as Tavi considered this. He may be of small size but his heart stirred with deep emotion. "I will return with help," he said finally.

Suddenly they felt a tremor in the ground as something massive approached from outside.

Tavi and Whitefeather turned in fright just as an enormous shadow covered the door and blotted out the sun. Terror gripped them both, even brave Whitefeather, as they stood there frozen at the sight. Before them stood a towering dragon so large they could see only slivers of the sky behind his form.

"Do not fear me," said the dragon in a low, rumbling tone. His fiery gaze was fixed upon them. "Usually it be death for any living creature who lights upon this place, let 'lone to venture into the sacred temple. That is...'til today..."

Gathering himself together, Whitefeather resumed his usual boldness. "And so what makes today any different dragon?" he asked loudly in his deepest voice.

The dragon lowered his great body to the ground and lay upon all fours before the stone stairs leading to the doorway so that he was eye to eye with Tavi and Whitefeather. "You call me *dragon* as though it were a curse, though I can hardly blame you. The stories handed down by the race of men usually begin with a hint of truth. But I am called Tëleios and it means quite the contrary. I saw your heroic arrival this past night in the storm, yet nevertheless I had intended that at dawn you would be a morning snack before I ventured out for a true hunt. Yet as I was approaching silently just a moment ago, words came to my ears which had not been spoken for many lifetimes and so I paused to consider. You spoke of Princess Lárwin as though she were still alive. If this is so, tell me now where I may find her."

"So you can have an even bigger snack for breakfast eh?" said Tavi stepping forward.

Whitefeather continued in the same spirit of protection. They would rather die than reveal their friend and companion. "What business would a dragon have with the Princess?"

"That is a long story spanning many thousands of your years," answered the dragon.

"You had better get started then," replied Tavi defiantly.

"Spare your defiance little one. I mean you nor her any harm. Quite the opposite, rather. Contrary to many beliefs, dragons hunt only for food and to protect their domain and think not of evil. A prideful race we are, but not evil. You see, unlike other creatures we dragons retain perfect memory. Over the long years since the beginning, it has been handed down from one generation to the next. Each dragonling is born with the memories of their parents in perfect clarity and order, and it is for this reason that most know that if you want to kill a dragon you had better do it before they bear children lest their children seek revenge. An offense made a thousand years in the past is just as fresh in the mind of new born dragon as it was in the dragon who lived it." He paused, and then lowered his tone as he continued.

"At the dawn of creation, there was born a mighty dragon who was betrayed and tricked into committing an evil act when he was still young and naive. My ancient grandsire, Fanglóriun he was called, was deceived into aiding Darkness and carrying away Lárwin to his realm in Gorgon. There she stayed imprisoned until the first Great War when the king buried that realm in the fires of Alária, sealing all beneath the rock until the rise of the Dark Ones who now rule that region of the world. Fanglóriun had watched the battle with shame from afar and then hid himself for the remainder of his days revealing himself to no image-bearer until the day of his death. His progeny carried with them this same guilt and shame until near a millennia later when Bularius, faithful servant of the king, arrived here in his flying vessel with the hope of awaking his queen. By then this island had become well-known to the race of dragons and the line of Fanglóriun frequented here often. It was then that one happened upon Bularius before he died and recognized him in his ancient memory. Bularius commissioned him to guard this sacred place until the return of the chosen king and thereby restoring purpose and honor to a line who had only known shame. That was many lifetimes ago and his body now still lies there just in the doorway faithful to his queen. Lorwin is her name, mother of Lárwin and queen of Everfall. It is she who protects a power I am sworn not to reveal yet always guard. And now, you say Lárwin lives! And you are traveling with her! This I must see with my own eyes. If it be true, I and my line shall devote ourselves to her as penance to the wrongs committed in the past." He finished his tale in a humble tone which seemed odd for a dragon.

Tavi and Whitefeather pondered on his words for a long time before either of them spoke.

"Very well," spoke Whitefeather finally. "Tavi shall show you the way."

Tavi stepped forward and with a fearsome look and a gleam in his eye he strode up to the dragon who lowered his head to see him levelly. Tavi fearlessly climbed the metallic scales of his face and perched himself on his nose right between his eyes and spoke, "If one hair falls from her head because of you, rest assured that I will be the last thing you see before sudden death overtakes you."

"You have the word of a dragon that I, nor none of my line, shall harm her," he replied.

"Go now," began Whitefeather. "She shall be worried for us."

Having flown often on the back of a hawk, Tavi had no problem nestling into the scales of Tëleios' gigantic shoulders. As the dragon strode to the edge of a cliff, Tavi began to wonder what he had meant when he called this place an *island*. Perhaps it was part of the island chain they had seen before the storm, he didn't know, but it didn't take long for him to find out.

"I shall return soon," came his little voice as he looked back to his friend. Whitefeather stood proudly upon the highest step and nodded. With that Tëleios launched them out into the open air and Tavi felt a gut-wrenching feeling he had never experienced with Whitefeather as the dragon dove toward the ocean to gain speed. He then spread his wings and turned to circle the mountain and sure enough it was indeed an island, but one like no other. Whitefeather had been right to assume that he was higher than any mountain peaks and that it was odd that one should be there among the clouds. Tavi gazed in wonder as he took in the sight of the floating island, ever so much higher than any mountain peak, though it appeared that it had once been one. The same enchantment which held the pillars and stonework in place within the acropolis must also be at work setting this mountain peak aloft and soaring higher than the clouds. Had he set out for Lárwin on foot, his journey would have been short indeed.

*   *   *

Tëleios covered the vast distance across the sea in what seemed like minutes. Soon they were upon the desolate shores of Gorgon near the place they had parted from Lárwin. It was agreed that Tavi would go to the camp first and introduce their fearsome guest so as not to raise alarm. When Tavi had left, Tëleios laid down upon a rock to bask in the sun beside the sea.

Unbeknownst to either of them, Lárwin's keen eye had caught the sight of Tëleios' shadow as he crossed the sun and she had hid herself carefully. *I'll die before I let myself be carried back to Ahriman*, she thought. Gathering the tattered sword she had collected she made for the shore where she thought he had landed. If she caught him unawares, she could put her blade in his neck before he could attack.

Meanwhile, Tavi arrived at the camp to find it abandoned. He searched and called but to no avail. There was no evidence of a struggle and everything seemed the way they had left it the day before, yet Lárwin was nowhere to be found.

Lárwin crept behind the rocks cautiously as she made for the beast. She was just beneath the rock where his massive body lay bathing in the sun and his breath was loud in her ears. She produced her blade silently and closed her eyes as she took a deep breath. She had seen before the only hope of killing a dragon with a sword lay under the neck where the scales are smallest. She would have to be quick. She suddenly leapt upon the rock to strike, but as fate would have it, her foot slipped on a rock tumbling her to the ground rousing the giant beast. She struck with her sword but not before the dragon parried the death blow with his iron-like forearm. His thick scales turned the blade and knocked her to the ground but not before its tip tore into the soft tissue of its intended target. It was not a fatal blow however, and she knew that she stood little chance now in a full fight.

She poised defiantly awaiting his strike. Tëleios however recognized her from Fanglóriun's ancient memories and backed away humbly, bleeding from his wound and bowing his head low to the ground. Lárwin stood there perplexed, sword in hand, wondering what trick this may be when she heard a familiar little voice behind her.

"Lárwin! He is a friend!" shouted Tavi from above, nearly out of breath. He had searched all over and then heard the commotion on the shore and feared the worst.

"I *knew* a dragon once," she began coldly without taking her eyes off her enemy. "And he carried me away from all I ever knew and loved."

"Then take your vengeance upon me," replied Tëleios meekly. "For I am descendant of Fanglóriun, the one who brought this upon you," and with that he lay down upon the rocks and stretched out his neck for her to strike.

"What manner of trick is this?" she wondered aloud.

Tavi came alongside her and crawled up to her shoulder as she held her sword, still at the ready. "It is no trick my lady," he began. "Whitefeather and I discovered him when we were blown out to sea and landed upon a floating island. And there is more. He was guarding a chamber where there rests an enchanted woman with features like yours and holding a sword nearly as long as she was. The dragon Tëleios called her Lorwin."

"Mother!" she gasped, and tears quickly filled her eyes forcing her to look away from Tëleios to wipe them away. She staggered back and let her sword fall to her side. "Is it true?!" she shouted as she struggled with her emotions.

"It is true," replied Tëleios rising slowly. "And I have come that I may repay the debt owed to you by giving you my service. Kill me if it pleases you, yet even still, I am your servant for life."

Lárwin approached the dragon slowly and Tëleios again bowed his head. She reached up with her left hand and touched the wound she had dealt him which still bled between his scales.

"Forgive me," she said tenderly.

"It is I who need the forgiveness my lady," he replied.

"Then let it be known henceforth that we are forgiven. If indeed your word is trustworthy, then there is no need for you to be my servant, but a friend."

"I accept," said Tëleios softly.

"Now, be true to your word and take me to this place that I may see it with my own eyes."

With that he bowed low that she may climb upon him and the three of them rose high into the air upon his mighty wings.

*   *   *

Whitefeather stood upon a rocky precipice at the edge of the floating island and waited patiently in the light of the evening sun for the return of his companions. The pain in his wing had diminished slightly, but even still, he knew it would be a long time before he would be able to fly again. Then, off in the distance, his sharp eyes picked out a black speck moving against the wind toward him. It moved ever closer and took the familiar shape of Tëleios and something more. Sure enough, there upon his back rode the unmistakable shape of Lárwin and Tavi was sure to be with her. His heart rose with joy and relief at seeing them again. Tëleios flew a wide circle overhead before landing and as he did, a large fish fell from his claws in front of Whitefeather.

"I thought you may be hungry," said Tëleios upon landing.

Whitefeather nodded in thanks but then looked to Lárwin who ran to him full of concern.

"You poor thing," she began. And she ran her fingers gently through his feathers. His pride would not suffer anyone else to touch him the way she did, but she had a special way about her that made him melt in her presence.

"I will heal," he said. "But in the meantime, you may wish to see what lies within the chamber."

She rose and looked toward the acropolis and its stone pillars. She walked toward it slowly, not knowing what to expect. As she entered the doorway she beheld what Tavi had tried to describe. There was an empty stone table covered with centuries of dust. Beyond, there in the reflection of a grand mirror, shone her mother Lorwin in an enchanted sleep upon the same table and cradling the sword. She could see her mother was protecting it, but that also meant another thing. Her father had died. She had feared this ever since her escape but upon hearing about her mother she had secretly hoped against all hope that he may still live. Now she knew. Beyond that, the Great Doorway must still remain locked also for here lay the key, undisturbed for all this time.

She suddenly felt so small and overwhelmed, as though all the time she was imprisoned suddenly descended upon her and threatened to crush her. She had lost everything. And now, the one thing that still remained of her past lay here so close, but impossible to touch. She knelt down at the alter in the fading sunlight and wept. She let lose all the tears she had held back since the day she was taken and they fell heavy upon the stone floor. She gripped the edge of the empty stone table where her mother should be and beat her fists upon it, screaming as hot tears ran down her face.

"Wake up!!" she screamed wildly toward the mirror. "Mother please! *Wake up!*......... Please wake up......" Her last words fell quietly like a drop of water into the waves of the sea.

She collapsed onto the floor and wept until there were no more tears left to cry and her body shook with exhaustion. She drew her legs to her chest and let the waves of grief wash over her.

After a long time, Tavi and Whitefeather slowly came in to comfort her; Tëleios was just outside guarding the door. Whitefeather reached out with his good wing and brushed her tearstained hair from her face as she lay there. She was fast asleep. They both lay down beside her for the night.

*   *   *

In the morning, Lárwin awoke to a warm fire and fresh fish broiling just outside the chamber.

Apparently dragon's fire has more uses than I thought, she thought tiredly to herself.

Tëleios had also taken the liberty of burying the body of Bularius there upon the floating island sometime in the night. He marked his grave with a giant round stone. The dragons had left his body there in the acropolis to honor his last wish to gaze upon his queen but now times were changing. Tëleios had saved the leather bag he had cradled though, and Lárwin discovered it quickly. As she opened it, she realized that it was the book her father had written,

his personal journal and proverbs. She too cradled it against her chest and cherished it as one of the last links to one she loved. Throughout the rest of the morning she scoured every inch of the island searching for anything which may uncover the riddle to her mother's enchantment. Finding nothing, she returned to the stone stairs and sat before the threshold. Withdrawing her father's book, she opened it and it quickly fell to the last page. It had obviously been opened to that page often in times past. Bularius had probably gazed upon it until his dying breath. The writing there upon it was in her native language which had apparently died many thousands of years ago but, curiously, it was not her father's hand writing. Instead, it was long and flowing like that of her mother. She must have written this before her enchantment. There on the page was the riddle.

As I lay me down this I write,
That the chosen king should find me still
And bear our plight.
There is war yet to be but in his sight
Is the peace of soul that is his right.
He is the boy who became the king
The chosen one of the Enduring Light.

There is a friend that is closer than a brother
It fills this house, and we have each other.

His heart shall then answer and bring at last
The other half of the reflection in the glass.

Lárwin stared blankly at the page after reading it. She read it again and again but nothing came to mind. She searched the chamber again from top to bottom for any clue that may help, but came away empty. Finally, with a heavy heart, she starred longingly at her mother's reflection and came to a conclusion. She must continue her journey alone.

"No, not alone," she said quietly to herself as she looked upon her companions.

They departed shortly after on their way to the west.

XV.

Aliquis ad Consoletur Me
Someone to Comfort Me

She ran swiftly through the forest like summer wind over an open plain. Her heartbeat was loud in her ears, yet her footfalls were like that of a ghost as she darted between trees and over rocks. She had left the others behind earlier that morning and had determined to start off slowly as she scouted ahead herself to see what had become of her ancient city, yet as she neared, her body breathed in the familiar air of home and beckoned her onward. Her heart yearned to see her home again and the thought drove her ever faster as she plunged through mist which parted quickly before her.

Despite time and the dimness of the forest, she knew her home well. Every tree, every rock, every stream had been a friend to her and she recognized them even now, though much time had passed. She began to sense that she was near and slowed her pace, breathing hard though concealing the sound. She came to a stop and rested in the shadow of a great oak tree a stone's throw away from the city gate where she could see its great ramparts firmly locked. She placed her hand upon the scarred bark of the old oak, leaning upon it to catch her breath when suddenly she felt the tree move beneath her hand. She looked up in astonishment to see the great height of the old tree bend down as if to bow toward her. She heard another sound and looked about her. Sure enough, all of the oldest trees around her began to bow as well as if welcoming her home. She was deeply moved by the gesture. Here were some who remembered her. Placing her hand gently on the old tree and looking upon it with loving eyes she whispered to it in her ancient tongue.

"You honor me with your kindness," she began quietly. "But honor me now and hide me so that I may know the truth of this place."

When she had finished speaking the old oak slowly straightened to its full height as well as the others. The rustle of their branches however created quite a stir and the guardsman upon the wall called to see if anyone was there. The call however, was answered only by silence and mist.

*　　　　　　　*　　　　　　　*

Early in the morning, Quinn walked slowly beside Namír far outside the city. He had become familiar with all the hidden ways in and out of the mist which concealed Everfall and as his mind wondered so did his feet. Kôdaï had given him much to think about these past few weeks and he pondered these thoughts deep within his heart. He had wondered into the north seeking shelter from an enemy he could bear no longer, yet upon reaching the end of himself his new 'teacher' claimed that he was to be the one to lead these people against that same enemy.

What Kôdaï failed to understand was that the fight had gone out of him. There was no more war within his spirit. He only wanted peace and solitude now and it seemed that here he may actually find it. He felt the moving tide in his heart and he came to a decision. Whatever he was, he was not the chosen one. He was sure it would break Kôdaï's heart and those he had entrusted with his convictions among their council, but it was the truth. He would leave the city if he must and continue his sojourn alone if he had to, but he would not be leading more people to their deaths. He would build a home. A nice home made of wood and stone. One that was filled with sunlight and smelled of herbs like those of his mother. He would hunt and fish and maybe even be a farmer. Anything was better than living by the edge of a sword.

He began to wonder what that life would be like and it pleased him. It was simple. He imagined filling his house with children whom he would teach and be a good father to. He laughed in spite of himself at the thought. It had been a long time since he had had any happy thoughts, but here, in this place with these peaceful people, he was finally beginning to heal. *Of course I would have to meet the right woman first*, he thought to himself with a faint smile.

He began to daydream of the girl painted on his wall and imagined her reddish-brown hair and her singing as she prepared food in their home. It was the most beautiful sound he had ever heard. As he continued to daydream, he could not place the words that she sang. It was as though his own thoughts were creating their own beautiful song. Walking along, he was startled to realize that he did not know where he was. He looked around but all was shrouded in thick mist and forest. The very path beneath his feet had faded and he could not remember when he last saw a defined trail. That is when he heard a faint sound from far away. He couldn't quite place the words, but he could just make out the sound of someone singing. He was sure he was not daydreaming this time and he wondered if that was the voice he had heard in his thoughts just a moment ago. He led Namír quietly toward the sound.

As he approached, the mist parted and gave way to a most wonderful sight. There was a small clearing in the autumn trees filled with sunlight and in the middle was a small clear stream. Beside it was a young woman bathing her feet and singing her enchanting song. As he watched, the trees themselves seemed to sway with her words and their leaves floated happily though the air was still. Quinn was just taking it all in when Namír took a step and snapped a twig loud enough for her to hear. The spell was suddenly broken and she turned quickly to see them standing there. For an instant, her eyes grew wide as though she recognized him but then the moment was gone. There was fierceness and odd curiosity about her countenance as she rose and faced him. She approached him slowly, and he too took a step forward. When she was close enough that he could see the sunlight reflecting in her eyes she opened her mouth to speak but the words which filled his ears surprised him.

"Illúminatâr isîl nathánö. Ta Äon milshï aänothorn com illuvabét?" she asked in a serious tone.

Quinn was lost at the words and did not understand them. He tried to speak but did not know what to say. Just then a sound came from the forest which caught their attention and they both looked. When Quinn had looked back, she was gone.

"Quinn?!" came the sound of a distant voice. It was Kôdaï calling for him somewhere in the mist. Quinn looked around once more but found no trace of the woman. He took the reins of Namír and walked away slowly, wondering. The words she spoke playing in his mind.

When he had caught up with his teacher he buried his thoughts and spoke not of the encounter. Kôdaï however, was keen on reading the aspect of those around him and there was not much that anyone could hide from his searching eyes.

"Somethin' happ'n in the forest today? I near figured ya for lost," he said in a fatherly tone of concern.

Quinn thought of concealing the matter but then thought better of it. Kôdaï was sure to see through any falseness anyway. He recalled the words she had spoken and tried to recall how she said them.

"What does 'Illúminât isîl nathánö. Ta Än milshï *something* illuvabét' mean?"

Kôdaï came to a sudden stop and stared hard at Quinn who had walked on a few more steps. "Tell me'now…" he began in a low and serious tone which Quinn had not heard from him before, "where did ye hear such language?" he asked with narrowed eyes of suspicion.

"Suffice it to say that I heard it in the forest," replied Quinn, reluctant to reveal the mystery.

"Then suffice it to say that ye utter a tongue not spoken 'near five thousand years. Me fathers themselves be the only ones to recount the Old Words and even them be mostly scant pieces. I thought I alone knew that speech, but you young sir... Yee be full o' surprises."

"What does it mean?" asked Quinn again now even more curious than before.

"You tell me who spoke these words to ye, an' I tell ye the mean'n," he countered with a hard expression.

"I'll do better than that," replied Quinn. "I'll show you."

Kôdaï raised a curious eyebrow. It was rare to see him in this state of wonderment and it bemused Quinn, but this mystery needed to be revealed and they both held a piece of it.

They quickly arrived at the city and Quinn took Kôdaï into his room beneath the remnants of the White Tower. Pointing to the wall with a serious look he spoke only one word.

"Her."

"Ha!" laughed Kôdaï mockingly. "Surely it cannot be! She be dead an' gone long 'fore these walls crumbled. Ye be mistaken lad."

"As surely as the day is light, I speak the truth," said Quinn evenly.

Kôdaï studied his face long and hard. Beneath his face Quinn could see the struggle of emotion when finally he let out a sigh and sat himself down upon a chair.

After a long pause Kôdaï looked up at him and said, "It means 'I am with the Enduring Light. Do you come in His name or another's?"

Quinn pondered long on the words in silence. There in the firelight both men sat down and wondered. When the fire had burned down to mere embers, Kôdaï finally spoke.

"This changes a great many things," he said quietly to himself.

Quinn looked at him.

"She must've been trapped down below when the black towers fell and the king took her for dead...all these long years...trapped down below with that demon..." he trailed off.

"Ahriman?" inquired Quinn, referring to the few scant stories Kôdaï had told him.

"Speak not his name!" shouted Kôdaï unexpectedly. "Who knows what powers he might've conjured these past era's he's spent in darkness. No. Speak not his name." Kôdaï stared into the embers of the fire.

"In my heart, I feel I will meet this woman again...and it worries me."

"Sooner than ye think my boy," he said, turning again toward Quinn. The old lines of his face suddenly softened. "Things be not always what they seem lad. But be ye not burdened. Yer troubled mind rests upon yer prior loss, and ya fear it come again. But that darkness only be as near as ye allow...E'en in this world, Endur'n Light be closer than a brother if ye let him. Ye must let go the past."

Quinn looked back to the coals. The fire was gone. He suddenly felt he needed to go for a walk.

The day had passed quickly and now night had fallen. He walked along the abandoned ruins of the old city and came upon a fissure in the great foundation of what used to be a town square. Now clear water had pooled within the crack and Quinn sat beside it and wondered. It was a beautiful night and the sky was filled with stars. He looked up at them and let his mind drift among them. *If Light Enduring is real then why is there so much evil destroying my world?*

"If you're there," he said quietly into the sky, "then tell me *why*…tell me why you haven't sent someone to stop all this." He searched the sky to see if there would be any kind of an answer. He was met with only silence. He sighed and looked back to the water beside him. It was a warm night and he was suddenly thirsty. Kneeling over the water intending to scoop some up to drink he stopped short and starred in amazement. There in the water was his reflection among the night sky and hallowing his head were five faint stars reflecting in the water from high above. They were so clear he thought he could reach out and touch them. There in the water they seemed to float around his brow and head as though they were a silver crown made of starlight. He slowly reached into the water to touch one, but in the small ripples they disappeared. He was left looking only upon his dark shadow and the reflection of the night sky. The vision settled on his soul with a heavy weight of significance. He stored this deep in his heart and pondered its meaning long into the night.

*   *   *

The next morning Quinn rose early and set out upon Namír determined to unravel the mystery of his acquaintance from the day before. He traveled openly upon the main path which wound its way out of the mist and onto the main road where he first met Kôdaï.

After many hours of riding, he dismounted and looked about. There among the high mountains the red Sakurra trees had turned into a deep purple and light pink. The sun beat down upon him and he reached for his water skin. As he brought the skin to his lips a shadow crossed the sky catching his attention. He looked, and there riding high on the light breeze was a great hawk with wings unfolded, gliding effortlessly above the peaks. He had yet to see such a large bird in these parts and as he watched he became quite convinced that it was not native to this land.

It circled high overhead and to his surprise, dove silently down toward him. Quinn could feel the air from massive wings as it passed close by overhead and Namír took a step back as the great hawk lighted on the ground before them. He looked down from upon his horse and the hawk looked up to him with what seemed like a serious expression. Despite the foreignness of the beast nothing else seemed peculiar until another quite unexpected animal appeared.

A mouse. Not that a mouse is in anyway peculiar but it was *where* this particular mouse appeared. It seemed to have crawled up the hawk's back and was now sitting on its hind legs upon the hawk's brow. The hawk quickly shook its large head and the mouse fell back only to reemerge beside the hawk's wing. The hawk then turned and Quinn quite expected the hawk to eat the small rodent but instead, it turned its head toward it and they looked at each other.

"You embarrass me when you climb up like that," said Whitefeather.

"I just wanted to see better," replied Tavi. "We've come a long way to see our first Evealian."

"All the same, we must use caution," said Whitefeather looking again toward the man and his horse.

A very puzzled look crossed Quinn's face as he saw the hawk look back at him; seeming quite at home with a mouse on his shoulder. He had heard no exchange between them, but was convinced that something strange was at work. Just then the hawk spread his wings and he took off circling him once and then out along the road. Quinn, filled with curiosity, decided to follow and he and Namír began the pursuit.

They galloped along the road heading north and tried to keep up with the great hawk soaring above the tree tops. It turned away from the road where the trees were sparse and quickly Quinn was deep within the pink Sakurra trees. He was so focused on pursuing the bird that he missed entirely the sleeping dragon in front of him in the shadows. Namír had not! As his beloved horse came to a screeching halt Quinn was thrown violently over the reins and landed with a heavy thud on his back in front of golden scales. Startled, the dragon lifted his head and eyed Quinn with a deep growl as it rose to all fours and spread its wings beneath the trees. Quinn could say nothing and expected to die right then and there when another, even more unexpected thing happened.

"Tëleios!" came a loud female voice from among the trees. "Isìl toCóm!"

The dragon suddenly stopped its advance and, incredibly, backed away slowly. He lay back down among the fallen petals yet never removed his gaze from Quinn who gaped in astonishment. The silhouette of a slender woman stepped out from beneath the shadow of the trees. Her long, reddish-brown hair trailing in the gentle breeze revealing the same features he had seen the day before. She walked past him and confidently strode to the dragon. She put her arms around him and caressed his ear speaking soft words he could not understand and it was then that he finally turned his fearsome look away from Quinn and seemed appeased. The hawk he had been following also appeared and landed fearlessly beside the dragon along with the small mouse which leapt from his back into the leaves. It was then that Namír came to him and nuzzled against his neck in what seemed like an apology. The mare roused him to stand. He looked at her and brushed her mane, wondering if perhaps he and his horse were the only two normal things in this entire strange forest. He looked back at the woman, now somewhat sure that he was not going to be eaten by the dragon....*somewhat*....

"You are Lady Lárwin," he said finally.

She raised a surprised eyebrow at the mention of her name and she stepped slowly toward him. He stepped forward to meet her and she took his hand in hers and began to speak. At first, the words she spoke seemed all together foreign, but then as she continued, he began to sense words forming in his mind.

"I know what you speak, though I know not your words. It is the same way that I speak with all the creatures of the Light," and she gestured to the hawk, the mouse and the dragon. "But I shall learn your tongue when you speak with me that I may know your ways and learn what has become of my home."

"Shall I take you to the city then? Surely you came to be there," he replied gently.

She looked back at her odd companions as if to say something and then turned back to him and nodded. He led her by the hand to Namír and offered to help her up, an offer which she obviously did not need as she mounted swiftly in one motion and they quietly walked back toward the road.

At first he did not know what to say and they walked together in silence. At length, he finally spoke.

"I'm not one for many words," he said, suddenly feeling awkward. If she felt the same she hid it well as she looked on and continued to ride with stately bearing. He opened his mouth to speak again but then stopped. "Forget it," he said and looked away. Then he felt a warm hand touch his shoulder and he looked up to see her looking at him. She opened her hand for him to take. He gently did so and heard her clear voice in his mind once more.

"Sometimes silence is just as well," she said.

They continued on. Eventually however, he decided that he would say something. Not knowing where to begin, he started from the beginning. He told her of his home in Deiriador and of his family. Thinking she could not understand his words, he even told her of his father and his violent childhood. He spoke of the rising darkness and the black armies which forced him from his home and his efforts to avenge his family. He ended with his arrival in Everfall and meeting his teacher, but was careful to leave out Kôdaï's conviction of his destiny. All the while Lárwin remained silent as she listened. As they entered the mist around the city she finally spoke.

"It seems as though you have been through much in a short time and my heart is grieved for your loss," she said perfectly.

Quinn looked up in surprise. "You learn quickly, my Lady."

"It is an easy thing to learn when you listen with your heart," she said kindly. "You seemed surprised when I spoke with Tëleios earlier. Do your people not commune with your wild neighbors?"

"I don't think that it's just *my* people," he replied. "I've never heard of anyone being able to do that."

"It was a common thing where I am from," she said. "I remember the first time I spoke with another of the forest kind. Amara was his name and he was a magnificent cardinal."

"It would seem that your present company shares a likeness."

"You refer to Whitefeather? He has quite a different story. He, Tavi and even Tëleios all share in the grief that has come from the evil one. His darkness has fallen on many lands. Yet it was the Light who brought us together and He who leads us now to this sacred place."

Quinn looked up at Lárwin with a sad countenance. "My Lady," he began, "it may not be as you remember it."

Lárwin straightened. "Even so, as the Light Endures there are things here which must be revealed and I intend on revealing them."

*   *   *

When they arrived at the city gate, there was Kôdaï to meet them. If he were surprised to see Lárwin riding upon Quinn's horse as they neared he carefully disguised it. He greeted them kindly and when he had helped Lárwin down he kneeled before her. All who were near quickly followed suit. Unbeknownst to Quinn, Kôdaï had shared his revelation with the council and word of Lárwin's return spread like wildfire throughout the city and many had waited patiently at the gate to get a glimpse of her. She quickly bid them rise and as she pulled her hood to her shoulders to release her hair there was suddenly no doubt that she was of the First Born. At first he seemed caught off guard at her appearance and the fluid use of their language, but then it passed as she bid him rise.

"I was never used to that even then," she said humbly.

"E'en still m'Lady," he began reverently, "it be an amaz'n thing to be in the light of yer presence"

She was led to the steps of the White Tower and from within someone came with a fresh set of clothes for her. She at first felt troubled at the sight of the many ruins around her, and she fought down tears as she saw the rubble of what once was her home, but she smiled at the kindness of those who now lived there and set her heart upon the treasure that was within them. She accepted their kindness and after she had changed and bathed, she stepped forth with a noble grace and prowess the like of which had not been seen in Everfall since its beginning. She was given a fitted velvet dress of midnight blue which had the likeness of stars stitched into the hem about her waist and arms. It fell short of the craftsmanship of old, yet it was a priceless gift nonetheless and she was grateful to be in proper clothes again.

Shortly thereafter, the council was gathered and Lárwin and Quinn were called to be among them. Lárwin now sat among the council and her youthful appearance stood in stark contrast to the stone-faced men about her, yet she set her face as flint as she listened to their stories of old and carefully hid her emotions until the proper time. Then Kôdaï stood and took his place beneath the dome in the center of the room. There the floor gave way to a shallow round pool of crystal clear water and a small walkway leading to a platform in the middle. From high above, the light of the sun was channeled through a prism and directed upon the speaker illuminating him in light.

He began the long recount of history as it was told him by his fathers. He told of the death of the king and the Evealian Civil War which followed and lasted nearly a thousand years in which surviving servants of Darkness infiltrated the ranks of Everfall and slowly worked to bring about its destruction. How good men became corrupted with power and lust for money and eventually sought to enslave their own brothers. Many had turned away from the Light and instead served Darkness, albeit called by a different name. Eventually the kingdom shattered into pieces and its former glory sank into ruin. The people were dispersed and the city was destroyed. How Bularius himself set off in search of Queen Lorwin and took with him the Book of the King which contained his secret to the mysterious flying iron used in the flying ships and legendary armor never to be seen or heard from again. After he had finished his tale, he took his seat among the elders and motioned toward Lárwin.

"Until now," she said standing and walking nobly to the center of the platform. Her stature and confidence as she entered the platform caught many off guard and Quinn could not help but notice how the light illuminated her as though she were one with it.

Many of the old men leaned forward in astonishment as she produced an old leather book from a satchel at her side and held it aloft in the light. She then stepped down and placed it upon the curved table in front of Kôdaï where he and the other nobles sat perplexed. Resuming her place, she continued.

"Bularius had indeed taken the book with him in search of Windermere and I did not understand why, but now I know it was because the world had become unworthy of such knowledge. Be that as it may, he found it and died there. His body now remains buried in the soil of the floating summit above the Middle Sea where rests Lorwin and the sword Dorlimere."

At this there were many gasps.

"How can this be?"

"…the Sword of the king…"

"…it has been *found*?"

She now began her own tale by recounting to them the history of their beginning, her tragic captivity and her even more remarkable escape. There were many gasps of awe and wonder when she mentioned the discovery of the sword with Lorwin upon the floating island and to this many questions were asked.

Apparently, long ago their history recorded Lorwin's resting place as an ancient mountain marked by a swift river that carved away the rock as the years passed until the entire mountain mysteriously disappeared in a terrible flood. To anyone's knowledge, all that remained of that place was a clear lake of water. Unbeknownst to the world however, the same spell which enchanted the acropolis held its sway over the land which it was built upon and preserved it from the long years of erosion until its very foundations were swept away. Instead of being carried away in a flood, it was set adrift among the clouds. It was there that Lárwin had discovered the riddle of the sword.

She set the book before Kôdaï to read, opened to show her mothers' ancient words. She then took her place in the center once more. He was, after all, perhaps the only other one who might be able to read her language. He read it silently and then lifted his head.

"Only the chosen one of the Light can unravel this mystery. He must go at once to retrieve the sword and put right what has too long laid in ruins," he said confidently. He continued in a low tone. "Quinn, step forward."

Before aught else happened, one of the elders spoke up in protest.

"How is it that this newcomer among us has so suddenly been accepted as the *chosen* one of the Light? Are there not many of our own sons worthy of the call to hold this honor?" To this there were not a few grumbles of agreement.

Kôdaï's voice gave way to his long held frustration with the speaker as he spoke coolly. "Many are called, my friend...but few are *chosen*."

"It is written," broke in another, "that the moons would yield to the hand of the chosen king. Has this man ever reached to Heaven and moved the moons?" At this many voices broke in and a heated argument began as long rivals let out their claim to support their own interpretation of prophecy and exactly who should have the honor of claiming the sword.

The clamor rose and frustrations began to boil over into anger as the council went back and forth. All the while Lárwin stood silently among them and let her eyes drift across the faces of the elders as they continued. Finally, her gaze rested upon Quinn as he sat silently. His face displayed a man who didn't waiver despite what was being said of him. She searched his eyes and in them she found no deceit or hidden fault. Raising a hand she spoke gently and silenced the din.

"I am the one to choose. And I choose him," she said simply. "He will accompany me to retrieve my father's sword."

All were now silent as they fixed their eyes on Quinn; some still hot with anger, some with discontent, one with hope. He rose and crossed the room to where Lárwin stood. Facing Kôdaï he knelt to one knee and looked into the humble eyes of the old man.

Kôdaï spoke softly, "You be the chosen one o' the Light my boy. You be prepared to accept this task?"

Inside Quinn's heart was reeling. He was not this *chosen one*. He had determined to set himself apart from things of war and put all things of light and dark behind him. But here were these people filled with hope and confusion. Darkness was closing in around them and they needed to believe in something. Against all his reason, he finally spoke.

"I will," he said.

"Then it is decided," he said turning to Lárwin. "You an' Quinn will retrieve the sword o' the King an' with it we shall vanquish Darkness forever!"

She nodded amidst many cheers drowning out those who grumbled. Lárwin herself kept a steady gaze upon Quinn as he rose, eyeing him carefully. He felt like a fool posing as someone he wasn't and it was all he could do to keep from walking away. Lárwin continued.

"Before we conclude here this night, let it be known that all haste must be made to make safe the city. As I traveled to this place I could see the sea and the land filled with the armies of Darkness. His ships stretch from his coast to ours and those fallen under his sway will soon be upon this place."

"Then this world be lost if we not act quickly," replied Kôdaï. "Quinn, you an' Lárwin shall leave 'soon as ye be prepared."

"At dawn then," replied Lárwin coolly.

Quinn cast a wary eye upon Lárwin as the gathering was drawn to a close. After they had concluded, he did not see her again that night.

*   *   *

As the first rays of dawn streaked across the morning sky, Quinn was in the stables readying Namír. He had heard Lárwin's story of riding upon a dragon to this so-called floating island but had he not been nearly eaten by the same dragon he would not have believed it.

"You're gonna come back without me this time ol' girl," he said lovingly into her ear.

Just then, Lárwin appeared at the entrance.

"She will miss you as well," she said.

"So you can speak to horses too now?"

"Every creature has its own language, and not all are in words. It is easy to see that she is bonded to you."

"Aye," he said looking back to his horse. "And I to her. We've been through a lot together she and I."

"May I inquire something of you Quinn?" she asked, and the sound of his name on her lips struck him in a most unusual way.

He looked at her and nodded.

"There is a wall, a painting actually, within your chamber I have heard about. May I see it?"

"Of course my Lady," said Quinn curiously, and he wondered at her curious tone and expression.

As he led her into his stone chamber she laid her eyes upon the faded painting. Despite the wear, it was made with incredible detail and portrayed her standing in her own armor from long ago. By its likeness, it must have been made by someone who knew her before she was taken. She laid her hand upon the stone and touched it lovingly and tried to imagine the care the artist had taken to create it. Surely it was for this reason that no one had touched this wall until now. She looked at it longingly and then withdrew from the chamber.

Quinn stood puzzled, but then without warning she reentered with a rather intimidating hammer in hand.

Before he could react, she plunged the iron tool into the stone painting sending shattered pieces of the ancient artwork across the room. Quinn shielded his eyes as she swung again and again at the wall. As the stone crumbled at her feet he suddenly realized what she was doing. As the rock fell away, he could make out the ruins of an old doorway carefully hidden behind the stone. He stepped up to the wall and helped her pull the stones away.

When they had finished, Quinn and Lárwin peered into the darkness. Just inside the entrance of a dim and neglected stairwell revealed itself. Lárwin quickly entered and disappeared in the shadows. Quinn paused, listening to the sound of her footfalls as she descended confidently. He took a short breath, half laughing at her presumption and then followed.

They were not long stairs and at the bottom he found a short torch upon the wall which he lit with a match. The old room was derelict and forgotten. Dust hung thick in the air which had not been disturbed since Lárwin's time, yet it held a treasure of unspeakable value.

Walking quickly to a large chest upon the floor, Lárwin smashed the ancient iron lock with her hammer shattering it into pieces. She let her tool fall to the ground as she lifted the lid. Hot tears began to sting her eyes as she laid her eyes upon her most beloved possession. Quinn knelt beside her and his own eyes widened in wonder.

Within sparkled Lárwin's armor, perfectly preserved within the chest. Upon the top was carefully nestled her sword and shield. She reached in with a slow hand, gently raising the large blade to her eyes. It was balanced perfectly, just as she remembered. Feeling the wonder rising in Quinn's expression she released the blade to show him the true wonder of its design. As she removed her hand, Quinn's mouth fell open as the blade momentarily hung in midair before it slowly began drifting to the floor like a feather.

"My father called it VolFerrum," she said quietly. "At one time the entire army of Everfall was clad in metal such as this." She rose and led him to another chest. Upon its lid was engraved a giant maple leaf, the sign of her father. "This was my father's," she began. The lock quickly fell away and she lifted the lid. "If you are to wield the sword you must be properly clad," she said, making reference to his dingy Deiriadorian armor. He started to take offense, but after laying eyes on the magnificent armor inside, he agreed.

If the appearance and lightness of the silver armor was not amazing enough, the fit was even more so. As he donned the armor of the ancient king it felt as though it were made for him. When he had finished, he turned and there stood Lárwin in her own polished armor shimmering in the firelight as though it were just made. She had just finished putting her sword into its sheath when their eyes met. After a short pause, Lárwin finally spoke.

"When I first saw you in the forest, you looked so much like my father," she said with a touch of sadness, remembering.

"And now?"

She just looked at him. In her heart she began to feel that perhaps she was right after all to have chosen him.

"An' still more secrets be revealed," said Kôdaï who had descended the stairs without a sound.

Startled, they both turned to him as he continued. "When ye both be set, yer proud dragon awaits."

"Tëleios? He is here?" asked Lárwin.

"He 'rrived shortly after ya diss'ppeared an' brought interesting company. A hawk an' a mouse. They wait for ye to see ya off."

"Then we shall not delay," she said, and Quinn and Kôdaï turned and made to go up the stairs but Lárwin stayed behind. When they had risen from the secret room, Quinn was surprised that Lárwin was not behind him, but as he looked into the shadows of the door, she emerged into the light. There in the doorway clad in her armor, she looked so much like the painting which now lay in ruins upon the floor. Yet it was a dim image of things to be, and now here stood the real thing. Lárwin emerged with a magnificent white bow and quiver of arrows, her mother's she would later explain. She was indeed prepared for battle.

Quinn stepped out into the light of day and there before him was Tëleios, glowing like an enormous bronze statue as the golden sun reflected upon his metallic scales. Looking down upon Quinn from his great height, he spoke with a deep, rumbling voice in the tongue of dragon-kind.

Quinn looked back at him, perplexed.

"He says that you bear the Image well," spoke Lárwin.

"What image is that?" inquired Quinn.

Tëleios fixed his gaze upon him and with great effort spoke in the tongue of men. A language he had never uttered in his lifetime yet was locked in his ancient memory.

"The Image of the Creator," he began in his rumbling voice. "All of dragon-kind remembers Him and His fading glory as the first of us opened his eyes at the dawn of time." He paused and stepped forward with an intimidating stance. "Though you are a poor shadow, you bear the Image well." With that he turned away and said no more.

Quinn stood there feeling all eyes upon him. "Let's get this thing started then," he said finally, trying to shake off the weight of significance.

Whitefeather appeared beside Lárwin with Tavi and he nestled his feathered head against her side. She caressed and hugged them both lovingly. Then she stood and turned to Kôdaï.

"I commit them to your care," she said.

Kôdaï bowed his head in acknowledgement and outstretched his arm to which Whitefeather flew and perched upon, careful not to dig his great talons into the man's flesh. Tavi also stood at the man's feet and he picked him up and placed him upon his shoulder. He felt they would soon be great friends indeed.

"Ye bring many treasures with ye me lady," he said resting his other hand on the satchel which held her father's book. "The least o' them worth more 'an all the kingdom," he finished, looking tenderly at his new woodland friends.

Large saddle bags were also brought which were reluctantly tied about the girth of Tëleios by trembling volunteers above the wings as a way to store provisions for the journey. To these Quinn and Lárwin lashed their weapons and as soon as all seemed ready they climbed upon him to leave.

Tëleios spread his golden wings, faced the morning breeze and began to move into it. His powerful wings soon lifted them into the sky and they rose high above the city. *I am already leaving again,* thought Lárwin to herself sadly. Sitting in front of Quinn with his arms about her she looked back in silent longing and then turned and set her face upon the journey. It was an odd and unexpected thing, but Quinn's arms around her comforted her greatly and she wondered at this in her heart.

XVI

Insula Inter Celestia

Island Among the Stars

They were nearing the end of the third day of the journey and if Tëleios was tired, he didn't show it. At the onset, Quinn had seen sights he never imagined possible as he and Lárwin traveled high above the clouds. He had tried bravely at first to hide his anxiety. Lárwin had only laughed at him as he gripped her waist with a death grip. Gradually however, he began to trust in the beast and became used to seeing the world from afar.

During the first day they had spoken few words and that night after they made camp, Lárwin seemed oddly solemn. From across the fire, Quinn wished he had Kôdaï's ability to read people, but her thoughts were lost to him. He gathered that when she was ready to speak, she would. Instead, he stood to his feet, walked around the fire and sat next to her in silence. That is how they spent the first night. The next day was little different but in the morning Quinn was grateful for his dragon companion as he awoke beneath his wing which sheltered them from a light rain. Undaunted, Tëleios assured them it was safe and as they climbed through the silver clouds they broke out into the shining sun which warmed and dried them.

Quinn was amazed to see white clouds stretching out like an ocean beneath them as far as the horizon in every direction, their shadows dancing upon their misty tops haloed in a faint rainbow. It was then that he felt his fear slip away and he began to fall in love with the sensation of flying. Lárwin too felt freer and as they flew, she unconsciously leaned against his chest and let go of her sorrows. That evening was different than the rest as it was she who sat beside Quinn as they prepared their meal. They stayed up late together and watched the stars slowly stretch out across the sky as night enfolded them like a blanket. They leaned against the warm scales of Tëleios and stared up in wonder as the fire died.

Quinn looked down from the sky and studied Lárwin. Her clear eyes mirrored the night sky and he felt a shiver run faintly within her. He placed his arm around her and drew her close. To his surprise, she leaned into his shoulder and put her arms around him also, resting her head upon his shoulder. Tëleios too must have felt them respond to the night air and he drew up his wing as though it were a living blanket to cover them, and together they fell asleep.

Now it was the third day and Lárwin seemed to be determined to reach their goal by nightfall. Not all of their journey had been as peaceful either, as all too often they could make out massive army formations moving against the open plains in the direction of Everfall. Quinn began to wonder if there were any free lands left outside western Lanália or if all the world had fallen to the Gorgonian

Empire. As he saw their formations and the size of their battlements, the tides of his heart took an unexpected turn. He felt renewed anger that they could trample so easily into his world and felt ashamed that he would have simply walked away and let it all fall into darkness had it not been for Kôdaï. Unknowingly, he determined he would rather die than to let that happen.

As day turned to night Quinn and Lárwin became weary.

"We near the end," spoke Tëleios over his shoulder. "I can smell the soil."

The twin moons were shining brightly overhead bathing the sea in silver light and reflecting upon the waves far below. Ahead, Quinn could just make out a dim shape moving against the stars high above. As they neared and climbed up to its incredible height it appeared as though it were an island floating among the stars and the sight of it took his breath away. They soon landed upon the stone and the sudden stillness seemed strange. At this height it was very cold and Quinn could see his breath in the moonlight. To one side of the small summit were the short stairs leading to Lorwin's resting place and from within came a faint glow. Mesmerized, Quinn walked slowly up the stairs toward the entrance and could just make out the empty table in the middle of the room. As he reached the top step however, he could see the glowing reflection of the woman in the mirror bathed in moonlight. His eyes grew wide and memories came flooding back to him from his childhood; of a dream he once had. A faint shiver ran down his spine.

"I have been here before..." he whispered to himself.

A curious look crossed Lárwin's face. "How is this possible?" spoke Lárwin quietly, feeling the gravity of the moment. "She has been lost to history longer than the ages."

There was a pause as Quinn approached. "She spoke to me in a dream once," said Quinn finally. "I remember her face and her deep blue eyes like the ocean. She told me I would be here one day."

Lárwin looked at him. There was no way for him to know the color of her mother's eyes nor their deep blue radiance.

"There is a riddle I must reveal to you," she said after a moment. "Only you can answer this and if you cannot, our doom is sealed with the fate of the new star and all will end in bitter darkness."

Quinn looked at her and wondered what kind of riddle this would be. Turning his gaze back to the woman in the mirror, he listened to Lárwin as she repeated the words gently.

"As I lay me down this I write,
That the chosen king should find me still
And bear our plight.
There is war yet to be but in his sight
Is the peace of soul that is his right.
He is the boy who became the king
The chosen one of the Enduring Light.

There is one that is closer than a brother
It fills this house, and we have each other.

His heart shall then answer and bring at last
The other half of the reflection in the glass"

She finished and Quinn starred into her. Her eyes reminded him so much of his mother's. That is when a memory hit him and he laughed aloud but was then overcome with emotion. The same night he had the vision of Lorwin so long ago, he and his brothers gathered around his mother to comfort her after their father had left. Instead, she had comforted *them* with her loving words which arose from Quinn's long forgotten past.

"This house is full of light... and we have each other," he said with a distant voice, remembering.

Just then, the fullness of the room began to glow with a pale blue light that danced like fire upon the walls. Quinn and Lárwin took a step back not knowing what to expect and as they did so, Quinn saw the reflection of the sword and how it had erupted into a fierce blue flame which shone out from the mirror. Soon, the blue fire gave way to a pillar of blinding white light which reached high into the stars. Outside, Tëleios had to hide his face beneath his wing and at a much greater distance, the lookouts of Gorgon sent word that a light had appeared in the darkness in the north.

Quinn grabbed Lárwin to shield her from the light but as the light diminished, he tried lifting his face and guarded his eyes with his hand. There in the middle of the light upon the table sat a figure of pure radiance. The light lessoned and Lárwin turned to see her mother. The sword still rested lengthwise on the stone table as Lorwin stood and embraced her daughter. Hot tears flowed on both sides as they clasped each other tightly. The touch and smell of her mother was just as she remembered from so long ago and she didn't want the moment to end. Not wanting to disturb their moment, Quinn silently excused himself and walked outside some distance away and stood beside Tëleios. Together they looked into the chamber with wonder.

"It is a beautiful thing..." spoke Tëleios quietly in his deep voice.

"Yes it is," he replied softly as he looked upon them. Inside the chamber, mother and daughter held each other tightly and exchanged words beyond understanding. *The sword can wait,* Quinn thought to himself.

After a long time, Lorwin stood at the threshold and called for Quinn and even Tëleios to come near. Quinn stopped at the bottom of the stairs and bowed his head.

"Come up to us," she said in a kind voice in his own tongue.

He slowly climbed the stairs until he was there beside them but still could not bring himself to look into her eyes. In her presence he suddenly felt unworthy, dirty even, as though the magnificent armor he wore was merely filthy rags compared to the light of her countenance.

"Do not think so of me," she said. "For though I shine with this light it is a mere reflection of His glory."

"Forgive me my Lady," he began, finally gathering enough courage to look her in the eyes, "but I do not understand..."

She laid a loving hand upon his shoulder as she spoke to him tenderly. "You are not what your eyes can see but what your heart believes. Even now, you carry a great light within you and many will follow it, even into bitter darkness. Upon your brow *alone* has Light Enduring laid a crown to lead these people into a new world." She reached behind her and produced the sword Dorlimere and laid its long length across her arm to present it to him before she continued. "The sword that I now give you is powerful indeed, but its power is contained within the spirit who wields it. It is yours, and if you will not, then all will end in black despair."

He searched her eyes and felt the weight of all of his fruitless searches slipping away. Finally he could see and understand.

"I will use this sword to bring healing to our people and for no other purpose," he said finally.

"Then take it for it is yours," she said, and with that she extended the pommel toward him which he took and held up the blade admiring it.

"Our short time is now nearly over," said Lorwin.

"Mother?" replied Lárwin full of concern. "What do you mean? Are you not coming with us?"

"No my daughter," and Quinn could hear pain in her voice. "My task is now complete and the sword has been given. When I walk beyond the threshold my power here will be extinguished and I will return to the Light."

Lárwin embraced her mother tightly once more but she knew in her heart that she must say goodbye.

"We will meet again," said Lorwin through her own tears as she comforted her daughter. "Go now, our people need you."

She then turned to Quinn, embraced him and kissed his cheek also. Overcome with emotion he did not know what to say, but in the gesture he noticed that she had crossed the threshold of the doorway. She took another long look at her daughter. Just then a tremor shook through the entire chamber. The ruined pillars which hung mysteriously in midair now fell and shattered upon the marble floor. Pieces of the ceiling also began to cave in behind her and Quinn knew they must be leaving.

Lárwin refused to leave but as the island began crumbling around them Quinn grabbed her and began to drag her away reluctantly. Tëleios lowered himself and they both climbed upon his shoulders. As he spread his shimmering wings against the stars Quinn looked back and saw Lorwin, the last of the First Born, still standing upon the stairs with an uplifted hand...

...and then she was gone...

Tëleios pushed hard against the air just as the ground beneath him shattered and fell away. He flew a wide circle around the falling ruins as they fell into the sea. Quinn held Lárwin tight as she let out her cries of sadness into the rushing wind.

Their shadow fled silently into the night.

XVII.

Prælûdium ad Bellum

Prelude to War

Quinn and Lárwin rode high above the world upon Tëleios and were fast approaching the western slopes which marked the borders of Everfall. They were anxious to return and were troubled at the sights they had witnessed. The clouds had concealed much during their journey east, but now a strong north wind presented a clear sky and revealed the extent of the enemy's war path as it burned through the open plains and once lush forests of Lanália. Two nights before, they had slept out underneath a blanket of stars and spoke long into the night about their past and things to come. In her, Quinn felt a resolve and strength that he had never seen in a woman before and it felt strange that such an emotion of comfort could come from another.

Yet he feared the memories it awakened. He had been in love once before and now he wanted nothing of it. He sighed and leaned back looking up at the night sky. Feeling a soft gaze upon him he turned and saw Lárwin looking at him with her large dark eyes. In them he could see the reflection of the stars burning brightly against the darkness and for what seemed like a long moment he was filled with wonder. Then, in her eyes he saw many shooting stars streak across the sky and they both looked up.

There in the heavens the sky began to fill with first just a few, then many shooting stars. Most of them were small but some were much larger and they lit up the sky and cast a diffused light upon the shadowy ground so much so that even Tëleios was aroused and looked. As all three of them looked up at the sky it seemed so beautiful, but Quinn knew in his heart that it marked the beginning of the end.

"It has begun," said Quinn quietly to himself.

"Quinn," began Lárwin with a curious tone, "the Light has chosen you to bear the sword, and so I must tell you of the thing which it unlocks."

Quinn turned and looked at her, and her face bore a serious expression. He had wondered what Lorwin had meant when she said that he would 'lead them to a new world,' but he had figured that she we simply being metaphorical.

"There is a doorway," she continued, "hidden near Everfall which leads to a different world. One free of Ahriman and his evil and untouched by any man. My father constructed a gate to guard it and protect it from any evil that may try to escape the Doom of Ahriman through it. It has been a secret that has been well hidden until now, but I fear that Ahriman may now somehow know of its existence and that is why he moves against Everfall with such haste. If he were to unlock the gate and pass through the door, then the age of Men would fall into an eternal darkness under his rule."

"And the sword is the key," replied Quinn.

"My father designed the gate to only be opened by he who bears the sword that he may stand guard and let no evil pass through. You are that guardian and it is you who must open the gate and protect those who pass through."

"Where is this gate?" he asked.

"When the doorway is opened and the bridge between the worlds is made, a white fire should appear upon a mountain and reveal its location. Beyond that, even I myself do not know."

Quinn lay back and took in the sight of the falling stars and pondered.

That was three days ago and now they could see plainly the resolve of the enemy as they burned their way across the country. They overflew massive battle formations and soldiers clad in black armor and their numbers were beyond counting. They spread out across the landscape like a dark shadow leaving only fire or ashes. Even out upon the waters between Lanália and the Southlands, they had seen vast ships innumerable laden with an evil cargo fast approaching the shores which was sure to birth new terrors.

As they crested a large ridge, they were surprised to see a small village, a once proud settlement surrounded by the enemy. There was some distance between this attacking force and the main body. The brave men within the barricades held their defenses nobly but when the main force arrived, Quinn knew they would be laid to waste quickly.

Quinn shouted over the wind. "We have to do something!"

"What do you purpose?" replied Lárwin.

Quinn looked down and saw the vast numbers of his enemy attacking these innocent people and he was reminded of the assault on his own home which set him on his course. Only one plan came to mind.

"Kill them," he said plainly.

"And what of Everfall?"

"You and Tëleios will continue on to the city, I will stay here and aid these people."

Lárwin turned and looked at him over her shoulder, her long hair whipping wildly in the wind. "As you wish," she said finally.

They turned a wide arc and swooped down upon the besieged village. From deep within, Tëleios began a low growl which soon erupted into a roar and a fire lit in his eyes. The village was being assaulted from every direction, but the main body was formed to the east just outside the wall and it was this that Tëleios targeted.

As they neared, black arrows began to whistle through the air and one glanced off Lárwin's armor followed by hundreds more. Their barbed tips however were no match for Tëleios' metallic scales and he turned them easily. As he flew overhead, he took in a mighty breath and Quinn could feel in his legs the beast's lungs filling with breath. There was a pause and, just when he was close enough that he could make out the terrified expressions upon the men's faces, Tëleios poured from his mouth a fire unquenchable.

For a hundred yards long and nearly a hundred feet to either side, fire engulfed the land and all who stood there. Their wild screams faded as they climbed away and Quinn looked back to see hundreds of men running on fire like living candle flames within a furnace. They turned again and as Tëleios descended upon them they scattered and began to run in every direction. Tëleios extended his talons and bore down upon a group of riders and snatched them up with his massive claws smashing bone like glass and digging into their flesh; three men, one still upon his horse. With a flick of his wing, he carried them with him and flew over the village wall.

To the men inside, they marveled at the panic which ran through their enemy and wondered what manner of sign this was. In the middle of the village, Tëleios' mighty wings kicked up a thick cloud of dust and even the bravest most battle-hardened men were intimidated by what they saw as the golden dragon landed hard upon the ground, his wings and belly stained with the blood of his enemies, and smashed the bodies of the men which lay dead in his claws. The horse also lay broken in his talons and let out a loud cry. He lifted it up with a powerful arm, its dead rider still pinned to his saddle, and bore down upon it with his mighty jaws, rending its flesh and instantly silencing the creature. The people watching let out gasps and both women and men cried out in terror and wonder as the remnants of its carcass fell to the ground.

Tëleios looked about himself fiercely as the fire in his eyes slowly faded. That is when they noticed the two riders upon it, one of which descended among the fallen bodies and walked by them as if they were of no concern. He wore strange armor and he carried a helmet and sword like no other.

"I am Quinn," he said loudly looking upon the stunned people. "I bear the Sword of the King. Who is in command here?"

There was a pause, then finally an old soldier emerged from the battlements in dented armor, the blood of his own enemies staining his breastplate.

"I am Nilrem, lord of this village. To who do you have allegiance?"

"I am ally to all those who would escape the coming darkness. What you have seen here has only been a scouting party of a much larger force which is following quickly behind. If you and your people wish to live, you will follow me into the mist of the Evealian Forest to the west. There you will find refuge and a fortified position. Your women and children will also find safety. All those who can carry a sword however, must swear that they will do so in its defense."

"You're saying we must abandon our village?" he asked longingly.

"Yes," replied Quinn, feeling the man's sadness.

There was a long pause as the man looked about at his remaining people. The village walls were nearly breached and were falling apart in many places. Half the village had already been burnt to the ground during the siege and hundreds of his brave men had fallen. Ash and smoke was all around. All the villagers and remaining soldiers fixed their gaze upon him desperately looking for hope. Finally, his face fell and he looked to the ground. His shoulders slumped and he took a deep breath. Looking at Quinn, his face appeared to be carved of stone and a fierceness appeared in his eyes beneath his grey eyebrows. He straightened as he spoke.

"To the west you say?"

Quinn looked back at Lárwin and met her eyes, his affection lying hidden behind his resolve. He gave her a short nod and with that she pressed her heels against Tëleios who then spread his shimmering wings out against the sun. As they launched into the air behind him, Quinn turned back to the soldier.

"We must leave as soon as you are ready," he said shortly.

There was another pause and the man sighed heavily.

"Prepare to abandon the village!" he finally shouted. "We make for the western mist! Take only that which you can carry!"

"How many men do you command with a sword?" asked Quinn.

"Three thousand," he replied, then added gravely, "but that was before this morning. I fear only two and half thousand remain."

"I am sorry for your loss," replied Quinn. "But I fear many more will perish if we are not swift to be on our way."

They did not take long. Within two hours the women and children were prepared to leave, some on mules and donkeys, others on the carts which they pulled. The faces of both the young and old appeared ghostly, as if they had already surrendered themselves to their fate and had not the strength to grieve further. Quinn realized that this was his own expression which he had carried for so long after the loss of his own home years ago. He would help these people or die trying.

Nilrem approached him with one of the few horses which remained in the village.

"You come bearing hope," he said. "The people must see you and be encouraged," he handed him the reins.

Quinn mounted the steed and rode to the head of the crowd forming at the gate which they were unbarring.

"We go westward, to the city of Everfall where there is hope!" he shouted. "Be brave, and do not look back at the homes you are leaving. Be of good courage and fear not the coming darkness!" he looked down at a young soldier who was barely older than a boy looking up at him. "You are the light of the world and even the smallest light overcomes the greatest darkness. Be strong!" he said again, raising his sword high and looking out across the people. Incredibly, he sensed hope in the crowd and a small light return to some faces. He turned and began the long march to Everfall. They would have to cross nearly fifty miles before they reached its walls, but it was a chance they had to take. There was no turning back.

The enemies that Tëleios had scattered were sure to regroup and Quinn was determined to put as much distance between them and the people as possible. To either side of the long caravan he directed the troops to station themselves in case of an attack. They readily obeyed. They were good men, brave and loyal, and now they had hope which they were willing to defend. On they marched without stopping. In the distance to the east at the end of day, Quinn stood beside Nilrem and watched as smoke billowed up against the fading rays of the sun, the burning remnants of their homes. The enemy had arrived.

"We must keep moving," said Quinn finally.

"Aye," replied Nilrem.

They traveled well into the night until it was too dark to see. What they could see through the black clouds and drifting smoke revealed the falling stars Quinn and Lárwin had seen days before, but now there were many more and much brighter. The sight brought urgency to Quinn – they would have to set out very early.

Before dawn the next day they were on the move again and it was raining. It was a cold hard rain, it slowed them considerably. Many things people had once thought valuable were cast aside as being a burden now to carry. They also witnessed peculiar things as they traveled. Many deer, bear and other creatures of the wild traveled closely by them. It was as if they too could sense the impending doom and sought to flee from the destruction of the enemy. They fled as if running from a wildfire and filled the forest floor and the very air with their quiet desperation.

Quinn led them through the foothills of the western mountains and they made their way through its gentle passes. Upon reaching the windward side, Quinn stood on a high precipice and looked out. The enemy was far greater than he had imagined. Far to the north he saw smoke rising from the forest marking where demons descended upon the northern mountains. This could not be the main body which he had seen from the air, yet it was a formidable force indeed and it threatened to cut him off from his advance toward Everfall. If it did, he would be trapped between it and the main body and his people would be crushed as if in a vice. They had no choice but to continue.

Nilrem spurred his people onward and they moved with great haste and with desperation. They covered more miles than Quinn thought possible with such a large group of women and children, but necessity and survival proved to be a great motivator. At dawn on the third day he again looked out and considered the situation. The enemy had also moved swiftly. They now occupied the lower region of the misted forest and were preparing their assault on the city. Quinn felt his heart drop as he considered their position.

"We will not make it," he lowly mumbled.

Nilrem stood by and he too considered. "We shall meet them regardless," he said finally, looking upon their vast numbers.

Just then, a purple mist appeared and out from it stepped Kôdaï in his thick fur cloak and Ténmei hidden underneath. Despite the circumstances, a warm smile appeared beneath his beard. He looked upon Nilrem and the other soldiers standing by before returning to Quinn.

"I see you be chosen to lead these people," he said kindly. "That is good. Many more be in need o' such leadership."

"The enemy is great," replied Quinn, revealing his doubt.

"Aye," said Kôdaï. "You must finish what's been started. No more can I teach ye. The rest be up to you."

Quinn looked out over the enemy to the mist, beyond which waited the city.

"The men cannot fight in such a mist," he said.

"Indeed, nor can mighty Tëleios. The mist has served its purpose for long enough. It shall be no more an' come dawn, the forest shall once again see the sun." He turned his grey eyes toward Quinn and set his hand upon his shoulder. "I see you in the battle," he said simply.

Quinn nodded. "Tell Lárwin I will meet her in the middle."

"Aye," he said, and with that he disappeared once again and the mist that remained drifted away.

For the rest of the day they traveled as far as they dared without alerting the enemy and made a cold camp for the night. The morning would prove to be a red dawn.

*   *   *

It was an odd thing, but even in the morning light Quinn was amazed to see the faint streaks of shooting stars continue high above the clouds, the sign the end was near. He sat upon his horse and looked down upon the enemy. The mist which had concealed Everfall for over a thousand years had cleared. There in the open he could see the dark armor of his enemies radiating malevolence and death with an evil darkness swallowing the sunlight. It seemed unnatural against the fairness of such a beautiful forest. Much of the sacred wood lay in ashes or burning behind them now, yet for all their numbers they failed to surround the city. The terrain coupled with many ancient and massive trees which had moved close together in the night prevented their advance. Still, many trees had been either pulled down or burned, yet they refused to move and slowed the advancing tide of evil. Their numbers filled the space between Quinn and the gate and it was here that he knew the battle must be fought.

He sent the women and children who were too small to fight with a small escort to the main road leading south, the same road he had happened upon when he first arrived, and ordered them to seek refuge among the Sakurra trees in the valley where he had found the ancient rock painting. There, the enemy would have great difficulty finding them if they failed.

When they had gone, Quinn rallied the men and he and Nilrem organized them into battalions and companies. When all was in order, they marched from their concealment among the trees into the open. The enemy had cleared a wide expanse between the city wall and what remained of the forest and it was here that the battle would be fought. Amongst the ashes, his small army spread out to face the enemy. Ahead, Quinn saw that the armies of darkness had already begun the siege and estimated their number to be more than ten thousand. Volleys of arrows poured from within the city and fell among the horde taking many to the ground.

Tëleios could not be seen, but he was sure to be near awaiting his chance and readying his strength. Quinn raised Dorlimere and looked upon it. Though it was a magnificent sword indeed, he had yet to see anything supernatural about it. Its blade reflected the sunlight like a perfect mirror and it felt good in his hand, yet for all its craftsmanship he doubted its ability. *At least it's sharp.* He looked over at Nilrem who stood nearby and nodded. Quinn then turned and galloped along the front lines of his men holding Dorlimere high. *He* needed the encouragement just as much as they.

"Sons of the Light!" he began. "Fear not this darkness! You are the glory of this world and have the right to claim the blood of your enemies! Even if you fall this day, do not be troubled, for you shall be with Light Eternal, and your enemies shall see your glory as they weep in Hell!"

A great roar erupted with shouts and battle cries. Quinn spurred his horse into the middle and dismounted, smacking its rear and sending it running off. There was no need for a single rider in this battle, it was better for the men to see him on the ground with them.

"With me!" he shouted boldly, and he donned his helmet and began to step forward slowly. All along the battle line, his men followed and they began a slow advance. Meanwhile, the enemy ahead had seen them emerge from the forest and had prepared battle lines of their own. They were forced to divide their attention between the wall and this new force yet even so their vast numbers gave them confidence. These were not the Dark Ones who led the ancient battles of the past, or even plundered the ruins of Everfall long ago, these were men who freely chose allegiance to Darkness and allowed themselves to be seduced by its power. By wickedness they had grown into a powerful force indeed and their minds were ruined long ago. Even so, it was blood which flowed through their veins and it was this blood which beckoned Quinn to war.

As they neared Quinn picked up the pace followed by the men behind. As they gathered momentum and bore down upon their enemies they suddenly broke out into a run. At a hundred yards, deadly arrows fell upon them and many valiant men fell to the ground.

Quinn continued undaunted and the men which followed took heart in his charge. With a wild and frenzied cry he fell upon the dark army and as their lines met a great crash was heard as sword, spear and shield smashed together in battle. Quinn had brought Dorlimere down upon his first man with a fell swoop which split his breastplate cleanly in two followed by a thin line of blood which streamed from his body as he slid in half.

Quinn and his men went to work at their bloody task and suddenly red was everywhere. The ground drank deep of the life of fallen warriors from both sides until it could contain no more. Blood ran in streams between the bodies. From beneath his bloodied helmet, Quinn could see the enemy overwhelming his men and knew his losses were rising. On he strove, pouring himself out like water with all of his strength, but still it was not enough. For every one that he slew, two more sprung up to take his place.

He began to take hits as his body tired and soon he was simply trying to stay alive. Suddenly, he felt a blow from behind and pain shot through his left arm as a blade hit its mark and he was thrown to the ground. His helmet had also fallen and for a moment he laid there among the bodies.

He was tired and beaten, and his heart quaked under the pressure of battle. How could he have grown so weak so quickly? He was not a king. He suddenly felt all hope slipping away as the battle raged around him. Just then a shadow crossed over him and through bloodied eyes he saw the silhouette of a man standing against the sun. He knelt down and extended a hand to Quinn who slowly reached up and clasped his wrist when he heard him speak.

"Can you stand boy?" said the man.

He nodded and with a powerful arm the man pulled him to his feet and looked him in the eyes. This was a man Quinn had never seen before and the look of him carried a kingly virtue. His appearance and countenance was more striking than any he had ever seen and his eyes spoke of pure confidence and ability. Still grasping his wrist the man spoke again.

"Victory is not to the strong, but to those who trust in the Light! Be strengthened!" he shouted over the roar of battle with a commanding voice. Quinn could feel renewed power flow into him and he was encouraged by this man's boldness. He blinked and the man was gone. For a moment he stood there confused and wondered about the man who helped him, but the maelstrom surrounding him called his attention. It was time to turn the battle.

He looked up to the wall above the gate and let out a loud cry, "Kôdaï, *NOW*!"

With that the gates of Everfall flew open as Tëleios, eyes aflame, broke out into the fray followed by thousands of Evealian soldiers. With a long breath Tëleios let loose his raging fire. Though Quinn stood some distance off, he had just enough time to raise his shield against the intense heat of the fire, which he could feel burning through to his arm. Having cleared a path, the Evealian's ran to either side of the dragon giving him a wide birth and their spears began taking their toll on their enemies.

Men reeled back at the sight of the dragon and panic began to rise in their faces as they saw that they were now caught in a vice. Tëleios' tail and talons swept away men and horses and his powerful jaws made the strongest armor break like straw. Quinn paused and marveled as he saw the body of a man thrown far across the battlefield.

Seeing this, the hearts of his men were encouraged and the tide of battle began to change. Far off, Quinn saw through the fighting and beheld another sight he would not soon forget. Lárwin was raising her sword against an onslaught of dark warriors as they descended upon her in waves. She moved through the battle slowly but purposefully leaving bodies piled high in her wake, their blood running from her armor and staining her skin, her red hair moving like a flame as it trailed behind her from beneath her helmet.

Soon, Quinn's men were meeting with the Evealians as their two armies met. Even the bravest of the dark ones fell back and retreated, fleeing for their lives. Quinn stood there in the middle of the field leaning against his sword, breathing hard and recovering his strength. Around him, his men and those from the city brandished their swords and erupted in great cheers of victory. Here the fighting had been fiercest and as he looked around, there stood Lárwin, wiping the blood from her blade. She saw him and walked slowly over to him, carefully stepping over fallen warriors and removing her helmet.

When she was near, Quinn could see in her eyes her strength and prowess, but behind them, sadness and pain for those who fell at her hands. He reached out for her and took her in his arms and embraced her. The danger had passed and as her intensity melted she put her arms around him also.

"Looks like we met in the middle after all," she said with a faint smile.

Quinn nodded. After a moment he replied, "I would move the moon and stars to get to you," he said softly.

"This battle be over now," said Kôdaï emerging from the soldiers, "but there be greater darkness on the horizon." He gestured to the east were Quinn and Lárwin had seen the main body of the enemy. Ahriman himself was sure to be among them and they knew that the coming battle would be much different than the one they had just won. Far away, the horizon was already filled with black smoke, marking the enemy's impending arrival.

*   *   *

In the evening, the survivors gathered themselves within the city and prepared for the second siege which was sure to come. The falling stars were fewer now but larger, and the sound of them began to reach the ears of men as they burned through the air like distant, rolling thunder.

Quinn sat outside the ruins of the White Tower and lit a pipe as he watched the sky. Soon, he was accompanied by Kôdaï and together they watched the comings and goings of the men around them.

"It was just a sword," said Quinn finally, breathing out a long wisp of faint smoke.

"What do ya mean?" asked Kôdaï passing the pipe.

"The sword...it was only a blade. A piece of metal," he said, and Kôdaï paused as he continued. "I guess I was expecting more than just a sword. I thought...I thought I could do more to save these people with it but now, now I know I cannot. Even a sword as sharp as Dorlimere cannot be raised against such a force as Ahriman's armies. It is only one sword against so many..." he trailed off.

After a moment Kôdaï spoke. "The man who wielded the sword before you, he too was only a man. But he was a man who knew that the *true* sword was the one within him. It was his *spirit* which came through to his blade. When he awoke the spirit within himself, he became something ever so much more."

"And what's that?" asked Quinn.

"A king."

Quinn took a long drag from his pipe as he considered this.   Just then, far off on the horizon, something broke out against the night. A giant white flame appeared upon a mountain top and its brilliance illuminated the clouds from below. It grew in intensity until it cast shadows off the people who watched upon the ground.

"The doorway opens," whispered Quinn. He quickly jumped to his feet nearly dropping his pipe and ran for Lárwin's quarters. He burst open the door to find her sitting next to the fire sharpening her sword next to Tavi and Whitefeather. They all three looked up at him unexpectedly as he caught his breath.

"The doorway opens!" he said finally.

"A little *too easily* it seems," replied Lárwin raising an eyebrow at his intrusion. Then her eyes widened as she understood. She responded with a serious tone. "We must leave immediately."

"I am ready for battle!" came Tavi's small voice as he looked up at them.

"That is not what I mean, brave one," replied Lárwin in a kind voice. "We must discover how to open the gateway that leads to the door first, before Ahriman does. Only then can we be safe. It must only be the two of us. Ahriman's spies are sure to be lurking in the darkness and if we arouse a stir then they are sure to discover the gate. It must stay a secret as long as possible."

"It will not stay a secret for long with a fire like that," said Whitefeather as he peered out the window at the mountain.

"That is why I have a mission for you," spoke Quinn, and Whitefeather cocked his head in curiosity. "I have spoken with Tëleios and Kôdaï, and if you will accept, you will go to the eastern cliffs which lead to the islands of the Middle Sea and summon Tëleios' kin. Tell them of our need and ask for their help. Explain that Lárwin is with us. Hold them to their honor because they will remember her. With any luck, they will prove to be great allies.

"More dragons?!" burst in Tavi. "Even Tëleios nearly ate us when we met him and you want us to walk into a whole family of them?"

"What do you mean by *us*?" asked Whitefeather. "If you do not wish to come, you do not have to. As for me, I would be honored to serve the king," he said, bowing low with an outspread wing.

"Far be it from me to be counted out," he retorted. He let out a sigh. "Another adventure…when do we leave?"

"At first light. As for Lárwin and I, we will leave for the doorway tonight."

They prepared to leave, and Lárwin gave a fond farewell to Tavi and Whitefeather. With any luck and fair winds, they would return within a few days' time with a great company. In the meantime, she and Quinn had other matters to attend to. After meeting briefly with Tëleios and Kôdaï, they set out with Namír and another strong steed upon the Southern Road.

Kôdaï had voiced his concerns about them setting out by themselves before they had left.

"A dangerous risk sett'n out without a guard," he said. "Hidden in the dark beyond the sacred forest the spies of Ahriman are sure to be hidden."

"Someone once told me to follow a compass despite the danger along the way," replied Quinn, placing his hand upon the shoulder of his friend. "Tonight, I must follow that compass." After a moment, Kôdaï nodded.

Kôdaï watched as they left and whispered quietly to himself. "It may be that he is finally beginning to understand."

They made their way by moonlight and starlight, and before sunrise the next day they had made it as far as the base of the burning mountain. Even now, in broad daylight, the white fire upon the summit was incredible, so bright that its shafts of light poured through the forest like the sun.

They traveled quietly, tired from the long night but also to listen for any sound of the enemy. Eventually, Quinn could hear the faint sound of running water. In the dim light of morning, to his surprise, he realized that it was the same spot where he had fought the white Tiger. To the west was the ravine Namír ran to with the great rock wall with the ancient painting. He looked up. Far above the trees, the summit was still burning brightly like a great lamp refusing to fade. He and Lárwin dismounted and walked into the shadows beneath the rocks and Sakurra trees.

Unbeknownst to them, a shadow moved from behind the trees. A shadow darker than the rest which had followed them during the night. It now moved nearer to watch.

Pink and purple petals had piled high along the ground against the walls and the scent of them was a welcome aroma. As the narrow valley widened, it opened to reveal the vast wall that Quinn had seen before. The painting was still there, and now it was Lárwin who stood amazed to see the likeness of Quinn in the ancient image. Above were the engraved words he could not understand. But now, standing beside him, was one who could.

Lárwin studied the writing carefully. "It was the hand of my father who wrote this," she said finally, reaching up and touching the words gently, remembering him. "It reads *'all who enter here shall be saved.'*"

"So how do we open it?" asked Quinn looking upon the stone. Stretching along its length high above, ran a crooked, narrow crack long eroded by wind and water. Near the base, at about the height of a man's shoulders, it widened slightly creating a small nook. Quinn ran his fingers along it and brushed out the dirt and small rocks which had collected inside. Within, there was a narrow slit about the width of his sword.

"Could it really be that simple?" he asked himself quietly. He unsheathed Dorlimere and to his amazement its mirrored blade glowed with a pale blue light all its own. The shadow behind them shrank back in fear at the sight of the sword, but then lay still seeing they were unaware of him. They did not know that the sword burned to alert them of his evil presence. Quinn placed the point of it against the opening and after a quick glance at Lárwin, pushed it hard into the lock up to the hilt. He twisted it to the right like a latch and paused. Nothing happened...a long moment passed. Then, from deep within the heart of the mountain, an echoing boom was heard as though an ancient machine had been set in motion. The ground began to quake and rocks began to fall from the face of the mountain. They stepped back cautiously but as a boulder fell from high above. Quinn jumped and grabbed Lárwin, pushing her out of the way as it broke upon the ground. They rose to their feet and ran as dust and rocks fell around them. From within, giant gears which had lain dormant for five thousand years began turning slowly and pushed hard against the stone which turned on massive iron hinges and broke free with a deafening screech.

Quinn and Lárwin looked back in awe to see the entire rock wall breaking at the crack and slowly hinging into the mountain like a massive door over a hundred feet high. As it did, wind and air were pulled into the opening with a great rush of noise like a storm and Quinn pulled Lárwin close to shield her face from flying debris.

The shadow, having seen all it needed to see, retreated and fled into the forest to return to his master.

When the door had fully opened and nearly stopped, the massive hinges which held their weight for so long finally broke and both of the stone doors fell hard against the wall within with a deafening sound. So heavy was their fall that it shook the ground. Eventually, the great noise and wind subsided and all became still once again. The imposing stone doors now stood silent and as the dust settled, Quinn and Lárwin peered inside. Within, a giant cave stretched through the heart of the mountain and something glowed faintly on the other side. Even in the broad light of morning it was hard to tell what it was, but they were determined to find out. They stepped cautiously toward it not knowing what to expect.

As they crossed the threshold, Quinn came to the door which held the sword and he pulled it out easily. Inside, they found a smooth stone pathway straight as an arrow and as level as still water. It was broad and wide and ran the entire length of the cave. Along the walls were brilliant paintings of animals and men, some he recognized immediately. The first was a woman in white with features like Lárwin's mother, the second was a mouse with a noble look about him. The third was a great hawk with a single white feather upon his wing. The fourth was a golden dragon that bore an intimidating look. Lastly, a young woman stood looking up toward the stars with a sad expression. As they walked together, their footsteps echoed from the walls and Quinn could hear the sound of Lárwin breathing. It was not a far walk, and as they neared the other end, something more amazing than anything they had yet seen dawned upon them.

The opening was tall and wide; at least one hundred feet in every direction. As they approached, Quinn began to make out silver clouds and stars shining brightly in a night sky. He looked back through the tunnel from where they had come and saw sunlight still pouring in through the open doorway, yet here, in this place, it was nighttime. As they stepped out into the new world, they saw they were on a low precipice which led down gently into a grassy plain beside a large starlit lake. Beyond lay a silent forest bathed in moonlight and illuminated with the soft glow of strange blue fireflies. Quinn was taking it all in when Lárwin pointed to the sky.

"There," she said, pointing toward a bright green star high above.

"What is it?" asked Quinn.

"That is Alária," she said after a moment. "Our home."

"It's so far away. How can you be sure?"

"I just know."

They both drank in the sight of it for a long moment before returning. They walked back through the tunnel and across millions of miles with a few short steps taken in silence. When they reached the other side they retrieved their horses and walked back out to the road. Quinn took a long look around at the landscape and felt his heart stirring. He would not suffer evil to sneak in behind them and steal into their new world.

"I will stay here to guard the gate," he said at last. "Ride ahead and tell Kôdaï what has happened here. It is here, in this place that the final battle against Darkness will happen."

Lárwin rode off swiftly toward the city.

Quinn spent much of the rest of that day in concealment with Namír among the shadows of the ravine. Though the door was large, it was mostly hidden by the tall Sakurra trees save for the very top which stood out against the mountain. Toward evening time, Quinn heard the faint sound of many footsteps approaching along the road from the south.

"The enemy approaches," he said quietly to Namír.

He drew Dorlimere but was discouraged to see that the pale blue flame he had seen when opening the door had faded and was no longer there. It didn't matter. He was there to defend the doorway between the worlds and only over his dead body would evil enter therein.

There's nothing for it, he thought to himself and stepped out onto the road to face whoever approached. He was thrown into confusion when he saw the advancing group. Here was not his enemy, a vast army clothed in black armor, but instead, simple peasants both young and old wondering together in a long train stretching off into the distance.

They carried with them what personal belongings they could, some with hand drawn carts, others with horses and mules. They looked like a beaten and tired people, survivors of a land long laid to waste. When those at the front saw Quinn standing there in his armor and his sword drawn, they stopped and gazed at him in silence and fear.

"Who are you?" asked Quinn, bewildered.

"We are the survivors of the war in the south," began a middle-aged man in the front. "We come from many towns and cities, all burned and razed to the ground. Most of us were scattered abroad when the Lady called to us."

"The *Lady*?" asked Quinn perplexed.

A younger man spoke. "She appeared to all of us in dreams and visions calling us to this place. She's the Lady in White, Lorwin some call her. Surely you've seen her?"

"I have," said Quinn finally. Apparently Lorwin had one final card to play before her power was dispersed and she used it to gather these people who were scattered far and wide together to find shelter from Ahriman's Doom. He sheathed Dorlimere and spoke loudly. "If you have come to find a place of refuge, you have found it. Here through a doorway I will show you, you will find a new world free of evil; a place to start anew. I only ask that those of you who can, will stand with me to defend it."

With that he led them to the doorway and to the other side where the sun was just cresting over the horizon. There were many gasps of wonder and amazement as they emerged, and Quinn was pleased that many brave men, upon seeing their chance of hope, pledged to follow him in its defense. When he returned, there stood Kôdaï with his back to the cave and Ténmei in hand.

"Our men be apprach'n," he said, looking toward the east. "But perhaps just barely in time." And no sooner had he finished speaking than Quinn heard a faint sound echoing through the mountains, a deep war drum announcing the arrival of their great enemy.

XVIII.

Apocalypsis
Apocalypse

That night, Quinn lay in his tent outside the gate and dreamed. The war drums had continued beating their slow rhythm long into the night and steadily grew louder as they approached. In his mind, he saw faded images of people and friends long dead and he felt a dark spirit around him but could not see it for it was like black clouds against a night sky, yet he knew it was there. He was standing upon an open plain laden with snow and small snowflakes gently falling from a clear night sky. Above, a sea of stars and a single moon illuminated the darkness yet far out toward the horizon and all around was a ring of silver clouds framing the window of night, beyond which poured brilliant sunlight bathing a far green country in radiance.

Before him stood a mirror made of shimmering water and in it was the reflection of a man he did not recognize at first. In the dim light he looked like a stranger, but when he looked closer he began to recognize features he had long forgotten. He was a tall man with heavy rounded shoulders and a grizzled beard. He wore a simple tunic and dirty breaches and his face told the story of a hard life of labor. It was his father. Quinn took a step back and suddenly felt very small like a child. As he did, so did the reflection. He reached up to touch his own face and the man in the mirror followed. Dread came upon him and crept down his spine like icy fingers reaching within and pulling at his darkest fears. He heard a sound and he turned. There was his brother Eldïr standing beside him in the gentle snow. He still bore the grievous wounds which had claimed his life and blood flowed to the ground staining the white snow with red like paint upon a canvass. He had a soft, loving look about him and he reached out with a scarred hand toward Quinn as if to embrace his brother. Quinn couldn't move and he stood there blinking. His brother paused with his hand outstretched and looked upon Quinn with affection in his eyes.

"I forgive you," said Eldïr in a distant, loving tone.

Quinn wanted to speak but could not find words.

"I forgive you for leaving me and letting me die," he said.

Eldïr had chosen to follow Quinn freely when their home was destroyed and he remembered fighting bravely beside his brother and holding him in his arms as the life drained from his body. It somehow felt wrong to accept responsibility for his death, though the pain was great. Even so, he couldn't find the words to speak.

Just then he saw his brother's eyes waver as he caught sight of something approaching behind him. He turned and saw the silent, shadowy silhouette of a great lion coming for him. Its footfalls sounded like the drums of war and echoed far off into the distance. The body of Eldïr stepped back in fear and he began to tremble. When he looked back, the mirror and his brother were gone and even their marks in the snow had disappeared. He looked upon the lion and could feel its power as its massive body circled him and came to his side. Looking out toward the distance it took a deep breath and raised its head as if to let out a deafening roar...but in that moment Quinn began to wake as if his roar were the thing waking him. Only silence ensued as Quinn opened his eyes.

*   *   *

Early in the morning, Lárwin walked to Quinn's tent seeking to discuss plans for battle and defense, but as she approached she heard him speaking softly and paused at the entrance. She did not mean to spy on him, she could just see him through the curtain and hear his whispered words. He had removed his armor and was dressed in his plain clothes kneeling to the ground with his head bowed.

"I just don't understand," he said quietly. "Kôdaï says that I have the power to awaken the sword but I do not feel it. How can I conquer my enemies when I cannot even conquer the memory of my own father?" He let out a long sigh. "It is his blood which flows through my veins and this I fear, that I may become like him and abuse those around me as he did my family. What is to stop that from happening? What would save me from becoming just like the darkness I now face? These questions weigh on my mind and burden my soul. Perhaps that is why the sword sleeps. Teach me your ways that I may know the path I should walk and feel your light upon my face."

Lárwin was deeply moved by the words Quinn spoke privately, and she departed in silence. Some distance away, she met with Kôdaï speaking with Nilrem. They informed her that the enemy had stopped unexpectedly and how they might use this time wisely.

Already the women and children of Everfall along with those refugees from the south had crossed over through the great door and they estimated their numbers neared fifty thousand. All that remained now were those willing to defend the gate. At first they had sought to repair the hinges and remount the giant stone doors, but that would require work which would take many weeks and they had not the time. Instead, they began fixing defenses around the natural terrain to slow the enemy and provide shelter. The land already provided good defense as the road itself wound through a narrow valley between the mountains and the ravine leading to the doorway was narrower still. They made long spears from the Sakurra trees and dug them into the ground to the north and south along the road; this would be their first line of defense. The cliffs guarding the ravine would be their second. Lastly, the tunnel itself. Within it, Kôdaï placed men with shields and spears as a last line of defense. They were fifty men across and ten rows deep, five hundred brave men in total. Outside the tunnel, the Evealian soldiers and those which remained from Nilrem's village numbered nearly forty thousand and they lined their defenses with noble ambition.

All that day, an eerie silence had crept through the world as if in anticipation of the finality to come. Even the birds which usually sang their cheerful songs throughout the day lay silent and refused to venture into the open sky.

Quinn knew this respite was simply Ahriman gathering his full strength before his assault on the gate. He would be as desperate as they were to leave this place before his doom fell upon him from the stars. Every resource at his disposal would be committed to their destruction and the taking of the new world. They had good defenses but even so, he knew many good men would die. He tried to think of a way to destroy the gate. Perhaps seal it from the other side or somehow destroy the bridge altogether. In his heart he knew there was no other way. The same power which forged the bridge between the worlds would continue to hold it open until the time of passage ends. He and his men would have to defend those who had already crossed, or die trying.

As the sun set that evening Quinn, Lárwin, Kôdaï and Nilrem shared a feast with their fellow soldiers. They ate and drank to their hearts content for they knew that the morning may find them among the fallen. When the enemy would attack, how long they would be able to hold, how many would perish; all of these questions arose in the hearts of each and the uncertainty was written upon their faces.

Quinn looked around at the men beside and across from him and his heart went out to them. "Gentleman," he said in the firelight as he stood up at the long table. "In the morrow we may all perish, and I along with you, but I am honored to fight alongside such noble men and women." He tipped his glass toward his friends. "We will hold the gate for as long as the last free man draws breath and we will strike our enemy with such a blow that it shall be recorded for all time." All eyes were fixed on him as he spoke and in them Quinn could see the faint embers of hope rekindled at his words. "This is the history that our children's children will speak of, and they will live in a world free of darkness because of us who fight here today."

"Here here!" they all said loudly and they too raised their cups in toast.

As Quinn finished his drink and set his cup upon the table it seemed to let out a deep sound which echoed off the mountains. Everyone paused, then it came again. The war drums of the enemy had returned. Each man stood and quickly returned to his station to prepare for the impending battle.

"It be the sound of the Lûctus Nöcturn, the immortals o' the enemy from the ancient past," spoke Kôdaï coming alongside Quinn. "They've waited for the fall o' night to begin their terror."

Suddenly, Tëleios landed behind them bringing with him a great whirlwind as he folded his wings.

"I have seen the enemy and their war fires stretch as far as the horizon to the north, east and south. Their numbers are beyond counting."

"We only need to hold. You have done well Tëleios, you are a good friend," said Quinn.

"Where would you have me?" he asked.

Quinn considered his advantage to have a dragon at his disposal and felt a debt of gratitude for his loyalty. He decided to put him where he expected the enemy to be strongest.

"Take the road on the north side," he said finally. "The enemy will be strongest there as they approach from

Lanália south of Everfall. I will move my men back to give you a wide area."

Tëleios nodded with a serious expression. "Be sure that you do image-bearer."

Quinn nodded back and Tëleios stalked off parting the formations of men before him. Quinn could see that his very presence inspired awe in his men and his great strength gave them courage. He was grateful for his friendship. As he departed, a white shooting star thundered across the sky and its noise rumbled through the mountains. As if to herald the attack, a small flame was lit atop the eastern slopes high above the road followed by another and another. Soon torches lit every cliff and slope around them and the men knew they were surrounded.

Quinn and Kôdaï positioned themselves along the south facing road with Tëleios behind them to the north. Lárwin led the defense of the ravine and Nilrem stood at the head of his men within the tunnel. In between and to either side stood the brave men of Alária standing fast in the defense of a world they had never seen yet trusting Quinn and his companions with their lives.

It took a long time, but eventually the sound of marching met their ears and the night revealed thousands and thousands of torches advancing along the road from either direction. The war drums beat loudly in their ears until suddenly a distant horn sounded and all fell silent as the entire force on both sides halted just beyond archery range. As another falling star illuminated the sky and rumbled through the clouds, Quinn could just make out the appearance of men clad in dark armor. Ahriman had decided to throw at him his own kind first before he risked his Lûctus Nöcturn against the sword. To him, men were disposable.

A giant of a man stepped forward and his men parted to let him through to the front. He stood a head and shoulders above the tallest man and his appearance was striking. In his hand he bore a spear like the trunk of an iron tree and its point was over two feet long. He held a shield larger than a common doorway and the sword at his side must have weighed over fifty pounds. He called out in a loud voice challenging them.

"You are surrounded by a force larger than any the world has ever known!" he began. "Surrender to the lord of this world, and he may yet have pity upon you! If you do not..." he was suddenly cut off as something whistled by Quinn's ear and brushed against his hair. Mouths fell agape as a swift arrow pierced the man's helmet and struck through to the other side of his skull. He blinked once, fell to his knees, and then collapsed upon the ground with a heavy thud. Quinn looked behind him with surprise to see Lárwin lowering her white bow and casually walking back to her post. She, for one, would not hear any terms from the enemy. Quinn agreed. The others standing near the fallen body of their commander looked down in shock and then back up at Quinn and his men.

"You were saying?" spoke Quinn mockingly.

A shout arose from Quinn's men as they joined in defiant battle cries which eventually fell into uniform 'HOORAH's. The enemy too began letting loose their war shouts, and their voices echoed loudly into the night. They began to move forward and the ground began to shake as their numbers buffeted the ground with their feet.

Quinn signaled his archers to let loose at will and volley after volley poured from their ranks, each one finding its target and felling its man. Untold numbers continued the charge however and they trampled their fallen comrades in the stampede. Behind him, he felt the heat of Tëleios as he went to work defending the rear and knew that he could hold his own...for now. As the enemy bore down upon them in a frenzied charge, Quinn could sense the anxiety of his men building and see the blood pulsing in their veins. He took a deep breath and gripped his shield and spear alongside them.

At his command, the Evealian's lining the front locked their rounded shields together to form a solid phalanx. If one were to fall, another would step forward to take his place. Those behind also braced the man in front as to absorb the impact of the charge. He and Kôdaï stood at the center of the line and looked down the length of their spears hungry for blood. He could hear the steady breathing of the men beside him quicken.

"Steady," Quinn said loudly. "Steady!" he shouted again over the sound of the charge. To him, all else seemed quiet now, except for the sound of his own heavy breathing beneath his helmet. Just prior to the impact, he let out a loud battle cry which the rest repeated and dug his feet into the ground.

Shield met spear as the armies of light and dark clashed for the final time.

Body after body fell before the spears of the Evealians but still the enemy poured in. Cries and hollers of victory and pain rose high into the night. As if to join in the fighting the sky illuminated the battlefield with a new wave of falling stars. The skill of his men created a new hazard as the bodies fell and mounted high in piles before them. It slowed the onslaught however, as his enemy now had to travel around to his flanks or risk going over at a slower pace. Incredibly, after a time the din of battle descended and their enemy retreated back into the dark. His men let out a great cry of victory but Quinn also heard something else. Something like whistling.

"Night arrows!" he cried and shielded himself followed by all those around him. Many were not so lucky however and fell to the ground dead or dying as thousands of black arrows rained down upon them. When the last of them had fallen, Quinn rose to his feet.

"Tëleios!" he called, seeing how his dragon friend had also held the northern road with little to no injury. "Use your flame for something useful," he said pointing at the piled dead along the front. With that, the dragon looked at the fallen men, some still moaning in pain or begging for mercy, and let out a long blast of his fiery breath instantly consuming all who lay there and reducing them to smoldering ashes. Quinn nodded at Tëleios who said nothing and resumed his post.

Before long, they heard another charge of men and they repositioned themselves. The second charge was much the same as the first though lasting much longer. The enemy decided to throw at them even greater numbers. On and on this continued through the night as the enemy descended in wave upon wave.

The maelstrom of clashing men and armor rose and fell like the tides of the sea and Quinn began struggling to keep up with replacing his men with fresh troops. He tried to let those who tired or became injured fall back and let others take their place, but as dawn approached the next morning he realized that his replacements were faces he had already seen before, and some many times. He too was feeling the strain.

Finally, the first rays of dawn broke over the Alárian horizon for the last time and gave strength to the fading men. With it came a new terror however.

In the sky far in the east and approaching quickly were dark flying creatures Quinn could not make out against the sun. Their screeches came echoing over the landscape however, and Tëleios looked up from his bloody task recognizing the sound. Ahriman apparently had loyal dragons of his own, long kept hidden within his fortress until they had lost their sanity and were bent to his will by torture and cruelty. Upon them rode tall warriors pulling hard at harsh bits chained to their mouths and steering them toward their target. Quinn could see half a dozen of them and if they were anywhere near as strong as Tëleios, they would be in dire need.

To his surprise, Kôdaï broke from the line and stepped forward before the men and unchained Ténmei from his belt. Quinn had never seen him without his beloved blade fastened to his side and he wondered what the old man was doing. With his right hand he drew back the length of his sword behind him and took a long step forward, hurling the blade with all of his strength at the largest of the beasts as they descended upon them. Ténmei whirled wildly through the air but instead of falling to the ground it gained incredible speed as it flew toward its target. The first and largest of the black dragons twisted violently out of the way but the one behind was not so swift. Ténmei shot through its metallic scales and iron bones like paper leaving a trail of red mist in its wake. The beast fell to the ground with a great crash. Kôdaï's blade then made a wide arc and circled back to him and he caught it from the air with a shout.

Quinn looked at him with a raised eyebrow. "You never told me you could do that," he said.

"You never asked," replied Kôdaï with a sarcastic tone.

Meanwhile, the rest of the dark dragons aimed for Tëleios and he braced himself for the impact. Just before they were upon him, Tëleios lunged into the air with his powerful hind legs and caught the first winged opponent with his claws and sank his teeth into its neck. Blood flowed in great showers as the black dragon writhed in pain. Its brethren were soon upon him \however, and the men around them ran back as their giant bodies wrestled upon the ground. Great trees snapped like toothpicks as they fought and Quinn marveled at so many teeth and claws. He wished there was something he could do for his loyal friend. He threw his spear to the ground and produced Dorlimere. Its blade shining in the morning sun and reflected the trails of the falling stars as they filled the sky...but nothing more.

"I need you now!" he shouted vainly at the blade. Behind him, a fresh wave of enemies began to pour in and he was forced to turn his attention away from his friend. Anger consumed him and he broke the line stepping out in front of the men alone. He looked at the man bearing down on him with his spear and drew back Dorlimere as he step forward. With one hand he parried the spear and with the other he swung a long arc with his blade and split the man from hip to shoulder with a spray of warm crimson rain.

"Quinn!" yelled Kôdaï over the fray. "The northern line is failing!"

He looked, and there hundreds of men were beginning to pour in around the wrestling dragons trying to avoid being crushed. Many not so lucky as the great reptiles slashed and tore at each other with such violence it shook the ground. The few men he had there were no match for the numbers bearing down upon them and so he moved to reinforce them. If they breached the line, then even his phalanx toward the south would be cut down from behind.

He looked and there upon a cliff archers had ascended and were starting to rain down deadly arrows upon the men he intended to reinforce the line with. They had to be stopped but he had no one to send. Just then, Lárwin appeared at his side. She had been flinging her deadly arrows since the beginning but now she came forward with a look of concern.

"Tëleios needs our help!" she cried, looking at his struggle. Even Quinn could tell that he was beginning to succumb to the fight as his great strength began to wane.

"Only he can fight such beasts," replied Quinn with longing for his friend's suffering. "If you want to live, do not approach them or you risk being crushed yourself. He is on his own."

"You are the king! You alone bear the sword and are the only one who can help him!" she shouted, her red hair flying back in the wind of battle. "You can do anything! *Anything*! But you must believe it!"

Just then another volley of arrows decimated a group of Evealians running to reinforce the northern line. Their cries of pain stole his attention. He looked back at Lárwin and their eyes met. Quinn's face took on a grim expression and set like stone as he searched for understanding. He turned and made for the cliff. Lárwin watched him go and her heart went with him, but as Tëleios was thrown to the ground with a heavy blow her attention was averted. She had to do something.

Quinn dodged arrows and spears and cut down all who stood in his way. He began to climb the rocks to where the archers stood slaughtering his men down below. As he climbed he heard a sound like thunder followed by a tremor in the rocks. He looked around him but saw nothing. Suddenly there was another and then another. From the corner of his eye, he saw a white flash and then fire off in the distance. The falling stars had finally begun to strike. They were all around him on every side of the battlefield, large and small falling upon both the enemy and his own men making no distinction. They appeared as white spears of light with tips of fire as they streaked across the sky and impacted the ground with terrible force. He continued to climb the rocks until he came atop the precipice overlooking the battle. Coming from behind, he gave the archers no quarter as he slew them, twenty men in all.

From this vantage, he took in the vast and wild world around him. He stood there for only a moment, but in that moment he saw what no other man had ever seen before or will again. He saw how thin his ranks had become and how his front lines wavered not being able to keep up with the onslaught of men being thrown at them. The vanilla sky overhead was painted with the giant crescents of the double moons and rounded white clouds being pierced with celestial arrows as they fell from above upon his world as far as his eyes could see.

High above, far beyond the battle, the clouds and even the moons themselves, he saw the New Star approaching from a great distance, yet for all its subtle movement he knew it came at incredible speed and marked the end of his world. Beside it, a smaller star moved also and seemed to be ever so much closer and larger than any that had yet fallen and would be upon them soon. His men, and his world, now had little time.

He heard a loud roar of pain from below followed by Lárwin's distant battle cry as she lifted her sword against the dragons attacking Tëleios. She ran valiantly toward them without fear as meteors exploded all around. As she neared she aimed her sword and dug it in deep between the scales of one of the dragons. As she did it whipped its tail around wildly and smashed into her breastplate sending her flying and landing hard upon her back. Quinn's eyes grew wide at this as he looked down upon her fallen body amidst the battle. His defensive line too was nearly broken and his heart shook within him. The enemy advanced upon Lárwin's motionless body. The stars were bearing down on them. His men were dying. Just then he heard a voice, whispers of his own memories echoing up from his spirit.

"*You can do anything if you just believe it,*" said the voice of Lárwin. Then he saw the face of the ancient king who had helped him and heard his voice also. "*Victory is not to the strong, but to those who trust in the Light. Be strengthened."* Finally, he heard the voice of Lorwin as she spoke to him before she perished on the floating island. *"You are not what your eyes can see but what your heart believes. The sword's power is contained within the spirit who wields it."* He sheathed Dorlimere and paused, blinking, and felt a stirring deep within his soul. It felt like he was remembering something long forgotten or perhaps simply understanding for the first time. It rose up within him like a sudden storm and he stepped forward to the windswept edge of the narrow precipice.

Lárwin lay either dead or dying and the enemy had broken through and now descended upon her. She was too far for him to get there before the enemy and the lesser star was bearing down upon them, streaking past the smaller moon with white fire in its wake. He needed more time to get to her.

"Contained within the spirit who wields it," he whispered to himself. Looking up at the giant crescent of the closest moon he let this new fire in his spirit rise to the top and he dug his toes hard into the ground to brace himself for what he intended to do. There was no other way. He reached out his open hands toward the sky and finally believed.

Kôdaï looked up from the fierceness of battle to see Quinn standing upon the windy cliff with his arms outstretched toward the moon and cried with a great voice, "Our king at last!"

Quinn put both hands around the crescent of the great moon and pushed with incredible strength not his own. A great force flowed through him in waves as he did the impossible. Despite the fighting, men and beasts on both sides felt a change within themselves as distant gravity pulled at them as if the entire world were tilting. Many looked up to see the moon itself subtly moving toward the path of the blazing meteor. Quinn let out a wild cry, straining as he felt the weight of it and the power to move it as faith rose within him.

Suddenly, as he stood there upon the cliff, the largest of the black dragons swooped over the battlefield and up the cliff side to where he stood with breathtaking speed. Opening wide its massive jaws, it came up from beneath and engulfed Quinn whole with its giant mouth, swallowing both him and the rock he stood upon.

It rose high into the air in a long curve as it turned back toward the battle. To those below, cries of shock and disbelief erupted from those who saw it. But then another thing happened. As the beast arced overhead, a flaming sword erupted from its scales with a raging blue fire as Quinn thrust Dorlimere through its rib cage and began to cut himself free from its belly. Torrents of blood and sinew rained down upon those below. The dragon cried out and writhed in pain throwing its rider out into the open air. When Quinn had torn a large enough opening he grasped the strap of the saddle and began to pull himself upon its back. They dove across the sky amidst the falling stars and high overhead, the lesser star impacted the backside of the moon he had sent moving. Great fractures split across the face of it as one half of the moon exploded silently in space. Rock and debris scattered across the heavens.

Standing upon the back of the dying dragon, he pulled hard at the reins and forced the beast back to the battle where Lárwin lay. The enemy was nearly upon her.

Careening over the battle, he smashed into their advancing line, crashing the dragon's corpse into a formation of fifty men, killing them instantly and sending himself summer-salting into the air amidst the maelstrom and confusion. He arose with momentum, most of his body and the right side of his face smeared in dark dragon's blood, Dorlimere ablaze in his hand, and a dazzling crown of silver stars above his head as he destroyed all those before him.

Lárwin sprawled in a daze upon the dusty ground as the battle raged all around her. She looked up through dim and narrow eyes to see a bird high overhead followed by the distant cry of a hawk. Whitefeather had returned. Behind him Tëleios' kin emerged from the clouds and filled the sky with golden terror as they dove toward the battle. In the fight, Tëleios had valiantly slain three of the black dragons but now the remaining two turned from their slaughter of men to finish him as he lay bleeding upon the stained grass. His brothers fell from the sky hurling themselves upon them, seven of them along with many smaller dragonlings which split off and flew toward the doorway, positioning themselves on either side of it. They made short work of their enemies and soon the last of Ahriman's dragons lay dead or dying. Then they turned vehemently upon the frail men below.

All the while, Quinn wondered where Ahriman himself was as he had not yet appeared, but his attention was now fully on saving Lárwin and he turned to come back for her. He picked her up in his arms. He felt how light she was and he treasured her as the most delicate object he had ever carried. Her helmet had fallen and her red, bloodstained hair swayed in the wind. He whistled loud and from somewhere in the battle emerged Namír, his faithful friend to the end. He placed her gently upon the saddle. He mounted also and rode quickly to the doorway, holding her tightly and dodging spears and arrows along the way. As he neared, he heard Kôdaï shout over the screams and clashing spears for the men to fall back to the doorway. The outer defenses had fallen to the enemy. Nilrem's men came forward and parted for those retreating and then locked their shields at the entrance. Nilrem himself stood in the front as Quinn approached out of the confusion with Lárwin.

"Take her!" he said, giving her gently to the man.

Nilrem looked down at her with the look of a loving father. "I'll keep her safe," he replied.

He felt a sudden wind from above, looking up he saw golden streaks fill the roof of the passage as Tëleios' kin retreated, Whitefeather and Tavi among them. They would have never fallen back without orders. Turning back to the battle, Quinn dismounted and looked for Kôdaï.

As he did, there upon the hills and mountains, descending from every open place the enemy poured in like dark ants covering the landscape and Kôdaï standing against them. Before him, a tall figure strode from amidst the soldiers, his massive frame hidden beneath black armor and a mighty sword in his hand. He had an air of power about him and his countenance revealed one who wielded great authority. Fear went out before him and terror filled his wake as those around him parted to give him room.

Ahriman would see to the breaching of the doorway himself. That's when Quinn took a closer look at his teacher and across the distance a startling sight met his eyes. The broken blade of Ténmei fell from his hand and he slumped to his knees upon the ground bleeding. Quinn's heart leapt within him for his friend and the image burned hotly into his mind. He saw Ahriman raise his sword to finish him and in that moment Quinn took a great stride forward drawing back Dorlimere. Pouring all of his strength into the throw, he hurled his blade at his great enemy and it flew wildly toward its target. Before he could bring down his blow, Dorlimere pierced the heart of Ahriman and drove through his armored chest and out the other side driving him back several paces.

To the horror of his officers, he fell to the ground flat upon his back with a great crash. The advancing troops suddenly halted in shock as Quinn strode forward and placed his foot upon their captain's chest as he withdrew his sword. To Quinn's amazement, there was no blood to stain his blade and he wondered what to make of it. He then looked to Kôdaï who had fallen among the slain. He lay there with grievous wounds. He had lived to be nearly one thousand years old and now he was in his final moments. Quinn knelt to the ground and cradled his head in his hands as tears welled up in his eyes.

"It be alright my boy," said Kôdaï in a quiet voice. "My eyes saw the fall of my enemy and the rise of a new king." He reached out and grasped Quinn's right hand in his own, shaking as his life ebbed away. "I give to thee now the length o' days me father's gave to me. That which ye were meant to have from the beginning. Share them well with yer love," he coughed violently and his eyes began to dim. "My soul...be at peace..." he said faintly. With that, he fell away to his eternal rest. Quinn reached up and closed his eyes gently.

Hot tears ran down his cheeks while he held his friend. As he did so however he noticed a black shadow creep along the ground extending out from the body of Ahriman where he had fallen. It flowed out long and dark, like liquid night refusing to reflect the sun. Up from the ground it began to rise like a man or a great demon standing, a black shadow rising above all who stood there and unfolding massive wings against the wild sky. Darkness himself towered above them now free of the human body he was imprisoned within and his appearance struck terror into even the bravest of his own warriors. His eyes flashed and a great cry went out from him. He raised his arms and made to strike Quinn and dash him to pieces upon the ground but as his shadowy fists rained down Quinn raised his shield and closed his eyes. To his great surprise however, he felt only a cold breeze flow over him like a winter wind. The power of Darkness had been diminished and held no sway over him. Enraged, he then drew himself up to his full height, more than ten times the height of a man, his countenance filled with fury, and then dispersed into thin air. The air was now still save for the stars still streaking heavily through the air and all marveled at what had happened and wondered what became of him.

Just then, the bodies of the fallen and slain who were loyal to Darkness began to groan and move upon the ground. There was no life within them and yet they were somehow reanimated and crawled toward one another with unusual motions as they were filled with a spirit not their own. Tens and hundreds of them reached out to grab the ones next to them and they began to crawl on top of one another in a grotesque pile of bodies.

Quinn watched in horror as he began to understand what was slowly taking shape before him. As hundreds turned into thousands and thousands ten thousands, the bodies began to move and writhe as one creature. It pulled in even those who were still alive and trying to escape. Ahriman's men backed away quickly and many ran to keep from being taken by the creature, but as Darkness filled the bodies of his followers and gained strength none could escape. It towered over the battle field and took the shape of a great serpent from hell as the bodies pulled and twisted together giving it power as it moved. Broken arms and legs created empty holes where eyes would be, and in its gaping mouth the swords and blades of the fallen reflected the sun and were held tightly in place by the morbid grip of the dead.

It let out a deep groan which turned to a roar, a torrent of voices as those who were still alive within it cried out in unison with pain and suffering. As its shadow fell over him Quinn was at a loss. How could he slay such a creature?

As he was thinking this, a new volley of falling stars began exploding all around as they impacted the ground. Fireballs ripped through the sky and he knew the closing of the doorway was soon to come. He secured the satchel Kôdaï carried containing the book of the king, taking care that it would not fall from his friend's lifeless body, and called for the last remaining Evealian soldiers to help him. They placed his body in their arms and carried him away as Quinn turned to face this new enemy. As he did, he thought he saw a face he had nearly forgotten among the writhing bodies of Darkness.

He was sure it was the face of his father, screaming with pain and regret only to be quickly consumed with the others. For a moment Quinn shuttered, but then steadied himself. He had already conquered those demons. Unsheathing Dorlimere he stepped forward, eyes blazing as he looked up at the creature.

"Let's dance..." he said bitterly and spit on the ground. But as he did, another thing surprised him.

A tall dark figure leapt from on high, the cliff he had once stood upon, and he saw the setting sunlight dance off the black armor of Ahriman as he fell upon the neck of the creature. He had removed his helmet as if to embrace the light for the first time and his hair waved wildly as the beast turned to reach him. He drove his blade deep into the bodies and hacked wildly at it, slicing off myriad hands that reached for him through the flesh of the serpent, but they were too many.

As the beast writhed hundreds of hands pulled at him and finally drug him down and held him fast. Quinn watched in horror as the serpent caught his leg in its mouth of swords and hands innumerable reached up from its throat and drug him screaming down into its fiery stomach.

It now turned to Quinn and its hollow eyes fixed upon him as its massive body coiled behind preparing to strike. It sprang upon him, driving its full force against him. As it did so there came a mighty streak of gold as Tëleios tore into its face and ripped at the bodies. He forced it away from Quinn with his fading strength and then fell to the ground and looked up with violent defiance. With his last breath he let out a long blast of fire, a heat all-consuming and blinding to the eyes. Even the hellish beast turned from the heat of it and the metal armor of the fallen soldiers in its flesh turned to liquid as it melted. Quinn raised his shield just in time to keep from being caught in the inferno himself. When it had subsided he looked again and there was the serpent, the great enemy of mankind towering high above Tëleios, its body aflame. The tortured souls inside cried out with one terrible voice of pure wrath as it bore down upon him.

Through the fire, images flashed into Quinn's mind. Images of a burning church and the screams within. Of falling to his knees in the ashes and holding his mother's necklace. Burying his family. He stole one last look over his shoulder at the doorway and there was Lárwin on the other side. She was standing against the backdrop of night with Nilrem and his soldiers behind. Silver moonlight illuminated her hair and reflected from her armor like water. The image burned into his soul. He knew this would be the last he would ever see of her.

He stood tall and turned to face his enemy. Throwing his blackened shield to the side he stood upon the threshold. He raised his sword high with both hands. Gripping Dorlimere tightly and clenching his fists around it he let out a great battle cry, long and loud; a legendary roar that rippled through time for ages to come...

Lárwin saw him run toward the great flaming serpent as it fell upon him, its terrible mouth open wide to consume him. Her heart leapt to be beside him. She ran to him down the tunnel, her feet like the wind and her heart pounding in her ears. But like the closing of a book, the dimming of a light, the waking of a dream; the sound of her love and the sight of him standing against the beast and the falling sky faded to a glimmer...until all was gone. The doorway between the worlds had closed.

She ran hard into the stone wall of the back of the cave and she fell back reeling in surprise. She looked up from the ground in shock with wide eyes.

"No..." she said not believing. "No, NO!" she screamed again as she stood and pounded the wall looking for an answer. She cried aloud and beat her fists upon the stone in vain as tears welled up in her eyes and streamed down her face. She felt a warm hand upon her shoulder and a soft gruff voice speaking.

"He's gone," said Nilrem sadly.

Burning tears fell from her eyes and landed hard upon the ground. "The star," she whispered suddenly. And with that she turned and ran from the cave.

Coming out under the still, moonlit sky she emerged to see a thick blanket of stars filling the void of night. She found the large green orb of Alária and its light reflected in her eyes. Somewhere on that world was Quinn, her love fighting to defend them.

Just then, high above in the silent sky, Alária exploded. Like the tears that sparkled in her eyes, her world shattered into countless shimmering pieces across the night. Her eyes widened and she fell to her knees not able to look away. From such a distance, it seemed like such a small thing. But far away whole continents, oceans and the very sky itself tore apart and drifted out into the void.

She looked on for a long time until there was nothing left. Only a long trail of faint debris reaching across the night.

She looked on for a long, long time...

XIX.

Infínitűs

Infinity

Quinn drifted along in silence and darkness. There had been a sudden flash of brilliant white light and then all had become still. How long had passed he did not know, but being there, wrapped in the embrace of the deep, he finally found rest and peace.

Presently, he discerned voices speaking softly. At first, they were too quiet to understand, but as he listened he began to understand their words and was surprised to find that they were talking about *him*. More specifically, the route of his eternity. A black and sinister voice claimed the right over his soul and recounted a long list of offenses he had committed throughout his life. He suddenly felt very ashamed and opened his mouth to speak yet could not find words to say. Was this a dream? Was he even there? He did not know. Then he heard the sound of another. A clearer and stronger voice pleaded in his defense to another still hidden and yet to reveal himself. Though he could not see, he perceived a judgment was made and all was silent once more. Then an even greater one finally spoke.

"He is to be returned to the world that is his, the world that I have given them," and his words were like that of the sound of thunder or a rushing river. At their sound his eyes were opened and there before him was a figure with the appearance of a man but radiated with such light that his face was hidden and he could not look upon it. To his right stepped forward another, a tall and kingly man with stately stride and bearing a familiar countenance. He had seen this man before.

Leánder placed his hand upon Quinn's shoulder and spoke. "My son, your adventures have only just begun..." and with that all was darkness once more.

XX.

Sol Etiam Oritur

The Sun Also Rises

He opened his eyes and suddenly felt a stab of pain as his senses came flooding back. As he looked up from the ground, he saw stars innumerable moving quickly across the endless black curtain of night. He stood and looked around himself. He was standing upon the edge of a cliff overlooking a landscape with no horizon. The ground simply fell away in every direction and he saw that above, below and all around were stars. He looked out into the void and saw the desolate debris of Alária moving silently and stretching out in a wide arc as far as he could see. High above, he saw the blue star of Ethália and the red sphere of Mur'alia passing in between. Ethália twinkled faintly and seemed so far away, but that is where Lárwin waited for him.

At his feet he saw his shadow moving across the ground and when he turned, he saw the doorway between the worlds open once more; the huge, ancient doors were broken upon the ground and the opening beyond them. Looking within, he saw the sun rising over distant green hills, the light of it warming his face. He looked once more at the heavens surrounding him and the beauty of its glorious desolation caught him unaware. A glittering object stole his attention and he looked down. There in the dust lay Dorlimere as though it were an ordinary thing, left behind and neglected. He reached down and picked it up gently. Wiping the dust from it he held it as something precious, though it felt different in his hands. Lighter perhaps. Perhaps not. But something...*something* was different. He then sensed that the fire within had left. It was no longer within the blade. He held up his other hand and saw a pale blue flame faintly cross between his fingers before fading again. *It...It is within me...* He stood there for a long moment, considering. Then, turning the point of the long blade downward, drove it hard into the ground with both hands. He stood back and marveled at its beauty as it stood out as a silent sentinel against the stars.

"Until another come with need of you," he said softly. He removed his mother's silver leaf from around his neck and hung it on the hilt of the sword deciding to leave the past behind him.

He turned, and walked through the door.

<u>Names and Pronunciations</u>

1. Aarondil [Air - ron - dill]: Quinn's third oldest brother.

2. Ahriman [**Air** - ah - min]: Brother of Leánder, deceived by Darkness through a vision of the future.

3. Bularius [Bul - **air** - ee - us]: Second in command under King Leánder in the ancient world.

4. Darkness: Archfiend of Men. Corrupter of the light.

5. DarMere-Itah [Dar - Meer - **Itah**]: Replicant of Dorlimere-Sissu. Sword of Darkness.

6. Deiriador [**Deer** - ee - ah - door]: Quinn's original home in the Southlands.

7. Dorlimere-Sisu [Door - lih - meer Sis - sue]: Sword of Leánder given by the Light Enduring. Means "Blade of the Light to overcome all adversity".

8. Eldïr [Ell - **deer**]: Quinn's fourth oldest brother.

9. Evealian [Eve - **eh** - lee - an], *plural* : Citizens or those belonging to the land of Everfall.

10. Everfall: First city of Men along the northwest coast of the continent of Lanália.

11. Fanglóriun [Fang - **glory** - un]: First prince of dragon-kind. Deceived by Ahriman.

12. Fáylinn [**Fay** - Linn]: Chief Stewardess of Ethália, Queen of the FáLlűmin, named after their luminous appearance.

13. Jädus [**Jay**-dus]: Returned captive from Ahriman's expedition.

14. Jahor [Jay - hore]: Quinn's oldest brother.

15. Kôdaï [Code - eye]: Last descendant of the Bularians

16. Lárwin: Daughter of Leánder and Lorwin, princess of the ancient world.

17. Leánder [Lee - and - er]: First king of Men in the ancient world.

18. Light Enduring: The Eternal Light (Lux Æterna) and Creator of all. Friend of all who pursue good and righteousness.

19. Lorwin: Wife of Leánder, first queen of Men, guardian of the Sword.

20. Lûctus Nöcturn [**Luck** - tis **Nock** - turn]: Shadow army of Darkness. Stole the form of men in ancient times.

21. Makïa [Mack - **eye** - ah]: Quinn's second oldest brother.

22. Merial [**Mare** - ee - ale]: Quinn's Mother

23. Namír [Na - **meer**]: Quinn's faithful horse.

24. Nilrem [Nill - rem]: Lord of besieged village. Ally of Quinn and Kôdaï.

25. Quinn: The Chosen One.

26. Tavi Quicktail: Friend of Lárwin and Quinn

27. Teivel [**Tie** - vel]: Henchman of Darkness.

28. Tëleios [**Te** - lee - oss]: Descendant of Fangloriun. Means "to be complete, whole, mature, to finish".

29. Ténmei [**Ten** - may]: Bularius' sword passed down to Kôdaï. Means "the will of God".

30. VolFerrum [Vole - **Fair** - um]: A certain metal discovered by Leánder. Means "flying iron".

31. VolNari [Vole - nahr - ee]: Evealian Flying ships of ancient times.

32. Whitefeather: Best friend of Tavi and friend of Lárwin and Quinn.

Ron J. McNutt was born in Ohio in 1982 and grew up in the Mohican Forest. He served in the U.S. Air Force during the second Persian Gulf War and afterward attended college to become a flight instructor. He currently works as a civilian instructor pilot for the Air Force and lives in Colorado Springs, Colorado with his wife.